The Beautiful Beast

"Insufferable prig!" cried Lady Caroline with indignance. "Lord Seabury is the greatest beast in nature, to serve his father so ill..."

But the father in question was looking past her so pointedly that Caroline turned to see what had caught his attention. The words froze on her lips when she found herself face to face with the greatest—and handsomest—beast in nature indeed...

THE AUTUMN ROSE

FIONA HILL

A BERKLEY BOOK
published by
BERKLEY PUBLISHING CORPORATION

THE AUTUMN ROSE

A Berkley Book / published by arrangement with
G.P. Putnam's Sons

PRINTING HISTORY
G.P. Putnam's Sons edition published November 1978
Berkley edition / November 1979

ISBN: 0-425-04224-3

A BERKLEY BOOK ® TM 757,375
Berkley Books are published by Berkley Publishing Corporation,
200 Madison Avenue, New York, New York 10016.
PRINTED IN THE UNITED STATES OF AMERICA

For my friend
Eugene Bier

"More exquisite than any other
is the autumn rose."

—THÉODORE AGRIPPA D'AUBIGNÉ

Chapter I

My Dearest Angela,

Here am I in London at last, and wonderfully pleased to say so. What a place of contraries, of wealth and poverty, grandeur and meanness! You will forgive my inelegance when I tell you straightway that it smells absolutely abominable, makes a noise like thirty cannon, and provides its inhabitants with water all but impotable for the taste. And yet it is London, inarguably London, the great Metropolis and heart of England. My kinsman Seabury's house, where I am now installed, is situated in Portman Square, which I am told is a very fine place indeed; but you would laugh to see what a paltry bit of land lies within its esteemed boundaries, and even more to survey the meagre strip on which the house is built. You would laugh, I say; but I cannot, for they are *my* windows which front so nearly upon the clamorous, noisome, narrow streets behind this splendid Rucke House. Not even a garden divides us from the saddest squalor I have ever witnessed; a mere cottager in Berkshire is a richer landlord than the mighty earl in town. So here am I in London, and cannot breathe for the air, drink for the water, nor think for the noise!

I exaggerate; but it is a place that encourages
hyperbole. My London relations seem to have no fear of
heights—nor breadths, nor depths, nor any dimension of
whatever magnitude; even the shawl in which I find
myself swathed is of amplitude sufficient to drape a
palace, or clothe a regiment at the least. Twenty could sit
to dinner at this desk—the very drawers produce an echo,
forsooth—and my host Lord Seabury's sleeves extend
beyond his wrists nearly half a dozen inches. Man may
have been the measure of all things in ancient Greece, but
in Rucke House Gog and Magog must be our yardsticks.

You will wish to know how our journey hither was
passed, having seen us climb into the coach after so
rotund a reverend, and so antiquated a lady. It was a
tolerable enough day, though scarcely what I should style
entertaining. Windle and I (our Windle is in high
fettle—more of her later) chiefly amused ourselves with
whispering nasty things to one another regarding our
fellow passengers. Windle naturally employed all the
restraint appropriate to a chaperone, but I had a fine time
wallowing in rudeness, and succeeded before our arrival
in thoroughly discrediting (though only in imagination)
our hapless companions. Frankly, had it not been for
speaking ill of them, I should have had no diversion
whatever, and for that reason I am almost glad my
brother's lady wife dissuaded him from sending us in his
carriage. I say almost, however, because the last stage of
our journey in the mail presented us with an incident quite
disagreeable to me, and all but fatal to Miss Windle.

No doubt you have read in the London papers of those
town bucks who bully the coachmen of the mail into
handing over the reins? They ride upon the box and bribe
or badger until they have their way—and then how will
they not abuse the horses, if only they may boast of their
exploits to their envious friends! Well then, at the last stop
before London our coach was entrusted to one such
admirable nonesuch, and thereafter it needed the courage
of a hero to remain tranquil within the carriage. My dear,
you know I am no Wellington, but I am not a coward
either; so you must believe me when I say we were in peril
of our lives. This maniac beat the horses till we thundered

down the road, squealing and lurching at every bend, and stopping for no man. Such was our velocity that I cannot be certain, but I believe I saw a little hare left wounded on the highway, trampled under our blind advance. The cleric for all his practice could not surpass the elderly lady in feverish prayers, and Windle, as you may imagine, huffed and squeaked and snorted to rival the horses; but ridiculous as she was, and disposed as I am to tease her, I am not even now of a mind to take the situation lightly. Our villainous captor dropped the reins and fled the moment we reached our destination, and since he had boarded the coach only after ourselves, none of the passengers saw his face, nor would the coachman (if indeed he knew) tell who it was; but I will close my account of this episode with a vow that if I can but find the mysterious gentleman, I will give him reason to regret his detestable prank.

So for my situation, and how I came to be here. I have given you a notion of the size of Rucke House, but nothing of its magnificence; nor can I hope to do so without taxing keenly my poor powers of description. I am almost sorry for Lady Lillian when I think she grew up in this fine house only to be stuck away with Humphrey and me at Two Towers, comfortable though it is, after her marriage. Rucke House is largely of brick, with a long row of windows facing the square, two, indeed, the bow windows which have become so much the rage of late. A vast oaken stairway rises from the entrance hall to bear the visitor up to the drawing-rooms (there are three), the library, the so-called Gilt Saloon, in which nothing but the curious ceiling is gilded; above this one may ascend another flight to find a perfectly tremendous ball-room, a music room with a pianoforte to make any music-fancier swoon, and numerous other apartments including my chamber, which is separated from Windle's by a very pretty parlour. At first when I arrived I found the bed monstrous soft, but I am ashamed to say that three nights passed upon it have left me a convert to its perfect cosiness. My windows, as I noted above, give upon a scene not overly pleasing, but beyond this complaint I have none. An abigail is being found for me; in the

meantime Windle does the honours. Oh how I regret my
deft little Jeannie! Lady Lillian absolutely promised she
would not turn her off in my absence, but I still fret; do if
you can go by Two Towers someday, and see that little
Jeannie is still there.

You must make shift somehow with this bare sketch of
Rucke House, for I am too eager to acquaint you with its
inhabitants to delay any longer. First there is Lady
Lillian's brother Lord Seabury, about whose character I
fear I was too sanguine. There is no love lost between
them you know—which goes some way to explaining why
I had never once met him in the six years since my
brother's marriage; of course he was fighting in Europe at
the time of their wedding, a cause for absence that no one
can fault . . . still, an affectionate brother must have found
his way to Berkshire ere this. I mention the matter because
it was my assumption that they could not be much alike,
or there had been more feeling between them; however, I
was wrong. There is little feeling *between* them simply
because there is little feeling *in* them; they are not
passionate souls. Not that Seabury is anything but
pleasant—far from it! Just like his sister, he is courteous,
intelligent, and reserved. It is the reserve, as you will
guess, that disappoints me. Also like Lillian, Lord
Seabury seems to be—alas!—just a trifle too
thrifty . . . more on this in a moment. As for the form in
which these qualities are enclosed, however, here the
family resemblance is less pronounced. If I told you he
was a man of nearly six feet, broad-shouldered and
slender of waist, with a head of dark curls in which Nature
anticipated the Byronic style, fine eyes brilliantly blue,
features emphatic but exactly straight and regular, and a
mouth like wine and winter snow, would you suppose him
comely? Never mind what you would suppose; he is
startlingly handsome, a fact as well established in London
as Edmund Kean's reputation.

Doubtless you will protest that (as ever) I judge too
soon, but if there had been any question in my mind as to
whether this gentleman might harbour some hidden fire,
it was erased yesterday by my introduction to the creature
whom all London expects him to marry, one Lady Susan

Manning. If Seabury is dry, Lady Susan is parched: an ocean could not humidify her. That she set her cap for his lordship seven years ago, and still waits patiently, says little enough for her spirit, in my estimation; but worse than that, her manner towards me yesterday was so impossibly correct as to be droll. "You are but lately come from the country, I think?" said she.

"Indeed," I smiled, "and green as grass."

"Surely not," was her answer.

"Oh but I am. I have been a perfect ostrich, with Berkshire for my sand."

Lady Susan would not hear of this. "Surely not," she murmured again.

"On the contrary, I assure you. I am not the least bit shy about it: I am a bumpkin, a country clown."

"I cannot credit it," she said, glancing uneasily about the room for her mamma (and this in a woman nearly thirty years of age!).

"But truly, I am! Rough, clumsy, lewd, untutored— how shall I say it else? I must throw myself upon your mercy, beg you to forgive my *naïvetés*, my *faux pas*, my cloddish foolishness."

"Surely it cannot be so bad . . ." said she vaguely.

"But I tell you it is! I am a lout, a boor, a ruffian! Earth stains my fingers, onions my breath! I am a Caliban in petticoats, my dearest ma'am, a Visigoth, a Barbar!"

Nothing, no matter how outlandish, could bring a smile to this lady; nothing tickled her; no epithet however crude suggested to her that I might be joking. I said more than what I record here, my dear Angela: I abused myself in terms the most cruel, the most outrageous. But still she regarded me mildly, still she insisted civilly, refused with the utmost gentleness to believe me! A woman who can stand firm under such a barrage of nonsense is a woman to be feared!

Even if that had not decided my opinion of her, when her mother did at last arrive at her side, Lady Susan turned to her with a countenance full of relief, indicated me with a wave of her hand and observed with perfect gravity, "Lady Caroline has been telling me how rustic her life has been till now; does it not sound charming? I should love to dwell in a simple cot, at the edge of a dewy mead. Should not you, Maman?"

We do well, dear Angel, to take so poetical and serious a nature in small doses, I believe. I shall do my possible to see as little of Lady Susan Manning as may be during my sojourn here.

I must return to the topic of Lord Seabury; forgive me, I ramble frightfully. I was arguing that his choice of a wife indicates something of his own nature, as I trust you will agree. And indeed he does exhibit that same cautious vigilance towards life which I have often remarked in his sister Lillian. In fact, they are almost as much a brother-and-sister pair as are Humphrey and I, and you know that is saying a good deal since (with one notable exception) we have hardly disagreed on anything. Seabury cannot be much older than thirty, and yet he is both stern and stately; he regards my visit here in the light of taking one's wares to market—which is to say, he supposes I am come to be displayed and, if all goes well, betrothed before the season is out.

Here it is a little difficult to fault him, I must confess, for I should be hard pressed to explain what I have indeed come for if not to marry. It is hardly an explanation, but I imagine my real reason for coming was so as not to listen to Lady Lillian's urging me to go throughout yet another winter. Since I was eighteen and refused Fred Manchester's offer she has been at me to pass a season here, as you must know; and every time I have discouraged your brother (my best love to him, by the way) she has behaved as if I buried a knife in her heart. From this I must conclude she desires me to marry, and from that, it is a mere skip to the idea that she would be happiest were I to leave Two Towers and take up residence elsewhere. Oh dear! I assign her ladyship such uncommendable motives; I know you will reproach me in your reply to this letter, but you must admit, she was peculiarly cheerful when Windle and I drove off. Anyway, there is something about London that encourages one to be blunt and spiteful. Perhaps it is simply the exhilaration of being in a new place; or homesick as I am, I feel a rush of spirit and independence. I do understand the naturalness of Lillian's wanting a home for herself, her husband and her children—though it was my home first. Oh fiddlesticks, I have done it again. I see I must leave this topic altogether.

There are three others at Rucke House, besides Seabury, Windle and myself. The most interesting of these is Seabury's father, the Earl of Romby, an estimable old man with one of the worst dispositions in Christendom. He came to Two Towers for the wedding naturally—and his sister too—but I was so much absorbed with my own sentiments at that time that I scarcely observed them. Besides, they were probably on their best behaviour then, and therefore not at all themselves. Here, how Romby drinks, and thunders, and swears! Everyone stands in dread of him (there are hordes of servants here) except his son. Romby is addicted to cards. His is one of the oldest members of Brooks's Club. He enjoys the very deepest play, and is well known to have lost £10,000 in a single hand during one particularly foolish period of his youth; but Seabury has put a stop to all that. Here is the thriftiness I referred to earlier. Can you believe it? Somehow he has got control of all the old man's money, and with that he keeps Romby very tightly in hand. This is not handsome in him, for I may tell you that Romby's fortune is immense, and my lord Seabury stands to inherit it all. Besides Rucke House and the county seats, there is a house in Hampstead (to which we may retire whenever London grows wearisome) and a shooting-box near Melton Mowbray. There is a good deal invested in four per cents as well, so it is not a question of being land-rich and cash-poor. No, it looks suspiciously like avarice, I must say, and does not endear Seabury to me in the least.

Oh but those blue eyes! I am a little in love with his eyes, as you see; I may say it to you, but pray burn this letter.

Romby, to return to my text, is the growliest beast on earth. He rants and raves and mutters day in and day out; he viewed my coming with profound disapproval and has scarcely said three words to me as yet, but I hope to make a friend of him, as I will need one in this household and cannot reasonably look elsewhere. You will know why when I tell you that the other residents here are a Miss Amy Meredith, nineteen years old and incredibly silly, and a Mrs. Henry, her chaperone. Henry, as she is called, is (like our Windle) a "lady of uncertain years." I suspect they are pretty much of an age, uncertain though that age may be; but Windle hints delicately that the other is older. A marked friction immediately sprang up between the two worthy women, which has already led to some amusing scenes, as when Henry attempted to learn Windle's ancestry:

Henry.   Windle, Windle ... Not the Ipswich Windles, perchance?
Windle. No, not the Ipswich Windles.
Henry.   Tunbridge Wells? Coventry?
Windle. (*Coldly*) Not those either.
Henry.   Not the Devonshire Windles, surely? (*To Amy*) Remember the Devonshire Windles, my dear? (*Amy shakes her head to indicate the negative.*)
Windle. No, not those either.
Henry.   I am so relieved. My life they were dreadful!
Windle. (*Chilly silence.*)
Henry.   Well, it is a common name, after all.
Windle. (*Frigid silence.*)
Henry.   Terribly common. There must be hundreds of Windles.
Windle. (*With icy majesty.*) Indeed. And your name is, I think, Henry? Not of the Tudor Henrys, perchance?
Henry.   Certainly not!
Windle. I see. Well, Henry is a common name too, I suppose.

Poor Mrs. Henry bit her lip with vexation upon this, and it must have been a very painful bite, for I saw her touching it tenderly afterwards.

I am sorry to say, however, that nothing so interesting as a friction has sprung up between Amy Meredith and me. She is the daughter of Romby's deceased sister, Lady Anne (about his very lively sister Beatrice I will tell you in a moment), and if death is contagious that fact will go some way to explaining Miss Meredith's character. Ridiculing orphans is very low behaviour, do you not think, but being one myself must give me some privileges, however dismal. In any case, Miss Meredith's father was alive until a few years ago, at which time she went to reside with a sister of his, a spinster. Apparently the sister grew weary of her company, for she has been sent to London very much as I have been, to see if perhaps she will return a married woman—which is to say, not return at all. I find, by the bye, that it is to this Amy that I owe my present internment at Rucke House; had it not been for her, I should have stayed with Romby's other sister, Lady Beatrice. She is a wonderful, wilful old lady, quite a *doyenne* of the *ton*, and it would naturally have been a good deal less awkward for me to have stopped on at her house in South Audley Street than at this bastion of bachelorhood—but I have learned that her ladyship declined to take me in because she would also have been obliged, in that case, to take in Miss Meredith—and that she would not do. You see, dear Angela, Lady Beatrice already knew little Amy, and to know Amy is to know how simpering, how contrary, how idiotish a young woman can be. She is the very soul of nonsense, and was therefore prime prey for Romby. Though she and Henry arrived only a week before I did, the earl has so thoroughly overwhelmed her that she lives in continual terror of him. He has but to enter the drawing-room for her to quit it; at dinner a single scowl from him produces headache in her, and sends her upstairs; I have even seen her blanch at the sound of his carriage arriving. Such is the state of affairs to which I have been introduced! A reign of terror prevails in Rucke House, and Romby is the tyrant.

He is trying to cow me into obedient awe as well, but I do not frighten so easily. Besides, I have perceived who really holds the power, and that is Seabury.

Miss Meredith, I may add, is rather pretty, except that she is pale. She is visibly Seabury's cousin, and has the same dark curls and emphatic features. Her eyes are brown, however. I suppose I may as well own, while I am at it, that Lady Susan Manning is a very well-looking woman too, and hardly shows her age (the devil prompts me to add), either in appearance or in behaviour. She is blond and light-complected, and except that she squints continually she is quite attractive.

I may truthfully mention, my dear Angel, that I have seen no one here at all pretty enough to rival you. You have a freshness no London toast can aspire to, so do not start thinking of yourself as a poor country mouse. All this talk of looks lead me to my first interview yesterday with Lady Beatrice. We visited her yesterday after mass (dreadfully tedious!), "we" being all of Rucke House save the impious Romby. Lady Beatrice herself must be near sixty-five; she is grey-haired, fat and frank. Like her brother, she is immoderate in her pleasures, free in her language, and really quite coarse (can such a stricture come from me?) in her notions and expressions. These are qualities of the last century, of course, and I daresay her ladyship and Romby consider themselves simply too old to change. Perhaps, I may even speculate, they would not if they could. Lady Beatrice is a widow since 1807, when her husband, the Marquis of Bree, died of the scarlet fever. The pair had no children, and so the marchioness has had nothing but her own pleasure to consult these past ten years, a habit she seems to have taken to heart. Though her fortune is but little more than adequate to her style of life, there is some considerable curiosity as to how she will eventually dispose of it. Seabury is the obvious choice, but she does not appear to admire him altogether; and Miss Meredith being the next most reasonable prospect, it will be interesting to see how she chuses.

What morbid considerations! Lady Beatrice continues quite alive for the moment, so let me concern myself with that. When she saw me it was all she could do to keep from sending me back to Berkshire straightway: apparently, my dear, I am no beauty by London standards. Where I am lean I ought to be plump; where angular, round; my back is too long, my cheek-bones too high... In short, everything is wrong with me, and nothing right. "You will be quite difficult; quite difficult, I am afraid," is how Lady Beatrice expressed it, waddling slowly round me and clucking with disapproval.

"I shall try to please," said I politely.

"You will need to do more than try. You will need to change."

"I beg your pardon, ma'am, but what exigence is this which requires my alteration?"

"The exigence of finding you a husband," said she, surprised. "I hope you had no other aims in mind, for this by itself will be hard enough."

"If it is all the same to you, I will spare you that difficulty," I replied. "I do not want a husband."

"That is very good; that will do for a start."

"I beg your pardon?"

"This business of not wanting a husband. It is an old trick—but it works more often than not, for all that. Yes, start with that line, and about mid-season—oh, by June at the latest—we will bruit it about that you have changed your mind. Or no, that Lord Such-and-Such has prevailed upon you to change your mind. Yes, that is very good." She paced around me as she laid out this scheme, for all the world like a general round his *aide-de-camp*. "Do you sing?" she snapped at me of a sudden.

"No. Not well, I mean. Though frequently I do sing."

"Never mind. Dance?"

"Somewhat."

"Lessons," was her decision. "Seabury, find her a dancing-master," she called over her shoulder—for you must understand that this evaluation of my prospects was going forward in a room full of people. She returned to the examination of my person. "Green eyes, thin cheeks, thick hair—it is thick, is it not?"

"Not too thick," I said, but she ignored me.

"High colour—that's something—and good large eyes; thin neck, long teeth, long hands... What happened to you in your youth, gal? You look as if you had been stretched on the rack. And speaking of youth," she continued, before I had answered, "how old are you?"

"Twenty-three."

"*Shh!*" hissed she, furiously. She glanced round to see if Lady Susan or her mother had been listening. Apparently satisfied they had not, she went on in a whisper, "Say you are twenty-one. *That* is bad enough."

This made me laugh, and Lady Beatrice grew friendlier. "I like you, my girl," she said, "and scrawny as you are, I shall help you find a husband. But you must promise me that when you and that husband have a daughter, if I have the astonishment to be still alive at her sixteenth birthday, you will *not* send her to me to make her come-out. It was I who brought out Lady Lillian, you know, for her own mother was a bumbler and a fool; and that was enough bringing-out for me. I only agreed to help you as a favour to your brother; I was always partial to Humphrey."

"So am I," said I, feeling a bit lonely.

"That speaks well for you; I wish I could think of something that spoke well for Miss Amy," she added in a murmur, "but I suppose at least she has her looks. You..." Her voice trailed off as she eyed me despondently.

"It is not so terrible as all that," I protested. "I have had offers in Berkshire, after all, so I cannot be so very plain." You see I had already bowed to her presumption that I wished to marry; at the moment it seemed as if it would occasion some amusing episodes, if nothing else.

"Country offers are a different thing. No, I am afraid what we must do," Lady Beatrice informed me, "is invent a character for you—develop a style which, though perhaps not the fashion, is particularly yours. For a start, let us dress you only in—what is your best colour?" she interrupted herself to ask.

"Yellow."

"Yellow! It cannot be yellow. What a very vulgar, tawdry hue. Think of another; what do you say to rose, a very dusky, muted rose?"

"Rose is pleasant," said I meekly.

"Then rose it must be. Seabury, send Lady Caroline here tomorrow, and I will have my dressmaker come at the same hour. Send her at four o'clock. No, not my dressmaker," she went on to herself. "Someone more modish. Lady Susan, who sews your—no, never mind. Never mind," she muttered twice, while Lady Susan looked questioningly in her direction. "I will find you a clever dressmaker, trust me," she whispered confidingly to me. "And do try to think of some acceptable eccentricities for yourself. You must begin to cultivate them at once, or no one will ever believe you."

I have given you this dialogue at some length in hopes it would divert you, and also because Seabury has very kindly offered to frank my letters—

Lady Caroline Wythe paused mid-sentence, her head tilted in a listening attitude. Had she heard a crash? Unlikely—but yes, and it was followed by a shout, then an unmistakeable wail in the entryway. Within instants her ears informed her unequivocally that positive pandemonium reigned below. Shrieks, halloas, keening—Lady Caro dropped her pen (it formed a perfectly enormous ink blot over her open, evenly drawn characters) and rushed out to the landing of the oaken stairway. From this vantage point she surveyed a sorry scene: Romby (bent with age though he was) poking his cane and shouting at Miss Amy Meredith, who stood amid a pool of porcelain shards, yelping and howling by turns.

"By God I will see you hanged for this!" thundered the old tartar. "You will finish in the workhouse, that you will, you vicious little thief!"

"Help!" shrilled Miss Amy, most pitifully. "Help me! Henry, Henry, he will kill me! Oh, someone! Oh, you fiend!" she added, dodging a thrust of the earl's ivory stick.

"Kill you? I will do worse than kill you, you wild young hoyden. Steal my vase, would you?"

"Heaven defend me!" squealed the pious Amy. "Why will you insist upon that, sir? I never stole your vase—"

"Because I caught you," he broke in, snarling. "I caught you—and your hurled it to the ground for spite, and smashed it."

"You startled me! It dropped," Amy contradicted.

"Dropped, did it? Startled? And what were you doing, pray, that you jumped when I came in? Only the guilty jump like that, my girl."

"But you stuck your cane in my back—you know you did!"

"And why should I do that?"

"And why should I steal your vase?" countered Amy, with a semblance of spirit soon belied by a renewed outbreak of tears and whimpers.

"Wretch! She-ape!" bellowed his lordship.

"Hartshorn! Sal-volatile!" pleaded Amy, looking indeed as if she might faint if these restoratives were not quickly applied.

"My dear sir," Lady Caro at last interrupted, still on the balcony above them. "My dear Amy! I must implore you both to put a period to this spectacle as soon as possible. It is well to be generous with one's servants, certainly, but to provide such an entertainment as this is doing it a bit brown, my friends;" and she indicated, with a nod of her head, the doorway leading to the kitchens, were half a dozen persons had assembled to view the interesting scuffle.

"Damn them," muttered Romby succinctly.

"Oh Lady Caroline, pray, pray do help me," begged Amy, adding in a loud whisper, "his lordship has gone mad again."

Lady Caro descended, sent one curious servant to fetch Mrs. Henry, another after a bottle of hartshorn, and directed a third to sweep up the fragments of the disputed vase. Lord Romby eyed her distrustfully through all of this but seemed unwilling to quit the scene, even when the officious Mrs. Henry (whom he particularly detested) appeared.

"Can you not keep your charge in hand?" he demanded of her, hobbling after the ladies as they assisted Amy to a couch in the nearest drawing-room. "I found her attempting to make off with one of my China vases, and now she has dashed it to the ground and destroyed it."

Miss Meredith moaned faintly.

"Merciful Heavens, listen to the man!" said Mrs. Henry, appealing to Caroline. "As if my poor angel could ever conceive of such a thing!"

Miss Windle, having finally heard of the commotion (she had been hopelessly lost in Mrs. Radcliffe's *An Italian Romance*) now flew through the drawing-room doors clutching a handful of feathers. "Here is help," she cried; "here am I. You, footman, fetch a glass of wine for the young lady."

"Wine?" Mrs. Henry repeated hollowly, looking up at Windle from where she knelt by the afflicted Miss Meredith.

"Yes indeed, wine," Windle insisted, proceeding to the fireplace, where a small flame burned steadily. Here she lit a candle, and over the candle singed the feathers she carried.

"Miss Meredith is in no need of your feathers, nor your wine either. In fact, she is so little in the habit of drinking wine, I should not be the least bit surprised if the draught you suggest to revive her killed her instead."

"What have you administered?" Windle inquired suspiciously, looking at the bottle Mrs. Henry held to the girl's nose. "Not sal-volatile, I hope?"

"Hartshorn," said Henry, with dignity, "and we will be most appreciative if you will stop burning those horrid feathers."

"There is nothing like burnt feathers to revive a young lady," Miss Windle said tightly.

"Save hartshorn, you mean," said Henry.

"Spirit of hartshorn or salt of hartshorn?" asked Windle, unwilling to give an inch. Lady Caroline turned their bickering to good advantage by leaving the room while they were so distracted; she took Lord Romby (though he resisted) along with her.

"My dear sir," she said to the old gentleman, when they were closeted safely in the Gilt Saloon, "this is really coming it a bit strong, I think."

Romby ignored this charge and took up the offensive himself. "I shall thank you not to meddle in my affairs, young lady," he said. "I do not like you, and I tell you so to your head."

"You do not know me," Caroline objected.

"I have no need to."

"Anyway, it is ridiculous to say you do not like me. Everybody likes me; I am universally liked."

"Gammon."

"It is not gammon at all. Even Lady Lillian likes me, after a fashion."

"Now I know you are talking gibberish, for I may remind you that Lady Lillian is my daughter, and I know she never in her life liked anyone above half. Except your brother," he appended grudgingly.

"And me."

"Rant."

"It is not."

"Fustian."

"Not in the least."

"Absolutely," said his lordship, rounding on her. "And even if she does like you, that is no reason why I may not."

"Then you are a silly dotard who does not know a friend when he sees one," said she.

The Earl of Romby was a tall, stooping, grey old man, but at this he leaped from his chair with all the spryness of a boy. "You will not tell me who is a dotard, miss" said he vehemently, waving a crooked finger in the neighborhood of her nose. "I shall know who my friends are when you are mouldering in your grave."

"The devil a bit you will."

"Devil a bit, is it?" he echoed. "Who taught you such words?"

"Humphrey," Caroline said calmly.

"Oh, Inlowe was it? A fine pice of language for a lord to teach his sister," Romby growled, but Caro could see he rather admired than deplored her mannish speech. "On that head, I may say I never did think it said much for your brother that he took such a fancy to Lillian. What a creature it is! Seabury is bad enough, but if I had to live with her I swear I should cut my throat."

"I suppose it is a mystery to you where she learned to be so hard," Lady Caroline observed coolly.

"Oh, you are a fine chit, my lady! Already all of twenty, I should guess, and judging your elders like the Lord on Domesday."

Caroline smiled sweetly. "Dreadful, am I not?"

"Worse." Romby, who had been stalking about the room, chose this moment to settle into a high-backed plush-covered chair. When he sat, his rounded shoulders fell forward even more, and since his neck sketched more a horizontal than a vertical line, he looked very like a weary vulture. Surveying him, Caro could see how handsome he must once have been; but time had dealt harshly with him and those traits which were formerly proud and fine were now sunken and painfully withered. His colour, as she watched, subsided from the heights to which anger had raised it, leaving behind an ashen complexion. He looked, once more, frail and old. Caroline thought he had tired of opposing her, but after a moment he said, "How should you like to go home again, and leave me in peace?"

"That I shall do," answered she, "in time. But do I truly disturb your peace so terribly much?"

"My dear ma'am," he said heavily, "before the arrival of your crony Miss Meredith—followed with such lamentable haste by your own coming—Rucke House was the home of two bachelors, pure and simple. There was none of the nonsense you see here now, no abigails running hither and yon, no bells ringing every quarter of an hour, no dressing for dinner—no dressing at all, on some days!—and most important, no niffy-naffy, mealy-mouthed, middle-aged ape leaders. Life was pleasant then! I could wake at eleven, growl at my valet till one, sip chocolate till two, rise at three, badger Seabury for money till five, dine—"

"Ah, but you see," Lady Caroline interrupted, "here is just the sort of thing I mean, my lord. I have no opinion at all of Seabury's pinching your pennies for you; it is most shocking! How can you have allowed such a monstrous situation to have developed in the first place?"

She had uttered magic words, it appeared, for now Romby answered freely, his blue eyes (the same almost as his son's) flashing as he warmed to his subject. "How indeed? How indeed? Ha! I shall tell you how indeed. Trickery! Villainy! Magistrates," he spat out with disgust. "Arbiters of justice plotted with my son, suggested, phrased, made legal this abomination of a budget. They schemed with him, advised him—barristers, solicitors, counsellors—rogues, rogues every blasted one of them! My note of hand is not worth the paper it is written on—all London knows that. And how they did it, since you inquire, was by encouraging me to consume, one night, four bottles of claret, then waking me at six the next morning to put my name to some papers. I might as well have signed my own death warrant, as it now appears. But

the worst of it—all this is not the worst of it, dear ma'am,"
he noted, glaring at her, "the most unbearable of all is that
Seabury has gone to my club, to Brooks's Club, to the
very place where I waited while his mother gave birth to
him—to Brooks's, I say, where wagers were once laid on
his turning out a boy or a girl—and had me barred from
the gaming-tables. Now that is a doleful tale if ever I heard
one, and I have heard two or three." Romby rapped his
ivory stick against the parqueted floor as if to punctuate
this conclusion.

Lady Caroline had listened to him with profound
interest; she sat in reflective silence for a few instants, then
declared, "This is even more horrid than I thought."

The earl *harrumphed* loudly to signify his approval of
her new estimation of his difficulties. He was surprised at
finding her so sympathetic, but not too surprised to be
pleased as well. "I omit a complete account of my
humiliations," he murmured, "and trust your imagination
to sketch in the details."

"They are very easily guessed," said Caro, with
growing indignation. "Sharper than a serpent's tooth
indeed; a good deal sharper. What an odious course of
action! It passes all bounds, truly. I hope you will believe
me your friend, sir, for I cannot hear such an history as
this unmoved. Such prodigious meanness! Surely there
must be some weapon to combat it. Seabury is the
greatest beast in nature, to rob his father of both pleasure
and power, and in full view of society as well! To be sure,
his bearing is not that of a tolerant man; indeed, I fancy
there is cruelty in the lines about his mouth... And yet, to
serve you so ill—" But Lord Romby, who sat facing the
doorway, had begun looking past her so pointedly that
she finally broke off her own sentence to see what had
caught his attention there. She whirled round, her next
words on her lips—but there they froze, for Lady
Caroline found herself face to face with the greatest beast
in nature.

Chapter II

After an agonising half-minute of silent confrontation, Lady Caroline realized what she ought to have known from the first: her host, if he had indeed overheard anything she said to his prejudice, was by far too courteous to admit it. True to form, he smiled pleasantly and informed her that the carriage to take her to Lady Beatrice's was being held in readiness at the door. "It is all very well," thought she to herself when, after a few hasty preparations, she had taken her place in it, "it is all very well to be polite; but now I have no notion whether he heard me or not." It was disagreeable to consider, but she rather fancied he had, from the look in his eyes. Besides, what other reason could he have had for hesitating before he delivered his message to her? And yet his voice had been every bit as smooth and even as it was habitually. There was no use in refining upon the point in any case, she concluded, as the coach bore her down South Audley Street. Either he had, or he had not; speculation could not change the fact.

Still, she was visibly preoccupied when Lady Beatrice found her in the drawing-room, and the venerable marchioness at once set about discovering what so absorbed her. "Not homesick, I hope?" she hazarded, while they walked side by side to the chamber where the dressmaker awaited them.

"No; or only a little," she amended. "It is nothing, really."

"I will not tease you about it, but please have the goodness not to infer from that that I believe your rather spiritless explanation," said the old lady agreeably. "And now tell me how you find my nephew. Is he not handsome?"

"Yes," replied Caroline, reddening. "Quite an Apollo."

"Yes. The great Sahara is also very handsome, do you not think?"

"I have heard it is," she answered, puzzled.

"It is; I have seen it. But it is a little dry as well; doubtless you have heard that too."

Caroline nodded, trying at the same time to look as much as possible as if she did not comprehend the reference. Lady Beatrice insisted upon continuing this interesting conversation even as the clever dressmaker, Mrs. Alsweet by name, took Caro's measurements and made her suggestions, although Caroline did everything she could to turn the subject.

"I have always dealt well with Lord Seabury," said that gentleman's aunt. "He is a good man, though austere. I shall be sorry to see him marry Lady Susan—you know he is expected to marry her, I suppose?"

"Yes. She seemed a very amiable girl to me," lied Caro. "Was not her hair dressed à la Titus? I should like to dress my hair that way. Do you suppose—"

"She is not an amiable girl at all," the marchioness interrupted, declining to leave her topic. "She is a fish. A trout, I would say, or a cod. Spiritually, that is—you understand, my dear."

"Actually," said Caro, smiling in spite of herself, "she did rather put me in mind of a fish."

"I am not surprised. It is the expression of her eyes, in especial. The resemblance is quite marked. And yet Seabury never sees it in the least. He professes to consider her a diamond of the first water. It is really ridiculous." Lady Beatrice now appeared to be thinking aloud, and she went on in this vein in spite of Mrs. Alsweet's actively seeking her attention. "Why will young people be so obstinate? It is extremely vexatious. I have as much as sworn to Seabury that a marriage to Susan would be tantamount to burying oneself alive, but he will not hear me. No, he insists, she is unexceptionable, entirely unexceptionable. He seems to believe that is the highest praise that may be given to a woman: that she is unexceptionable! Where can he have learned such a credo? Certainly not from Romby—and by the way, what do you think of my brother?"

This was a less confusing topic for Caro, and she went on at some length giving her impressions of the earl. Mrs. Alsweet, ever busy about her work, cried out as if with pain when she learned Caro's dresses were all to be of a single colour, but her objections were firmly overridden by Lady Beatrice. Her visit, which lasted above two hours, was thrice interrupted, first by the milliner and then by the corsetier. Later came a silk mercer, in company with the linen-draper who had been so fortunate as to have enjoyed Lady Beatrice's patronage these past forty years; and all these persons hummed and bustled about, disputing, comparing, and privately forming very low opinions of one another until Lady Caroline could bear no more. Just at the moment she thought she certainly must scream if her desires were consulted (and subtly twisted to agree with those of a tradesman) once more, Lady Beatrice dismissed them all and swept them out of the chamber. She was tired; she would dine. She hoped Lady Caro would dine with her.

This Caroline was happy to do, first sending a note round to Rucke House to explain her prolonged absence. Then she enjoyed a perfectly delightful repast, indulging herself (since there was no one but the comfortable marchioness to see) in three servings of a neat French pie very tastily prepared. Lady Beatrice's considerable girth was soon explained by observing her at table: she ate a very good deal, and she clearly preferred rich foods. Caroline herself was by nature slender, and was therefore never obliged to trouble herself about how much dinner she ate, but she could easily comprehend that with such a cook as Lady Beatrice had, even a slight person might grow large. She was praising the sauce on the turbot when the under-butler appeared in the doorway of the dining-room. He looked at his mistress, hesitated, coughed a little and finally came forward bearing a small silver tray. On it was a card, which he offered to the marchioness. "I was not certain—" he began, leaving the sentence dangling.

Her ladyship took the card, smiled, frowned, and looked up at Caroline. "It is Ansel Walfish, a particular friend of mine. He is, I fear, much in the habit of calling just at dinner-time. The poor man is a bachelor, and I suppose his income is insufficient to keep a cook. Will it disturb you if I invite him to join us? He is rather pleasant."

Lady Caroline of course replied that Mr. Walfish must on no account be turned away for her sake.

"That is a dear girl," said her hostess, giving the order to have the caller shown in. He appeared a few moments later, still carrying his stick. He was of middle height, fair-haired, about thirty years of age. Light-complected, with regular features and a mild expression, Mr. Walfish relied mainly on his clothing to mark him out from the other young men of quality. Tonight he wore Wellington Trousers and a blue frockcoat, two waistcosts (one striped, one plain) with gilded buttons, a gilded quizzing-glass, glossy highlows, a fob with three seals, and a cravat tied *à la Bergami*. Such splendour was quite unknown to Caroline, and if truth be told, she could not help but think it a trifle overdone; indeed, it was all she could do in the first few minutes of her acquaintance with this gentleman to keep from laughing aloud. She later learned that there were tulips with far greater pretensions to elegance even than Mr. Walfish, who dressed and behaved with much more pronounced affectation. She, understandably, had been using Lord Seabury as a standard for comparison, but since (as she came to realize) he favoured only the most understated of fashions, this had been misleading.

Mr. Walfish saluted his hostess with a graceful bow and a brief dry, peck at her hand; then he observed Lady Caro for the first time, quizzed her, and sank into a sea of courtesies. "Oh dear, my good, my most super-excellent friend, how horribly I have imposed upon you! If only I had known—! I am sorry beyond words; you know how anti-agreeable rudeness is to me—it is what I dislike above all things. But here am I, intruding with absolute hyper-coolness into what I now discover was a party of the most select character. Pray believe me, if I had had even the slightest inkling, even a micro-inkling I may say, I should never have—"

"In the name of all that is reasonable, I beg you will be still a moment," Lady Beatrice interrupted him. "Lady Caroline is my relative; she is but newly arrived in town; and if you continue at such a fever pitch of civility I am afraid she will also quit it forthwith. Now pray do sit down and dine with us—you see where a cover has been laid for you—and tell me what you have been doing."

The gentleman thus applied to obediently sat at table and allowed a few morsels of food to be placed on the plate before him. "But who is this glorious damsel?" he demanded. "You have kept her a deep secret, dear Lady Beatrice!"

Lady Caroline, who did not especially enjoy being discussed in the third person while she was in the room, replied to this question herself. "I am the sister of the husband of a niece of her ladyship; not a near relation, as you see, but Lady Beatrice had been very gracious towards me nevertheless."

"Oh, fiddlestick," said her ladyship. "I refused to take her in; judge for yourself if that is graciousness. She stops at Seabury's. This is a scheme of his, this bringing-out of young ladies."

"Oh, are you to make your come-out, then? How perfectly charming."

"I am a little old for it, I th—"

But she was hastily cut off by her hostess, who would not allow her to hang herself in such a manner. "We had hoped Caroline would come last year," she said mendaciously, "but it proved impossible in the event."

"The intervening twelvemonth has but placed a greater bloom on your cheek," Walfish remarked, "for the rose there now could not be improved."

New as she was to the world of the *ton*, Caroline had a pretty shrewd idea how her plain sarsenet gown and country toilette must appear to this town tulip. "You are kind to say so, sir; Lady Beatrice has been at considerable pains today to mend the deficiencies of my costume."

"Hardly necessary, my dear ma'am," said Walfish, but even he could not deliver such a falsehood as this without wanting to laugh, a desire which he camouflaged unsuccessfully in the guise of a cough. "You will have a dozen offers before the end of a fortnight, depend upon it."

Caro smiled. "My young friend is not interested in offers," Lady Beatrice said pointedly. "Are you, my dear?"

Caroline, her mouth full of roast turkey, shook her head.

Mr. Walfish raised his eyebrows but said nothing to indicate incredulity. "Will it be a very large come-out? I suppose it is hypo-delicate of me to inquire, but I know you will forgive me."

"Yes Ansel, it will; and you will be invited, so set your mind at rest. And while you are adjusting your mind, I wish you would remove all those little Greek flags from your vocabulary."

Mr. Walfish politely ignored the insult to his modish pseudo-classical terminology, asked when the come-out was to be, took out a little book, and made a note of the date. "You have no notion how full my calendar becomes sometimes," he observed apologetically, adding, "not but what the date is forever engraved in my memory already, dear ma'ams."

"Heavens no, we are certain of that," said the older lady, adding a moment later, "what date did I say, now? I did tell you the twelfth, did I not? I protest, I am positively in my dotage now-a-days, and can barely remember my name."

Mr. Walfish said yes. Mr. Walfish said no. Mr. Walfish said, "I think so." At last Mr. Walfish was obliged to take out his little book again and consult it. Lady Caro enjoyed the spectacle greatly and (reflecting that she was, after all, supposed to cultivate eccentricity) gave in to her impulse and laughed very long. Lady Beatrice joined her, and even Mr. Walfish yielded in the end and grinned at his own foolishness. The under-butler, unobserved, smiled silently into a napkin.

Rucke House, April 14.

My dearest, kindest Angela,

Well, I am launched, as one may say, and though it may seem odd I must report that I feel no different from when I was not "out" at all. What a pucker we were in, though, on Saturday! The guests were not expected until eight, but we were obliged to rise at ten in the morning—the crack of dawn in London!—and fuss and flutter about all day. I am told this is a part of the proceedings, and that I could not have been properly introduced into society if I had not passed that whole day in the most exalted agitation; if that is the case, I must be farther out than most, for I promise you there is nothing like ten women despairing over my appearance to set my teeth on edge. I was released at last (and not a moment to soon) in a ball-dress of ivory satin (even I, it was felt, could not wear rose at my come-out), veiled with Brussels net. A wide satin bandeau was placed upon my head, which was coiffed (you would not recognize me) in an hundred curls, and laced with satin ribands. The merest wisps of satin did for my slippers, and my stays (I may tell you) gave every sign of having been forged of steel, and ornamented with thorns. Lady Beatrice, who as I told you in my last letter is the dearest, roughest creature on earth, gave me a most extraordinary fan to carry—with a watch in the handle!—made of mother-of-pearl; and I wore the rope of pearls Humphrey gave me for my sixteenth birthday wound closely round my neck to complement it. My ministering angel also lent me a pair of pearl ear-drops, and a ring set with three black pearls (daring and distinctive, my dear) to wear over my gloves. The glovers here, by the way, are excessively careful in their measurements; I was two hours, almost, having mine fitted.

Lady Beatrice expressed satisfaction with the result of

all these efforts, especially congratulating herself on the sheen of the satin she had chosen for me, which she insisted improved the colour of my eyes from a mere common sea-green to a deep, vibrant, forest-green. Be that as it may, I was glad to have something to please her, since from her first estimation of me I thought I must always be a disappointment. I was not, naturally, the only one undergoing this torture: Miss Amy Meredith, about whom I have written before, was subjected to it as well for, as I think I mentioned, the come-out was for both of us. She submitted to the process with somewhat a better grace than myself, being (I do not think even she would contradict me on this point) a good deal more interested in fashion than myself; besides, she is finer material than I for this sort of thing. She issued from the hands of our tormentors looking considerably lovelier than I—for it is ridiculous to imagine that, with my excessive height and angularity, I could even appear lovely, or charming, or adorable in any degree; however, I will own to looking magnificent, so do not pity me. Anyway, this Amy simply sparkled her way through the evening. Windle said I was much the prettier of the two of us, but you know what Windle is. The truly shocking thing was, that compared to Amy I not only looked less precious I also looked—just the tiniest bit—old. This is a terrible thing indeed, and one to which we must somehow put a stop!

To continue with this fascinating history, somehow the day was survived by all, and the evening arrived at. There was an awkward moment just before the first guests came, when we all—I mean Romby, Seabury, Lady Beatrice, we two gorgeous young ladies and our chaperones—stood about in Lady Beatrice's grand drawing-room trying hard not to breathe and so disturb our finery. "You are an enchanting picture," said Seabury to Miss Meredith, though without much feeling.

"I thank you, cousin," said she. She is something in awe of him, I believe; as indeed she should be in awe of anyone who can say the alphabet backwards, or count to ten thousand, or perform any other useful and difficult feat which she cannot.

"I think Lady Caroline is very beautiful tonight too," said Windle loudly, to save what she fancied was my wounded self-esteem.

I thanked her and returned the complement directly.

To my astonishment she blushed up to her eyes! "Oh," said she, "I am sure no one else thinks so." And then she cast a glance at Romby!

Now this is something I did not expect, dear Angela. Let us only hope that my chaperone will not require a chaperone.

I was under the necessity, of course, of making the acquaintance of a very large number of people that night, for the marchioness is something of an institution among society, and seems to know everybody in the world, but I will not burden you with more details than need be. Suffice it to say that my hand was tired of being shaken, and my lips of smiling, long before the evening had ended. What I did not weary of, though, was dancing, for this I find is quite wonderful. Thanks to my dancing-master here, my feet are no longer the slaves of that miserable little set of *contredanses* you and I have so frequently walked through at the assembly-hall in High Bowen. On the contrary, they positively fly through the figures, skip and bounce and pirouette in a way most marvelous to behold. I always rather suspected I could dance, my dear, and I reflect with both complacency and gratification that I was absolutely right. It was my honour, too, to stand up with Seabury for the first dance, and I discovered to my surprise that he also dances wonderfully well! If I say this has made me a little more in love with him than his blue eyes had already done, you will think I am shallow and frivolous; but if I say otherwise I should lie; and so I think I shall not mention the subject at all, and thus avert misfortune.

One quite interesting episode I shall mention, however, and that is the following. I had just returned to Lady Beatrice's side after dancing a quadrille with Ansel Walfish, a particular friend to the marchioness, when a gentleman with a strangely lupine countenance came up to me and called me by name. I assumed I had met him earlier in the evening and forgot him, for he did not look familiar; so I offered my apologies, using the sudden rush of new faces as my excuse.

"But I made your acquaintance long before tonight," said the gentleman, grinning oddly. "Do you not recall me? Of course, if you prefer to deny the acquaintance, that is your prerogative..."

"There is no one in my life, so far as I recall, whose acquaintance I feel the need to deny," said I, "and yet I do not remember you, sir."

"Look at me again," he suggested, and (though I detest this sort of parlour-game—except in parlours, I mean) I obliged him. Let me tell you what I saw, and then you (for you know him too!) may decide if you blame me for forgetting him. He is about eight-and-twenty years of age; his complexion sallow and his hair jet black. His eyes, too, are black, and glint peculiarly. They are set rather strangely beneath his dark brows, which is, I think, what makes him resemble a wolf. He is half a head taller than I, narrow-shouldered, clean-shaven, and fastidious. His voice, though deep, has an odd edge to it, an edge which sometimes whines, sometimes accuses. Can you see him in your mind yet? The last details are these: a long nose broken just below the bridge; thin, pale lips—and yet for all this, he is not ugly! Indeed, if one admires savage things (and not a few do, now-a-days) he is rather well-looking.

Well, I am doing what a moment ago I said I loathed: forcing you to divine what I may just as easily tell you at once—though you have the luxury of looking ahead in the letter, or I should have stopped ere this. In any case, if you did not guess, I will be comforted, for I certainly did not. The man's name is Armand Mockabee—Baron Mockabee, since several years ago—and when you were twelve, and I fourteen, we used to hide by the road expressly for the purpose of watching him go by. Not only that, but I have some memory of leaving *billets-doux* for him where we thought he might find them, and signing them "*Incognita.*" Are you blushing? I would stake my life on it you are. Yes, my dear, I had found the object of our first, mutual love-fit. All would be well enough if we had

had more discretion, but if you remember correctly, you will recall that I cast caution to the winds one day and stepped forward in person to declare my ardent admiration of him. Now, I had forgot him entirely within months (for you know he laughed in my face at my confession) and, very sensibly, chose to continue to suppress the memory; but Baron Mockabee, alas, did not. When he finally told me his name on Saturday night, all of the above rushed back to me, as he could easily perceive by my sudden colour.

"I am relieved to see you do know me after all," said he, smiling not altogether pleasantly. "I trust you are as well as you look. How is Inlowe?"

I told him Humphrey went on very well, and then he asked after you. This brought the flush to my cheeks again, and finally I declared, "You may imagine my embarrassment before you sir; I hope you will be so kind as to forget the follies of youth. I am no longer half so sentimental as I once was, I assure you."

"Forget? That I should be loth to do," he replied, while Lady Beatrice listened in surprise. "Indeed the episode to which you refer was one of the most flattering of my life; I only regret I was too callow to turn it to good advantage."

"Nevertheless, you did well not to," said I, a little primly.

"I collect, then, that your feelings have changed?"

"You may be certain of it. But how come you to be in London?" I inquired, to turn the topic. "Have you been here long?"

"Oh, I am hardly ever in Berkshire," said he carelessly, while I wondered how his tenants withstood such neglect. "London is the only place that is gay enough for me. How do you enjoy it here?"

At this point Lady Beatrice interrupted, to beg an introduction to Mockabee. "Then you are not acquainted with Lady Beatrice?" said I to him, after obliging her. Methought at once he had come without an invitation, for I cannot tell you how unsavoury an air he has developed.

"No, it was your brother Romby who invited me," said he to her, laughing. I am convinced he knew my suspicions instantly, and that was the cause of his laugh, for there is something very sharp about him that suggests he knows more than he says.

"Are you a member of Brooks's, then?" Lady Beatrice hazarded.

The baron said that he was. "I have lost many a pound to his lordship, too," he added, showing his teeth.

"Well, this is quite a surprise to me," said I, as an uncomfortable silence ensued. "Imagine meeting you in town, after missing you so consistently where we are neighbours."

"To be candid, I must admit it is not a surprise to me," said Mockabee. "I had the honour of driving your carriage part of the way to London."

"I beg your pardon?"

"I say, I took the reins from your coachman during the last stage; do you not recall it?"

"Very plainly," said I, warning myself against a rash response.

"How the Reverend Roundbelly did squeal!" he exclaimed gleefully, recounting the incident to Lady Beatrice, and concluding proudly, "I took ten minutes off the coachman's regular time, you know; so you have had ten minutes more pleasure here, Lady Caroline, and all thanks to me."

I decided it was only fair to give him the opportunity of apologizing before I flew at him in a violent rage. "Dear Baron," I said, governing myself extraordinarily well, "I am afraid you caused more mischief than you know. I was uncomfortable, it is true, but that is hardly a disaster; my chaperone, however, was frightened half out of her wits. That is not even to mention the elderly lady who also travelled with us, nor how it feels to have a very large gentleman (clerical or not) thrown suddenly into one's lap."

But he still stood before me, shameless. "Heyday," cried he, "I begin to believe you do not care for a joke, my lady."

"Not for that joke, I did not. To put it bluntly, I feel it is unconscionable to play such a trick on an unoffending party. I am aware many young gentlemen amuse themselves in this way, but I have no opinion of it."

By now he had discovered I was in earnest, but instead of apologizing he grew surly. "It was all sport," he muttered.

"For you perhaps, but not for the passengers."

This conversation had gone on for so long, and I was so much the centre of attention (merely from the fact of its being *my* come-out), that the persons round us began to stare. "Your ladyship has led too sheltered a life; there is nothing objectionable in so mild a prank as this one."

"I object to it," said I, standing my ground admirably, as you will agree. "I rather expected an apology by now, than an argument, sir; but I see I judged you wrongly." At this point Lady Beatrice became somewhat alarmed by our vehemence, and whispered to me, that eccentricity was one thing, but unruliness quite another. When I ignored her—for I was too angry to listen—she beckoned to Seabury, who stood some little distance away from us with Lady Susan Manning. He came at once, and greeted Mockabee a trifle coolly, as it seemed to me.

I must say for Seabury that he took in the situation very quickly. "There is nothing amiss here, I hope?" he asked, giving Mockabee a stern glance that seemed to say, "My hope had better be answered."

"Baron Mockabee and I have had a disagreement," I told him.

"No question of an insult, I trust?" Seabury pursued. I realized then what he was getting at: he wished to discover whether he ought to call the baron out. The habit of fighting my own battles being deeply engrained in my character, I immediately said there was not. Lord Seabury then led me away to the supper-room and gave me a glass of orgeat (which I did not want), this being the simplest way to curtail the altercation. He did not inquire of me what the dispute concerned, even when we were safely away from the others. Doubtless he considers his discretion very fine and noble; I think it tedious, *mais chacun a` son goût*. Lady Susan by the way, who had no means of knowing why she had been so suddenly deserted, looked at me very cross when we regained the ball-room.

An enemy was hardly what I hoped to acquire in

London, but it seems I have done so, *nolens volens*. I have not yet hit upon a suitable means to settle with the baron, but I am gnawing and fretting at the question all the time, like a dog at his bone, and hope to have a really vengeful scheme invented before the week is out. It will interest you to know, by the bye, that Mockabee did not in the least have the grace to depart after this scene; on the contrary, I saw him dancing with Amy Meredith at two in the morning, by which hour nearly half the other guests had gone home. He avoided my glance, so I suppose he has a nodding acquaintance with shame.

We have received a perfect avalanche of invitations, cards, and visits since the come-out. Tonight I am to dine at Lady Mufftow's, and tomorrow night I shall attend my first opera. How gay it is! I am quite accustomed to the noise from the adjoining streets by now, and even the taste of the water here has become faimilar, if not pleasant. But I do miss you dreadfully, along with everybody else at home. I hope you will convey my compliments to Edgar. Sometimes I get terribly moped just thinking of my nieces. Did you kiss them at all? Theresa will always take a kiss you know, even if Delphina will not. It was so sweet of you to visit Two Towers to look in on Jeannie. My abigail here is named Mary; she is tolerably clever, but nothing so dear as Jean. I do not complain of Mary, you understand, but I wish I had a confidante with me.

I forgot to tell you the best of all (according to Lady Beatrice, at least): Lady Sefton was at my come-out, and she has judged both Amy and me acceptable to be allowed subscriptions to Almack's! What? Not overjoyed? Well my dear, I can only say that it shows a pretty frivolous attitude towards life, not to feel ecstatic when such a privilege is accorded your dearest friend.

Seriously though, it is a great thing to be admitted to Almack's, and may prove very convenient if I ever need to commit suicide, and desire to die of boredom. At least that is what every sensible person I have met tells me of Almack's; Lady Beatrice herself, indeed, confesses it is not the thing itself, but the idea of it, which is so precious.

You asked in your last letter what eccentricities I was to acquire for the benefit of the *ton*. As it happens, Lady

Beatrice and I had a most comfortable cose on that subject on Friday evening, and here is what we resolved: first, that I shall always wear rose, deeper or paler as I please. Next, that I shall develop my own mixture of snuff, carry it, and take it (oh horrible!). Third, that I shall ride every day in the Green Park, in spite of its being less frequented than Hyde Park, with a Newfoundland dog trotting after me. Fourth, that I shall profess not to wish to marry. Fifth, that I shall cultivate spirit and magnificence, while every other damsel in London strives to look languid and interesting. Sixth, that I shall be frank, blunt, or even rude, before I shall be missish. And last, I must somehow contrive to intimate that beneath all this self-assurance and forthrightness there hides a heart easily wounded, pure, loyal, and fierce in its affections. Such a scheme leaves little time for ennui!

Of course those are only the seven chief points. There are lesser ones, and small refinements, that develop every day, such as that I shall carry a walking-stick like a man, and sprinkle my conversation with the less vulgar kinds of cant. The aim, to be candid, is to make me look as far from innocent as possible, yet without permitting anything that might cast a doubt upon my virtue. At least that is what I divine the aim to be; almost every idea is Lady Beatrice's, so I can only guess. Have you any suggestions? We are at a non-plus.

The pen is fairly dropping from my hand, but I must paint one more scene. All night long on my come-out, Miss Windle made sheeps-eyes at Lord Romby. By some means upon which I shall not speculate, she managed to sit next to him at the supper table. He had brought in Lady Crowsley, who is an ancient acquaintance of his, but Windle did not give him a minute in which to address her. She kept up, instead, a ceaseless flow of remarks (completely neglecting her own supper-partner, naturally) directed to him, and seemed not the least bit daunted as his saying nothing but yes and no in reply. À propos of Romby, he and I get on better and better with one another, and have now formed an alliance which I hope will someday be strong enough to overthrow that self-appointed Chancellor of the Exchequer, Seabury.

And not so à propos, this same Seabury's hand on my
waist felt like heaven when we danced. I begin to agree
with Lady Beatrice: what a pity if he marries that Susan!
Adio my love; I must fly.

Ever most affectionately yours,
C. W.

"But my dear sir, I am expected to conduct myself
strangely!" Lady Caroline protested to Romby while they
waited for the remainder of their party to finish dressing.
More than a week had passed since the letter recorded
above had been written, during which time Caroline had
not ceased (during every free moment) to search out a
scheme whereby her revenge upon Baron Mockabee
might be effected. Her days had been so much taken up by
visits and calls—not a few of them from Mockabee
himself—and her nights so much absorbed in the pleasant
whirl of the season, though, that she had had but little
time to think.

Nevertheless, she had finally devised a satisfactory
scheme. Unfortunately, it required the active cooperation
of Lord Romby. She continued after a pause, "Indeed, I
am directed to conduct myself strangely; so la! for your
scruples."

"Still, I do not like it," growled the old earl. "If Lord
Seabury found out it would be the end of me, so do not
think of it further."

"What a stubborn old man you are!" cried Caro,
exasperated. "How could it be the end of you? What a
remark! Do you mean Seabury would murder you? Send
you away? Have you imprisoned?"

"No, naturally not, my fine little hoyden. But he would
be mighty angry; and when he is wrathful, he is most
unpleasant."

"Do you allow him to control you so closely, man? He
has you under his thumb, and merely because he lets you
roar and bellow, you think you have the upper hand!
Come, sir, this will never answer."

"But he would be right, Mistress Spitfire. Deep play
with a set of reckless gamesters is nothing for you to be

mixed up with. It is out of the question, so forget it."

"My lord, pray consider it a while longer," Caroline said more calmly. Her large green eyes, which had been flashing, became milder as they gazed at the elderly gentleman. "Both you and I might benefit from the game—and there need only be one!—and if Seabury does not gain too, at least he loses nothing either. For my sake, will you think of it?"

The door to the drawing-room in which they waited opened as Romby grumbled out a yes, and they were ensconced in Seabury's box at the Opera half an hour later. Romby, who would much rather have gone to Brooks's, sat at the back and coughed and mumbled through the whole of the first act. Caroline found herself flanked by Miss Windle on her right and Miss Meredith on her left. Lady Beatrice had declined to join the party, remarking that she had seen *Don Giovanni* too many times to go when nobody in particular was singing, but Caro had a suspicion that the marchioness was feeling her age more than usually of late, and had preferred for that reason to rest at home. Lord Seabury was on Amy's other side, and Mrs. Henry sat behind him. As the opera began, Lady Caro was sorry to discover that she could see but two thirds of the stage; later she learned that one had one's choice between the side boxes, where the view was obstructed, and the front ones, which were too far from the stage to hear the singing properly. Unhappily, she found it difficult to profit even by the acoustic advantage she ought to have enjoyed, for Miss Meredith—notwithstanding it was the first time either of them had been to the Opera—talked to her continually. "Who is that, I wonder?" she would whisper into Caro's ear.

"Why, it is Leporello, Don Giovanni's servant."

"No, no, my dear. Not on the stage; that man in the box across from us, behind the lady with the ostrich plumes." She pointed with her fan. "I wonder who is her plumassier; are they not lovely feathers?"

Caro did not answer, but Amy went on undisturbed: "See the gentleman in that box... that one... one two three four five boxes from the farthest on the left? Not the one with the curls, the other one. Is he not handsome? He has been quizzing us these past five minutes; do you think he is looking at me or at you? I suppose he might even be looking at Henry or Windle, but it seems most improbable."

"Most."

"Is he not handsome?" repeated Miss Meredith.

"Quite."

"Do you like the Opera? I do."

"Yes."

"Lord Seabury is very attentive to the stage. Look, he is nearly frowning, he is so intent upon the action. I should have thought by his age he would have seen *Don Giovanni* a thousand times or more. Should not you?"

"Quite."

"I like Lord Seabury very much, but he is most disagreeably stern. Also, I think he is too old. Did you know he is full thirty-three?"

"Yes."

"I met him several times when he was younger, you know, but he was just as stern even then. I like Lady Beatrice better, but I am afraid she thinks I am too giddy."

"Quite."

"I beg your pardon?"

"Yes, indeed."

"You have not been listening to me at all, have you?" cried Miss Meredith, stung.

"Most," said Caro. "Exactly. Indeed."

Miss Meredith fell silent till the first interval. Romby disappeared directly as the curtain fell, and a short time afterwards Mr. Ansel Walfish visited them and took the old man's chair. "If you will excuse me, I ought to call upon a few of our neighbours," Lord Seabury said, as soon as the other gentleman had arrived. The ladies gave his lordship leave to go where he would (though he would go to Lady Susan Manning's box, Caroline noted with something like dissatisfaction), expressing their conviction that Mr. Walfish would look after them in his absence, and then fell into easy conversation with that modish young man on the subject of the Opera, and the evening, and the woman with the splended plumes.

"She is not a lady of whom you ought to take note,"

Walfish told Miss Meredith, looking a little uncomfortable.

"But how can one avoid it when she is so very lovely?" Amy smiled. "Who is she?"

"I do not know her name."

"I think you are teasing me, Mr. Walfish," declared Amy. "Now pray tell me, what can she have done to deserve your pretending not to know her name?"

Caroline, who was sophisticated enough to grasp at once just exactly what the lady in question could have done, was about to cut a joke to make her naïve companion drop the subject when an all-too-familiar figure appeared in the doorway of the box. "Mr. Walfish," she whispered quickly, leaning forward, "is there any civil way to deny a person entrance to one's box?"

Ansel regarded her in surprise, then lifted his quizzing-glass and looked towards the door. The first thing he saw was a snowy white cravat tied in the style known as *Irlandaise*. The second thing he saw was the face above it: the sallow, wolf-like face of Baron Mockabee.

Chapter III

"I hope I may join you for a moment," Mockabee began, addressing himself chiefly to Mrs. Henry. "It is not often one meets with so beautiful a party as this; it would be too unkind to allow no one but Mr. Walfish to enjoy it." Even as he begged permission, he made his way into the box, bowing to each lady and speaking in deep, flowing accents.

"I protest, we are too crowded already," Lady Caro broke in, though this was a perfectly indefensible lie.

The baron would probably have bowed to this not very subtle intimation and retired at once, had not Miss Meredith suddenly proclaimed, "I do not feel the least bit crowded; come, sir, and sit next to me." Her brown eyes sparkled gaily at Mockabee, and she showed him a smile much broader than the one she had displayed to Walfish. To her discomfiture, the newcomer did not take the chair she offered, but remained standing.

"You are extremely good, Miss Meredith," said he, "but I cannot risk her ladyship's displeasure. She is sufficiently out of charity with me as it is, I think."

"Her ladyship—oh, Caro," Amy took up. "No, Caroline could not be out of charity with you, could you, Caro?"

"I rather fancy I could, yes, Amy."

The younger lady looked, in confusion, from Caroline to Mockabee and back again. The objects of her attention were staring at one another very steadily—far too steadily, the observant Walfish noted—but saying nothing. Lady Caro's gaze was positively grim; she was in fact at that moment wishing her eyes could bore holes into the baron. Mockabee was reading the expression of her face; he could perceive anger, but he could not guess its extent; nor could he judge how easily it might be dispelled.

"Then I will not intrude myself upon you," Mockabee finally said, very quietly. He bowed and vanished in a moment.

"Why did you do that?" Amy Meredith whined, as soon as he had gone. She looked seriously agitated.

"It was crowded," Caro said simply.

Miss Windle jumped into the fray. "Lady Caroline did very right. Lord Seabury had no idea Baron Mockabee might visit us; he might not have liked it."

"That is not why Caro turned him away," Amy insisted, accurately but rudely. "It was not, was it? Caro is not afraid of Seabury. Caro is afraid of no one. It was pure spite, confess it, Caroline. You did it to deprive me of some pleasant discourse."

"Merciful Heavens, why should I desire to spite you?" Caro said, sincerely puzzled. "In any case, we ought not to discuss it here; what a scene we are making for poor Mr. Walfish!"

"You are the one who is said to be so frank," Amy persisted maddeningly, even as Walfish mendaciously proclaimed his perfect ease. "Why will you not answer me?"

"My dear Miss Meredith," Mrs. Henry stepped in, "this is really not the time to pursue the topic!" It cost the poor lady a good deal to say this, for she doted on Amy despite all her faults, but the situation was becoming distinctly critical.

Ansel Walfish looked miserable, and the moment Lord Seabury returned—which fortunately for the dandy was well before the curtain rose again—he fled the box. Their only visitor during the next interval was Charles Stickney, by far too innocuous a man to be the occasion of contention, and the remainder of the evening passed without incident. On the way home Lord Seabury contrived—or at least it seemed to Caroline that he had had to expend some effort to achieve this result—to sit next to her ladyship in the barouche. Miss Windle was with them (the others were in a second carriage) but still there was some degree of privacy there. "What has put Amy into such high dudgeon?" he inquired, for the lady to whom he referred had indeed stubbornly maintained a dispirited air all evening.

"I cannot guess," said Caroline, as the carriage took a sudden lurch that threw her lightly against the viscount.

"My lady, it was very clear what disturbed—" Miss Windle began to object, but a glance from her mistress, even in the shadowy coach, silenced her before she completed her thought.

"I trust Lady Susan and her parents are well," Caro remarked, to turn the topic.

"Very well indeed. The marquis—Lord Safford I mean—is an admirable man, you know; he has done a great deal for me, particularly in helping me to act properly in Parliament. My own father, I am sorry to say, is very likely incapable of spelling the word, let alone speaking there."

"You are very hard on your father," Caro observed. The carriage lurched in the other direction, but Seabury braced himself immediately and remained where he was. His handsome, pronounced features were but dimly visible; still, Caro thought she saw a grimace of some sort pass over them before he spoke.

"My father has been a little hard on *me* in his time," said he, "but I will not seek to exonerate myself. I am not—" He paused for quite half a minute; then said very slowly, "I am not at all certain that what I did was well done—I mean, taking control of his fortune. If I had not done so, there is every likelihood we would be penniless today; and yet . . . I have turned over the question with the rector at Twinehame many times; he always assures me I acted for the best." The viscount was silent a few more moments; then, "It surprises you to hear me say such a thing, does it not?" he added heavily.

Lady Caroline was moved to speak frankly. "Yes it does, rather. Yes, indeed."

"You think I am a hard man all round, doubtless?" he suggested, smiling more ironically than she ever expected to see him do.

"I—I have thought so, yes."

"Yes." His lordship appeared to be lost in reflection. After what seemed, to the wondering Caroline, an eternity, "So I am indeed," he declared. "Very hard."

They drove on in silence a little while longer. "You will not take it amiss that I answered you so bluntly, will you, my lord?" Caroline suddenly blurted out.

"Do you care for my opinion?" His tone expressed surprise.

Caro, though she later upbraided herself for having done so, dodged the question. Forcing a smile and a lighter tone, she replied, "I care for anyone's opinion, who is near enough to do me violence, sir. One ought to survey one's enemies *à la distance*, I think—if one has any."

Lord Seabury was too polite to demand a better answer. Instead he inquired of Miss Windle how she had enjoyed the excursion. The older lady was only too pleased with this kind attention, and replied at some length, waxing poetical about the Opera, which she compared (it would be hard to say why) to a carriage. The singers were the horses, the audience the passengers, the stage-manager the coachman, and so on. Lord Seabury took the whole ridiculous oration with a profound gravity it scarcely merited; Caroline, immune to all but the most acute of her chaperone's absurdities, watched his lordship carefully. The sentiments he had just expressed in regard to his father were, she realized, frank, touching, and admirable. Yet they failed to move her; he was no more approachable after the admission than he had been before. On the contrary, he appeared if anything heavier, more solemn and sombre than usual. With a demeanour impossibly respectful he heard Miss Windle's every foolish word. Caro simply could not find him sympa-

thetic, though she knew she ought to do so. He was
certainly very handsome, however, she concluded: here
her feelings knew no division.

They arrived at Rucke House somewhat in advance of
the other coach. Mr. Hedgepeth, the butler, opened the
door to them with even greater alacrity than was
customary; the reason of this, they soon discovered, was
that a letter for his lordship had arrived a few minutes
earlier. Seabury scanned it and his brow gathered darkly.
He begged to be excused; the letter came from Lord
Safford and related to some legislation they were
concerned with in Parliament. Would the ladies be so
kind, as to permit his immediate withdrawal? Naturally
they would, and so the viscount retired to his study
forthwith, bowing his good-nights.

"Dear me," yawned Miss Windle, returning his bow
and watching his retreating back. "I am more fatigued
than I knew. Come, my love; you must be exhausted."

"No indeed, I am extraordinarily awake," Caro
disclaimed, striving mightily against the automatic yawn
Miss Windle's provoked. "I believe I shall go to the library
and see if there is not some volume there to lull me to
sleep."

"Very well, if you wish to," said the older lady, yawning
again. "I shall accompany you."

"Goodness no, I could not consider it," Caro said
firmly. "You are dreadfully fagged, it is obvious." She
took Miss Windle's arm and led her towards the staircase.

"I am not so tired as all that, I find," said Windle, ever
eager to do her duty.

"Nonsense, nonsense," protested her ladyship, casting
about wildly for some more persuasive line. "Ah!" she
finally said, triumphantly, "I hear carriage wheels. If you
tarry a moment longer, my dear ma'am, Lord Romby will
see how weary and haggard you are. I am certain you do
not wish that to come to pass."

"Dear me no!" cried the lady in alarm; then,
recollecting herself, added, "I do detest to appear to
disadvantage before any but my oldest friends, you know.
Any," she stressed.

"Oh yes, indeed, yes. I understand entirely," said her

charge, propelling her hastily up the stairs. "Good-night, good-night. I shall be along in a moment."

Miss Windle safely out of the way, she skipped into the library, this being the rendezvous appointed between herself and Romby. It would be easier to meet with him there if the others assumed she had gone to bed. In due time, the old earl ambled into the room, a peculiarly satisfied expression on his face. Later Lady Caroline learned that his gratification proceeded from his having styled Mrs. Henry a sow, and Amy Meredith a piglet, but she was too concerned with her own projects now to quiz him on any of his.

"Will you do it?" she asked at once, even before the old gentleman had sat down.

"Quite desperate, are you?" he said, amused. Slowly he drew a chair up to the dying fire and settled himself among the velvet cushions. "Revenge is but a thin repast, some say, no sweeter to the palate than satisfying to the belly. But you will have it, eh?"

Irritated with his deliberate pace, Caroline placed herself squarely before him and nodded decisively. "You will do it, then?"

Romby paused, then cleared his throat. "I will," he said finally.

"Ah, wonderful, wonderful!" exclaimed Caro, smiling with delight and just barely managing to refrain from throwing her arms around the old man's neck—a gesture that she fancied (accurately) he would not appreciate. "When?"

"All haste, my dear. Such haste!" he observed teasingly. "Well, for one thing, we must wait till you learn to play at cards."

"I can play at cards," she defended herself.

"Not to win, I think. You will be playing with experts, and a good deal more will be at stake than in your country gentlewoman's game."

"But you will teach me," she objected, her green eyes widening perceptibly.

Romby fixed her with a curious gaze. "No, that I shall not do," he said firmly.

"Do you mean you will not help me fleece him?"

"On the contrary, I shall provide all the assistance you can hope for in that line. I mean very simply what I say: I shall not teach you how to win the game of brag. You must learn for yourself; and mind you lose any silly mannerisms that may have answered at home, but will not here. I'll have no giggling at my table, no exclamations of distress or joy. You must learn to play hard, or not at all. You see, my dear, I have some interest in the proposition of doing Baron Mockabee a little mischief—indeed, there is hardly a member of Brooks's who has not some cause to complain of him—but I have no interest at all in teaching you to play at cards. In fact, it sounds rather dull. You must work for your revenge a little; that is my philosophy."

"This is odious," cried she. "Why do you consent, if you only mean to help me by halves?"

"If you do not care for my bargain, you have only to refuse me," he reminded her. "As to why I consent at all, I may tell you that Mockabee tried to have me blackballed at Brooks's some years ago, when Seabury first instituted my allowance. He failed, naturally, but I did not take the attempt in good part. I thought it very low. I feel I owe him something in return. As for the confederates we shall be needing, my friend Lord Deatherage was at loggerheads with Mockabee on that issue of the blackballing, and will be delighted to aid us, I trust. Of course we need a fifth, and I have been pondering all evening who ought to have that honour. I have finally settled, among the many who would seek the position if they knew it to be open, upon Lord Wolfus, on the principle that his grievance against the baron is the freshest. Not three weeks ago Lord Mockabee and Wolfus were to stage a race to Brighton; large sums of money were wagered on it, not only between them but among other members too. At the last possible moment before they were to set off, one of Wolfus' pair stumbled and contrived to throw a shoe. It was then Mockabee's choice, by custom, whether to name a new date or insist on the old one and declare himself winner by default. Everyone assumed he would choose the former, but he did not. Wolfus was astonished, as we all were. I never pretended to excel in matters of honour, but this even pressed *my* limits! There was no explanation for Mockabee's behaviour, unless he is desperate for cash. If he is, the circumstance may, come to think of it, aid your scheme considerably: a hungry man may forget his manners, and a gamester short on the ready sometimes makes mistakes."

"What an abominable man," Lady Caro could not help saying. "Why does no one blackball him?"

Romby shrugged. "For one thing, he is quicker than anybody else I know to accept a wager. That is a quality much valued among gaming men. But even if he were not, his conduct is never entirely reprehensible—at least, not so far as anyone has discovered. He treads near the borders of gentlemanly conduct, but he never deserts them altogether. Even in Wolfus' case, it was undeniably his right to act as he did; it simply was not very handsome."

Unmoved by this explanation, Lady Caroline raised her eyebrows. "All this merely increases my zeal," said she. "I am determined to find a teacher well versed in all the subtleties of brag, so kindly proceed with your half of the bargain with all possible despatch."

"Whom will you ask?" Romby inquired, with that look of amusement Caroline found so annoying.

"Seabury, if I must," she said, still piqued at the earl's refusal to be her tutor himself. "Mockabee, if need be. It does not signify; somehow I shall learn, depend upon it." Upon these words she took her leave of the old man and went, yawning, up to bed. It had been a very fine closing speech, she reflected as her abigail helped her to undress—but who indeed might she ask without arousing suspicion? She would not have been surprised to find that Lady Beatrice was initiated into the finer mysteries of games of chance, but any inquiry in that quarter would be shrewdly made note of, no doubt, and would end in the discovery of her scheme. The same was true of Ansel Walfish, for Caro had noticed that this delicate gentleman repeated almost anything he learned, on almost any head, to his particular friend Lady Beatrice. Seabury of course

could not be asked; that was mere prattle, nor
Mockabee... and so she must ask... must ask... Lady
Caroline dreamt that she asked a sphinx.

In the morning, however, a much more likely source of
intelligence presented itself, in the plumpish form of one
Sir Sidney Pettingill, Bart, who came most conveniently
to call at Rucke House. Despite the rotundity of his
figure, Sir Sidney was a widely admired man, with an
earnest air and such manners as must please. His nose and
eyes were good and his fair hair (only a little carroty)
waved very fashionably. If it had not been for his
chin—that dreadful, meaty, jowly round chin—he might
have been positively attractive... but there was, after all,
that chin. Set in its ample midst was a fleshy pair of lips,
which ever glistened rather strangely—repellently, one
might have said—and an excellent set of teeth. Besides
these attributes, Sir Sidney had twenty thousand a year,
no paltry sum. Between his manners and his purse, Sir
Sidney succeeded pretty well in making himself agreeable
aux dames, and could look nearly anywhere for a wife.
Though only two-and-twenty, he had come into full
possession of his father's estate in Dorset, and was even
(to the delight of numerous matchmaking mammas this
season) quite frankly of a mind to marry and return there
with his fortunate bride.

Lady Caroline did not care a pin for his excellent purse
or his excellent teeth, but she did seem to recall—could
she really be so fortunate?—that Pettingill played at cards
a good deal, and was in fact a member of Crockfords'.
They had met but once before this morning, at the
come-out, and her memories of that evening were all
jumbled together; but it did seem to her as if Sir Sidney
might have been sent by the gods.

She found Miss Meredith, Mrs. Henry, and her own
Windle already gathered in the drawing-room to which
Sir Sidney had been shown. The talk, as she entered,
appeared to be about the rain that had been falling
abundantly since dawn. Miss Meredith was complaining
of her hair, saying with some coyness that it always lost its
curl in the damp, a circumstance most vexatious to her. "I
suppose you know nothing of such difficulties, dear sir,

with your fine waves. I protest, they would put Lord Byron to shame!"

Pettingill's ordinarily pallid cheeks coloured at this sally, and he waved off the compliment saying. "You are a great deal too kind to me, and too hard upon yourself, Miss Meredith. Is she not, Mrs. Henry? I am sure any young lady in London would pay an hundred pounds, could she but look in the mirror and see such tresses as yours."

Amy appeared much pleased at this praise, casting her eyes downwards very prettily and declaring that Sir Sidney was only being gallant. A small flicker of interest which Caroline observed in his eyes as she herself came into his view seemed to confirm Amy's supposition to a degree the younger woman would probably have deplored, had she been aware of it, but Amy was never, as a rule, aware of very much. The flicker Caro thought she had seen flared up quite plainly as Sir Sidney moved with unusual alacrity to offer her a chair near his. This she accepted, bowing to the company, and sat quietly while she determined how she might best draw him away from the others.

It proved impossible at first, for Amy Meredith, with no inner strength or resources to rely upon in moments of solitude, had not the least intention of allowing their only, and very amiable, guest to escape her before she had a better diversion. On the contrary, she chattered at length about London, about her previous life in the country, about an injured lamb she had once found in a corner of a meadow, and nursed back to health (Caroline suspected strongly that someone else had done the actual nursing, while Amy only visited the animal when the fancy struck her), about everything, in short, that came into her head. Pettingill, who had really come to visit Lady Caro, was about to abandon the effort altogether and go away for the moment when a second caller arrived to distract Miss Meredith. This second visitor being no more overwhelming a personage than Mr. Ansel Walfish, Caro had no difficulty in contriving to leave him with Amy while she and Sir Sidney wandered across the room.

"I am very glad to see you," said Caro candidly when

they had moved a little ways off, "for I have a particular favour to request."

"Anything, madam," was the succinct reply.

Lady Caroline smiled. "I knew you were the man to ask," she murmured, using low tones to prevent the others' hearing. "I must ask you first of all to keep this in confidence—though it is but a trifling matter, after all."

"You have my word, indeed."

"How very obliging you are, Sir Sidney! Now, to the point: I have been playing at cards with my cousin Seabury, and have been losing all the time. You have no notion how conceited he can be in his victories—in a teasing way, I mean, naturally, but still it is most provoking—and I wondered if I might apply to you to teach me how to play better. I am sure the trouble is merely my own ignorance: I have never played before but under the most homely, least competitive conditions. If you could but give me a little idea of how a really good player proceeds—I am told you play marvellously well."

"Oh my, there is not so much to it; simply a little learning allied with a knack for it, you know. What is your game?"

"Brag."

"Indeed? Then you must have other opponents than Seabury, for brag is not a game for two hands. Who are they?"

Caro saw with alarm that she had invented her pretext too hastily. Whom should she name? After a pause of decidedly suspicious length, she answered, "Why, Miss Meredith and our lady companions; but it is not on their account that I am eager to improve my game. It is Seabury who crows over his triumphs."

"I am surprised to hear of such ungentlemanlike behaviour in him—" began Pettingill.

"It is all done in the best of good spirits," she assured him at once. "My object is merely to startle him a little by playing somewhat more wisely the next time we sit down together. You understand: no one cares to be the one who is teased and laughed at all the time. So will you help me?"

"Most assuredly; it is a profound honour to be applied to. I am only sorry the service you request is so trifling," Sir Sidney replied, smiling wetly.

She turned her eyes from that glistening mouth and smiled in return. "Must we sit down for our lesson? Shall I fetch the cards? Or will you merely tell me how I must go on to win?"

"The guiding principles of brag are nothing great," said he. "Most crucial is that you maintain an impassive countenance no matter what occurs. It is equally an error to show your cards are good, as to show they are poor. Say nothing and trust no one. So much for your own expressions."

"This is most helpful," said she. They were walking up and down the long room, and had now reached the fireplace. "I already begin to see where I have been making my mistakes," she added as they turned.

"Indeed, showing too much emotion is the commonest failing of the amateur, but there are subtler ones than that. Even when they do not smile or frown, card players tend to give some sign of pleasure, or lack thereof, when first they see their hand. Some may, for example, rub their temples or twist up their fingers if their cards are nothing worthwhile; whereas the sight of a pair-royal might induce a straightening of stooped shoulders, or encourage the taking of a pinch of snuff to celebrate. This being the case, it is essential that you observe your adversaries closely. Does Seabury have no little mannerisms such as these? A good sober player does not, but if he is careless or excited he may tell you all you wish to know about his hand."

"I have not watched him half closely enough to know if he has such habits or not, but I assure you I shall start immediately. I am most wondrously grateful to you, sir."

Pettingill would hear none of this. He hurried on with his instructions even as the rush of colour into his pale cheeks told of his consciousness. "The accomplished gamester understands the odds against him too. He does not depend upon luck to pull him through but rather disciplines himself to act as his hand indicates. If you have nothing, wager nothing. This requires restraint, but it is essential."

"I believe I can contain myself sufficiently to obey such a law. What else must I know?"

"If you do have something, do not rely upon it

overmuch. A pair with a bragger is very well, unless your neighbour holds a pair. Do you follow me? One ought never to forget, in the joy of receiving good cards, that better ones may be held. And it is much wiser to withdraw from the round at once, the moment one has such a suspicion, than to risk even greater sums by remaining engaged."

"I am indebted to you more than you know, Sir Sidney," she took up. "Is there any other thing I—" But she was prevented from finishing her sentence by Miss Meredith, who was calling insistently across the room.

"Caro, please," she was begging volubly, "Caroline, I pray you, what is the name of Baron Mockabee's estate in Berkshire?"

Her attention once caught, it ran too much against Lady Caro's breeding to answer her petitioner from a distance. It was most annoying to be interrupted before she could be sure of gleaning all she might from Sir Sidney, but it was more impossible still to answer rudeness with rudeness by remaining apart from the others. Instead, she dropped Pettingill's arm and returned to a seat near Windle. Sir Sidney drifted over behind her and sat down too. "I hardly recall," she said when she had at last settled herself again, "but I am almost positive it has an M in it."

"Mockabee? Mockabee Hall, perhaps, or—?" Amy suggested.

"Ah! Morton Hall. That is it," she said. "Why do you ask?"

"Oh, Mr. Walfish and I have been wondering, that is all," Amy said, with marked carelessness.

"I suppose you are acquainted with Baron Mockabee, Mr. Walfish?" Mrs. Henry asked.

"Oh, very slightly," said he. "Sufficiently to admire his cravats; not more than that."

"His cravats are marvels, I think," Amy blurted out suddenly.

"Goodness, such enthusiasm," Miss Windle murmured.

"I did notice, at the Opera," Mrs. Henry concurred heavily, "that Lord Mockabee's neck-tie was very well

arranged. Full of artifice, and yet with the appearance of
ease and accident: this is what I look for in a gentleman's
attire."

This brief speech did much to endear Mrs. Henry to
Ansel Walfish, for she had precisely given his own criteria
with regard to elegance. He took up her theme eagerly,
and the conversation very naturally left Lord Mockabee
behind. For this reason, Mrs. Henry's comment provoked
Miss Meredith just as much as it had pleased Walfish.
Miss Meredith would have liked to discuss the baron
further, a fact which her expression made clear to any
interested observer. Caroline, as an extremely interested
observer, took note of the circumstance and confronted
Amy with it the moment their visitors and chaperones had
left them *tête-à-tête*.

"My dear Amy," She commenced, with sincere distress
in her accents, "I do hope your interest in Baron
Mockabee does not proceed from any attachment you
may be forming—" No sooner had she said this much
than she realized her error. Miss Meredith's pretty face
had at once assumed an expression of the most perfect
resentment, the most complete contrariness: she supposed Lady Caro disliked her, and now addressed her for
spite.

"My dear Caroline," she returned in mocking tones,
"what reason could you have to hope such a thing? What
reason, indeed, have you for caring where I form my
attachments at all?"

"I see you find my concern intrusive, but I assure you it
springs purely from the most disinterested motives. I
merely wish to preserve your happiness."

"And to keep me from Lord Mockabee," Amy added.

"Only if I think he may injure your peace of mind, as I
fear he may. Baron Mockabee is not a kind man, my dear.
He really is not."

"Faugh," came the reply. "Merely because you have
taken him in dislike—for what cause I know not;
probably because he slighted you to dance with me
instead, at our come-out—whatever the cause, in any
case, I shall be grateful if you will not presume to burden
me with your disapproval again. I do not at all seek your

favour, so you may conclude from that how heavily your
disfavour weighs upon me."

Caro flew impulsively into the face of this rebuff. "I am
sorry for your lack of regard for me, but you must at least
give me credit for honesty. This Mockabee is a cool hand,
my dear; he is something of a rake. There are hostesses, in
fact, who bar their doors to him; Lady Beatrice told me so
herself. Truly, of all the gentlemen to whom you have
been presented, Lord Mockabee is perhaps the least
acceptable. Now surely there are other men among our
acquaintance who have shown you more diligent
attentions! Why, with my own eyes I witnessed both
Arthur and John Lanham falling over each other to
please you, not two days ago; and everyone knows Sir
Clement Haslett considers you the beauty of the season.
Come, my dear," she continued gently, "leave off this
curiosity about the baron, and bestow your favour upon
some more assiduous admirer, who deserves it better."

"If I had not seen you turn Lord Mockabee away from
our box last night," Amy said deliberately, "I should be
absolutely certain you desire him for yourself. Indeed,
even as things stand now, I wonder if you do not seek to
divert me, the better to approach him yourself." She
stared suddenly into Caroline's eyes with an intensity
almost ludicrous. "Are you my rival?" she demanded.

"Oh dear, this is more serious than I suspected!" cried
Caro in spite of herself. "Are you indeed so far advanced
in your infatuation? This is dreadfully unsuitable, dear
Amy; this is deplorable."

"You do not answer me."

"Not answer—do you mean, not answer your
ridiculous accusation?" said she, laughing involuntarily.
"How can you suppose me attracted to Lord Mockabee?
Me! After what I have been saying of him!"

"You still do not answer," Amy said, with deep
mistrust.

"My dear girl, of course I am not your rival. I am
nobody's rival, for that matter. I should have thought you
would know that."

Some of the sullen anger went out of Amy's eyes, but
she was not wholly satisfied. "Lady Beatrice thinks you
wish to marry," she said.

"Lady Beatrice is entitled, by rank, age, and purse, to any odd fancies she chuses to have," Caro said, hoping to mollify Amy be speaking lightly. "She is an old love, but she has more opinions than she has grey hairs, and most of them spring exclusively from the same source."

Amy responded sulkily, "I am to understand, then, that you chuse to end your days an ape leader?"

Shrugging, Caro said she thought she might very well.

"I should hate to die an old maid," said Amy. "There was a woman in the village near my father's house who had lived alone since she was twenty, and she was eighty years of age when I knew her! It almost made me weep to think of her."

"Was she unhappy, then?"

"She? Oh not at all; at least, not that showed. It just frightened me to think I might live that way; that was what made me cry."

Caroline had her own opinion of this account, but she kept it to herself. It had struck her forcibly that, for the sake of learning tid-bits about Mockabee, Amy was rapidly leaving behind her old habit of timidity, and entering a new phase of perhaps disastrous forwardness. Apparently the idea of the baron was working very powerfully upon her sensibilities, or else she could never have faced up to Caroline as she had just now. "I am sure there is not the least likelihood of your dying single, nor even of passing your twentieth year in such a state," she said, straining to maintain a conciliatory tone. "You have several of London's most eligible bachelors at your feet already, so by all means enjoy your position, and never fret over improbabilities."

This flattery was finally beginning to reach Miss Meredith's dim consciousness, and she dimpled up pleasantly. "Do you really think they are London's most eligible bachelors?"

"Oh, absolutely," Caro assured her, though this nonsense was costing her quite an effort by now. Fortunately for her, Amy was sufficiently taken with the notion of herself as a presiding beauty to wish to go upstairs and contemplate her image in the mirror. She excused herself therefore, making her way directly to her chamber, where she mooned at herself in the glass above half an hour. Caroline, hardly ever so glad to see someone's back, was left at last to release the laughter— both shocked and amused—that Amy's performance had provoked.

A quiet knock on the drawing-room door, which Amy had left half ajar anyhow, was immediately followed by the entrance into the room of Lord Seabury. "I hope I am not intruding—Oh! Lady Caroline, you are alone," he broke off, surprised.

"Pray sit down sir," said she, her fit of giggling still continuing, and filling her with good will towards all men. "I have not gone mad, I promise you, only Miss Meredith has been telling me such things!"

Seabury, gravely taking a seat, said, "I was not aware my cousin was so witty."

"Witty!" The suggestion sent Caro reeling into another peal of laughter, but the discourtesy of this to his lordship at last stopped her. Still choking, she murmured, "Perhaps she is a wit, as Molière says, in spite of herself. I apologise, my lord. I ought not to laugh so at private jokes," she added contritely.

"I do not suppose you mean to style Miss Meredith a joke."

"Not at all; not a wit, nor a joke." Her temporary euphoria wearing away, Lady Caro began to remember how irksome Seabury's company could be. "I pray you will have the goodness to forget all about this foolish scene, dear sir."

The viscount bowed. "It is forgot. And now I have a favour to ask of you, if you are not too much engaged."

Lady Caro would have taken an oath she saw a blush rising on his lordship's fine cheeks, and yet the proposition seemed so very unlikely. Still, that *was* a deepening of colour; indeed it was, and he was keeping his beautiful blue glance to the floor for all the world like a bashful schoolboy. Irresistibly intrigued, she said, "Anything, my lord."

"The rain seems to have cleared up, Lady Caroline. I should like—" He looked up at her for an instant, then glanced away at once, "I should like to drive out with you in the Park this afternoon, if you care to come. If not," he added fussily, "I am quite prepared to go alone."

The spectacle of this sober, handsome gentleman turned into an embarrassed pup was almost too much for Caroline. "Of course I shall be honoured to accompany you," she replied after a moment, "but I should like to go to the Green Park, if you do not mind."

"It is a matter of the completest indifference to me."

This heavier tone marked a return to his lordship's ordinary manner, a return that left Caroline strangely relieved. A few more phrases sufficed to fill in the details of their proposed excursion, which would take place an hour later, and Caroline quitted the drawing-room at last in order to contemplate this unexpected invitation. In view of her distaste for Seabury's customary demeanour, she was strangely pleased; and yet in view of this pleasure, she was peculiarly severe. Most of all she strove to conceal from herself any sentiments whatever aroused by his lordship's request. It was extraordinary; that was the limit of her acknowledged response.

Chapter IV

Rucke House, April 25th.

My Dearest A,

Forgive, I pray, the lapse of days since my last letter to you. They have been mostly uneventful; still, I shall attempt to give you some account of them. For one thing, I have made my first appearance at Almack's so it is now within my power to assure you it is nothing, of itself, to pine away for. On the contrary, I very much envied those so-called unfortunates who are denied admittance, for it is dull, dull, dull. The only redeeming feature, for me, was the dancing; but even this is unadventurous compared to what may be done at private balls and parties. And here is a bit of intelligence you will scarcely credit: the cakes laid out for the guests are two days stale at least! I found it a very tame evening; its main advantage to me was that our ancient friend the Baron Mockabee cannot be met with there. Unhappily, he is to be seen almost everywhere else—but I shall return to this text later.

Lord Seabury and I were accorded the privilege of leading off the first dance together. Oh my dear, he does foot it away beautifully! Your humble correspondent shows some improvement too, I may add, even beyond her initial brilliance. And while I am on the topic of Seabury, I must report unexpected news: twice now, in the last three days, my lord has invited me to drive out with him in the Park. Since you will not immediately comprehend why these tidings merit such emphasis, allow me to explain that during the five or six years previous to my appearance in this city, it was Lord Seabury's constant habit to drive Lady Susan Manning, and no other than she, out into the Park. Those habitual outings took place only twice a week, according to his tiger (who told my abigail), and so it is impossible for me to know whether or not they still continue when he does not escort me; but is this not a striking detail? He neither said nor did anything out of the way during our two excursions together, and yet I cannot help but conclude that his lordship enjoys my company. Lady Susan drives in Hyde Park with her mamma when Seabury does not claim her companionship, I am told, and since I insist on visiting only the Green Park it is beyond my power to know more than I have already reported. I wonder, though, if she is miffed. I would be. More likely she meets the catastrophe with complacency or indifference—these are more in her style. I did encounter her at Almack's on the occasion I have mentioned, and on that night, certainly, her manner was as bland as always. Of course, my lord had driven out with me but once before that, and she might easily not have known.

Idle speculation!

Lady Beatrice, by the way, is delighted with Seabury's altered customs. She drew me aside after dinner last night—we dined in South Audley Street—to tell me she had heard all, and was all approval.

"But surely it is without significance?" said I.

"You try an old woman's patience, gal," said she testily. "Obviously it is significant; if not, why should Charles Stickney have mentioned it to Arthur Lanham, who in turn passed it on to Mr. Walfish, who of course repeated it to me?"

"Why indeed?" was all I could reply.

"Come come! Is this the lady so much renowned for her candour? He has a *tendre* for you; confess it."

I was rather surprised. "If such a thing be true—and I doubt it very much—it is not for me to confess, madam, but for him."

"Now that is so," said the shrewd lady. "Well? Has he?"

Truly baffled, I answered, "Has he what?"

"Declared himself? Has he come out with it? Please, my dear, I am an old woman. I have not got all the time in the world any longer. Do not keep me in suspense; has my nephew talked of love to you?"

"My lady!"

"But has he?" she insisted impatiently.

"Certainly he has not," said I, "and if he did, I hardly think it would be cause for celebration."

"And why not?"

"Quite simply, because we should not suit. I could not return his regard."

"Oh, the devil fly away with your regard," said she, disgusted. "The point is, he may be turning away from Lady Susan, at last. If you disappoint him—well, you may cause him some pain; but it will be nothing compared to the disaster of his marrying Susan."

"Suppose—and we are supposing rather too much—he did offer for me, and I refused him. Would he not turn back to Lady Susan anyhow? Surely that would be most natural in him. And probably, he would renew his attentions there with greatly increased fervour—"

But Lady Beatrice cut me off. "Perhaps he may," she snapped, "but I know Lady Susan too well to imagine she would accept him after such an episode. Or rather, I know her father too well to suppose he would allow it, even if she chose to do so. Have no fears on that head: once Seabury is pried away from Susan, he will be obliged to stay away."

The discussion did not end here, dear Angela, though I will no longer repeat it verbatim. Lady Beatrice went on to say such things as make me very apprehensive she will now endeavour to throw me into company with his lordship whenever possible. I cannot but believe that, great as is her desire to help me succeed in the *ton*, it is a far greater object with her to detach her nephew from Lady Susan. To that end she will sacrifice even that achievement of splendid artifice which was to be my public character here; when I told her I was (following your inspired suggestion) attempting to learn to smoke cigars, she scarcely listened. I am forging onward in the attempt anyway, you will be glad to hear, though tobacco is of a foulness I would never have believed. The first time I tried it I was obliged to lie down for an hour, so much did it disagree with me, but I have smoked five cigars to date, and am improving all the time. I hope to enlist the aid of Sir Sidney Pettingill in this endeavour too, as he has been known to take a cigar after dinner. They are not much the fashion here yet, as you noted, but perhaps my taking them up will set a style.

Sir Sidney has already been of considerable use to me in another venture: I mean, he has taught me how to play well at brag. I was obliged to ask him for aid when Lord Romby—contrary man!—refused to assist me in that wise. Everything else, however, he consents to: he is enlisting confederates, and promises to teach me a system of secret communication that he swears is impossible to detect. Further, he will help me to deceive Miss Windle and the others on those evenings when I must escape from the usual round of social activities in order to pursue my scheme.

I *have* told you about the fleecing, have I not? Oh dear! What a terrible correspondent I am; I cannot recall! Lord Mockabee is my target, of course, and a very good broad one he makes thus far. Do you know, at Lady Harleigh's rout party the other night he actually had the audacity to wink at me! I was most astonished, as you may imagine. He did it very slyly too, which is what I hate, slipping it in between an unctuous compliment on my gown and an even oilier one on my hair. I cannot think what he meant by it. Certainly I contemplate my revenge with ardent satisfaction, if there can be such a thing.

Of course, you are not to suppose that I am utterly heartless. On the contrary, I have every intention, when the proper time arrives, of—

A clamorous knocking at the library door interrupted this sentence and prevented Lady Caroline from saying, for the moment, just what she had every intention of doing. She bade her unknown visitor enter at once, and was burst in upon by Miss Cecelia Windle, in a state of extraordinary excitement.

"Lady Caroline! Dear Lady Caroline! Look at what I have discovered!" she cried, with many more similar exclamations, all the while waving before Caro's face a crumpled square of muslin.

"My good Miss Windle, pray be calm! This untoward excitement is surely of no use. I see what you show me, truly I do, but I do not know how to interpret it. Please, a little less agitation and a trifle more sense!" So saying, she took the middle-aged lady by the arm and guided her towards a sofa. Miss Windle became a bit more tranquil, particularly after Caroline rang for a glass of wine, and tried once more to tell her tale.

"This, my lady, is—or was—a handkerchief I was embroidering for Lady Lillian. It was to be a gift, for Christmas—I always make all my presents early, you know. I begin in March; I find it best. Of course if I had sufficient funds to *buy* my gifts I should not be under the necessity of reserving so long a period for their creation; but I have not, as you know, a very great deal of money. Not to say—not in the least to say!—that I am not perfectly satisfied with my—oh, thank you," she finally interrupted herself to add, as Lady Caro handed her the promised glass of wine. Miss Windle took a sip and then another, then smiled up gratefully at her ladyship. Her upper lip fringed with glistening purple, she remarked, "I am so little acquainted with wines as hardly to know one from the other, but I think this is—claret? A very good claret to, I think."

Caroline had not troubled to ask the footman what sort of wine he had fetched, and therefore did not know. She said as much to the older lady.

"Oh, indeed," said she, nodding her head rather too many times, while a faint flush appeared on her nose. The tip of her genteel tongue appeared from between uneven teeth to lick, with the utmost niceness, the purple fringe away from her upper lip; it was immediately replaced, after another delicate swallow, with a fresh one. "Oh my," said Miss Windle. "A *very* good claret."

Anxious to return to her letter, Lady Caroline did not think it too unkind to prompt, "My dear ma'am, the handkerchief—?"

"Ah! Indeed! Well then, imagine my astonishment when, upon opening my work-box this morning, I found the handkerchief in this condition!" Again she displayed the object in question, dangling it before Caro. Her ladyship took it and examined it. The embroidery which had, clearly, once been a feature of the thing had been carefully snipped in the middle of every stitch, leaving tiny threads sticking up all over it, more like a Turkish carpet than a muslin handkerchief.

"This is most unusual," Caroline said quietly. "You are certain—forgive me, but are you certain you did not do this yourself, and forget? We all have small lapses in memory—"

She could not blame Windle for appearing indignant. "Merciful powers, my dear, why should I do such a thing as that? Let alone forget it!"

"Yes, of course you are right," she agreed. "I only inquired because it is so very—puzzling. Who would do such a thing? When did you last see it whole, by the way?"

"Last night," said Windle, with a tearful choke in her voice. Now that the excitement of first discovery was over, she had leisure to reflect upon how much damage had been done. It would take days to do the work again; and she would have the trouble and expense of replacing the materials too. Her courage damped by the wine, she was beginning to feel extremely sorry for herself, and was about to launch into a sobbing account of all her woes, when the library door once again opened and Amy Meredith flew in.

"Save me!" was her first remark, as she slammed the door behind her and flung herself against it. Her breath was short, her breast heaving, her thick, silken hair crept out of its coiffure, and her cheeks were as red as Cecelia Windle's nose.

"What in Heaven is the matter?" Caro demanded. She

was immediately out of patience with Miss Meredith: it was just like her to rush into a room without knocking and enact high drama. "What do you need to be saved from? You look as if there were a hurricane in the front hall."

"There is," panted Amy, turning the key in the lock. "Romby."

"Lord Romby?" asked Windle brightly, and hiccoughed.

"Yes, quite. He will kill me before the season is out, depend upon it. He said so himself!"

"Dear child," Caro said, with an emphasis on the second word, "Lord Romby will certainly not kill you, and if you would face up to him only once you would know that. You allow him to bully you; you play right into his hands. If you would not shriek and run, he would be obliged to leave you in peace. Your fear of him is the only weapon he has against you."

"Do not forget his stick!" Amy cried, finally daring to leave the massive door unguarded and collapsing into a chair.

"His stick!" Caro pronounced with scorn. "His fiddle-stick, you mean. How did this nonsense arise again? With what has he charged you?"

"He says I have hurt the mouth of one of his bays," she answered, beginning to retrieve her composure. "He calls me a savage rider and swears he will have me sent to Bridewell. May I have a glass of the wine?" she added.

"Certainly not," Caroline told her.

Amy stared. "You speak as if you were my governess, or my guardian. I shall ring for it myself, if you do not care to," with which declaration she did indeed pull the rope.

Lady Caro shrugged. "As you like. And did you, after all, hurt Lord Romby's horse?" she pursued.

"I never even rode it! I told him so."

"And—?"

"And he insisted I did, and that I harmed it."

"And you let him chase you about for an unfounded accusation?"

"His lordship is a violent man," Amy asserted, looking

to Windle for confirmation. Unfortunately for her, Miss Windle did not agree.

"I am persuaded that Lord Romby is an excellent, admirable gentleman," she brought out. "A trifle rough, perhaps, but never violent. No, never violent," she repeated, draining her glass and asking the footman, who had just entered in answer to Amy's call, to replenish it.

"This is ridiculous," Caroline observed. "Amy, I think it will be best if you seek out Lord Romby at once, and confront him with his bullying."

"Lord Romby a bully! Oh no, I could never say that," Miss Windle remarked, exactly as if she were an eminent Rombyist, called in particularly for her opinion. Lady Caroline ignored her.

"I shall go with you, if you like," she offered, still addressing Miss Meredith, "but you must make up your mind to stand firm."

Amy, however, was very far from agreeing to this course. "I thank you, but no," she said sulkily.

"But what can you fear if I am with you?"

Amy merely eyed her and pulled her lips into a deeper frown.

"Good Heavens," her ladyship exclaimed, thoroughly exasperated. "I must excuse myself then, *mesdemoiselles*, and attend to the matter myself. I trust you will enjoy yourselves heartily with your bottle of very good claret." With this she swept out of the door and, simultaneously berating herself for such rash behaviour, banged it shut behind her. A few inquiries informed her that Lord Romby was in the breakfast room; and there she found him, placidly eating a muffin.

"Can you credit it, he absolutely denied the whole incident," she complained to Lord Seabury an hour afterwards as, perched beside him in his grey phaeton, she surveyed absent-mindedly the foliage of the Green Park. His lordship had interrupted the *tête-à-tête* in the breakfast room to invite Lady Caro to drive with him, and as her interview with Romby had been most unsatisfactory, Caroline was disposed to harangue Seabury on the subject. "It was all I could do, indeed, to force him to admit he was even acquainted with Miss Meredith! I call that doing it a bit brown, do not you, my lord? I hope you will forgive me for speaking ill of your father, but if I ever met a more obstinate gentleman I am sure I cannot recall it."

She was surprised, when she finally glanced at her companion, to find that he was smiling. "Has my lord remembered something amusing? If so, I wish you will share it with me, for I am sadly in need of diversion."

"It is not amusement, dear ma'am, but pleasure," said he slowly, "that makes me smile."

"You enjoy my frustration?" she demanded.

Lord Seabury hesitated. It would not be gallant, and yet—"Yes," he replied.

"I beg your pardon?"

"I say, it is indeed your frustration that pleases me. It is so very like my own. No one but myself, you know, is obliged to deal with my father in a general way—at least, not on the sort of issue that arises naturally within a household. It is that sort, by the way, which I have often thought to be the most inflamatory. One's political party members one may leave behind at Parliament; one's club members, similarly, at Whites' or Boodles'. Servants may be dismissed, and tradespeople sent away: but one's family goes on forever."

"You never said a truer word," Caroline interjected warmly.

The viscount laughed. "I am obliged to own, too, that this display of temper in you particularly appeals to me in light of our discussion a week ago—as we returned from the Opera, you remember? You took me to task so severely for my treatment of my father that I fairly blushed for shame. Now, perhaps, you will understand me better."

He had spoken with more liberty than he had ever exercised with her heretofore; but that circumstance, instead of gratifying her (who had been, after all, so critical of his reserve) seemed somehow to pique her anger. "I do not consider that the cases run parallel. I am not proposing, you will note, to restrict Lord Romby's powers. I am only—venting my feelings with regard to him at present. By evening I daresay I shall have forgot all about it."

Lord Seabury, whose sensibility was vastly more delicate than his companion imagined, heard the call to retreat blast loud and clear in his head, and was obliged to obey it. "I am desolate," he stated evenly and quietly, "if I have had the unhappiness to offend you in any way. I beg you will believe it was the farthest thing from my intention, and forgive me. If you do not object overmuch, I shall turn the carriage towards Rucke House again. There is some business I must attend to there, which I have just this moment recalled."

Of course she could not object and still preserve her pride, so Lady Caroline merely nodded and murmured her acquiescence. The little speech, modest and quiet though it had been, had done much to humiliate her, however. She was ashamed of her previous tone, which now seemed boisterous and graceless. Lord Seabury, stung, outraged, distressed, or misunderstood as he had perhaps been, had not for an instant deviated from the course of a gentleman. Why, she demanded of herself, why had she been rude? So thoughtless, so careless! She had abundant leisure to pursue such inquiries, for during the whole of the ensuing week Lord Seabury never spoke to her but in the most succinct and purposeful terms. Most of all, worst of all, he did not repeat his invitation to drive with him in the Park. Lady Caroline had herself to thank for the change, as she grimly reflected: her rashness, her impulsiveness, her ingratitude. To be denied anything—even what one does not desire—is unpleasant, and Caroline suffered not a little during her fall from his lordship's (albeit uncoveted) favour. Mostly what dismayed her, she told herself, were her own too hasty, too proud words. Even if they had not effected the loss of the viscount's newly-sprung regard, she would have regretted them in retrospect.

And yet, it may be noted, if that were all, a simple apology to Seabury would have undone the wrong. She had no more to do than to take back her words, if she rued them—but she did not take them back. Indeed, the possibility did not even present itself to her worried mind:

it could not penetrate her immediate, instinctual sense that irretrievable damage had been done.

She had other things to occupy her anyhow. An important evening in the life of Baron Mockabee (though he did not know it) was soon upon her: Saturday night, the first in May, an evening on which Lord Seabury's party was supposed to attend the Opera. Miss Windle, apprised that Lord Romby did not mean to accompany them, sat, late that afternoon, before her looking-glass and accomplished a sad, sketchy toilette. She was in the sitting-room that joined her chambers to Caroline's in plenty of time, therefore, to wait for that lady, who was engaged within with her abigail. The minutes passed by, then half an hour, however, and still her charge did not appear. Dusk had fallen some time before, and they were expected at Lady Beatrice's for dinner before the performance; where was Caroline? Just as Miss Windle was about to knock on the communicating door to ask this question, Lady Caro issued thence. Though beautifully coiffed, and robed in a splendid gown of rose-coloured satin, her ladyship did not look at all well. In fact, she looked quite ill: her cheeks were pale, her fine green eyes heavy-lidded and rather pink, and her shoulders were positively stooped.

"My dear Miss Windle," she brought out in a hoarse whisper, "I am sorry to have kept you waiting."

"Not at all, my pet," said the good woman, "but are you feeling—quite fit?"

"Fit?" she echoed, in the grating whisper. "Certainly, very fit. Save . . . save for a little headache," she qualified, leaning heavily on Windle's arm. "Shall we be off, then?"

"My dear, I am not at all sure you ought to go!"

"Not go? But I must! I confess, I have felt healthier in my day—but I could not think of depriving you of the evening." With this she began feebly pulling Miss Windle towards the corridor.

Miss Windle, reflecting privately that Lord Romby could not stay at his club (his stated destination) forever, gladly disabused Lady Caro of this notion. "But of course you may deprive me of the evening," said she lightly. "How should I enjoy it with you in such a state?"

Caroline groaned faintly. "May I be frank, dear ma'am?"

"Naturally! I should be shocked if you were otherwise."

"Well then, it is not for your sake, nor for mine, that I beg you to attend the Opera tonight. If is for Amy Meredith's sake," she said solemnly.

"Miss Meredith?"

"Precisely. Do you know, Miss Windle, I have often pitied poor Amy? And do you know why?"

Breathless, Miss Windle posed the question, "Why?"

"Because, my dear friend, poor Amy has not so fine a chaperone as I."

Miss Windle blushed and started to refuse the compliment.

"No, no; I do not speak to flatter, but simply to inform. You are the sort of chaperone a girl like Amy needs; you are the sort she ought to have. What is this Mrs. Henry after all? Is she meticulous? Is she trustworthy? Is she honourable? We do not know, Miss Windle! We do not—oh, pray," she broke off suddenly, "I should like to sit down for a moment, if I may."

With the utmost solicitude Miss Windle helped her to a chair.

"We do not know," Lady Caroline resumed after a moment. "And yet, on occasion after occasion, Amy's happiness and reputation are entrusted to her care; day after day, her whole future is risked at every moment. I cannot rest, indeed I cannot, when I think of it! And so, shall I, because of a paltry indisposition—" she paused to cough for forty-five seconds or so—"shall I refuse her the shield of my own Windle's unassailable dignity? Her flawless judgement? Shall I selfishly sacrifice her happiness on the altar of my own convenience?"

Her dramatic pause formed a breach into which Miss Windle jumped with both neatly shod feet. "NO!" she cried fervently, continuing with a triumphant, "I shall go without you!"

After this there fell a hush in the snug sitting-room. "I could not permit it," Caroline rasped at last. "It is too kind of you."

"No, no, I see it is my duty. I see it perfectly," exclaimed Cecelia Windle.

Caroline gazed at her as if she had been a certified martyr. "You are very good," she said at last.

Miss Windle protested, but she rather agreed in secret. Tenderly, energetically, she bore the failing Caroline back to her bed. With many instructions she handed her into the care of the abigail, Mary. When all was done—Lady Caroline undressed and tucked in, and rhubarb and calomel sent for—then and only then did Miss Windle march bravely off to the Opera. The moment she was gone Lady Caro leapt from her bed.

"You must slip downstairs, Mary," she said, "and see if anyone has arrived as yet. Then come back to me."

Left alone, Lady Caroline rinsed her smarting eyes with water from her basin. The lavender drops had done their work well: she was sure Miss Windle had no idea whatever of her being in perfect health. The fine dusting of powder on her cheeks had succeeded too; but there was no need of it any longer. She washed it away and began, hurriedly, to take the pins out of her elaborate coiffure. By the time this was done Mary had returned.

"Mr. Hedgepeth says yes, a Lord Wolfus is arrived, your la'ship. Is that all ma'am?"

"Thank you, Mary. I need your assistance tonight, my dear. I hope you will give it to me."

"Naturally, ma'am," said the biddable Mary.

"Help me out of my gown, first of all," she instructed. "There is a suit of man's clothing in the wordrobe, just next to my redingote. Do you see it? A blue coat, and black pantaloons? Ah, exactly," she cried, as Mary at last located the missing articles and brought them to her. She sat on the edge of the bed now, pulling on a pair of striped silk socks, "There is a waistcoat too, and a cravat in the drawer with my ribands."

"Your la'ship!" Mary brought out breathlessly.

"Yes?" She looked up.

"Dear madam, you are never going to wear these clothes!"

"But of course I am. And you must help me and never

breathe a word of it anyone. Will you? Pray, say you will;
it is for a very good cause."

"Oh, laws!"

"Mary, please," she begged. She had waited until now
to secure Mary's assistance on purpose, for it struck her
that the abigail was more a girl to win over on impulse
than to conspire and collude with. She was too honest to
accept hush-money, and Caroline could not bear the
thought of commanding her to do something she might
consider a betrayal to her employer; and so she had left
this last detail till now. "All you need do is to help me
dress, then go downstairs and distract Hedgepeth while I
slip into the Gilt Saloon. Then, later, lock the door to my
bed-chamber, and when Miss Windle comes—well, I am
afraid you must lie a little. You must tell her I complained
of head-ache all evening, and at last fell asleep, leaving
word I was not to be disturbed by anybody until eleven
tomorrow morning. And that is all, except, to be secret
about it. Will you do it? It means a very great deal to me."

Mary, though perfectly aware that Lord Seabury, and
not Lady Caroline, paid her wages, was yet far more eager
to help the lady before her than the absent gentleman.
After a moment's hesitation she bobbed a curtsey and
expressed her complete willingness to serve Lady
Caroline. Jubilant, Caro told her where to find the leather
pumps she hid hidden among her boots and sandals.
These donned, she sat in front of her mirror and
attempted to tie her cravat.

"Dear Mary, have you any idea how to arrange a
neckcloth?"

"How should I have learned such a thing, ma'am?"
asked Mary, shocked to her toes.

"No, of course not," Caroline said. "Well then . . ." She
set to work with the unwieldy fabric herself, folding and
pleating and half strangling herself before she had done,
but at last emerged from the efforts with a result not
entirely risible. There remained only her hair to be dealt
with: most of it could be swept away behind her ears and
concealed under her enormously high collar, but the
crown—the crown looked very silly, and gave her away at

once. "Oh Mary," she exclaimed, in deep anxiety, lest Mockabee be made to wait overlong, "see if you cannot coax a few little curls on top, something like my Lord Seabury's. Can you?"

The abigail's clever fingers darted quickly through Caro's dark hair; when she took them away the effect was striking.

"Good Heavens!" Caroline cried. "I look just like a boy."

This was rather more unnerving than she had anticipated, but her eagerness to be off bore her up and away from the glass. "Run downstairs, my dear, and if you find no one between here and the Gilt Saloon, come back to me. If there is only a footman, tell him—tell him to fetch a cordial for me. If Hedgepeth is there . . . you had better return and let me know. I shall follow you in an instant. And remember, you are to lock my door from without, and be absolutely certain nobody enters until I come. Do you understand?"

Mary gave a quick recital of all her instructions, and slipped down the corridor. When she did not reappear, Lady Caroline went after her, leaving the door to her chambers shut. She found Mary at the head of the staircase, and being told that the only servant posted near there had been sent on the designated errand, Caroline ran down the passageway and into the Gilt Saloon. She discovered she was the last of the party to arrive: Deatherage, Wolfus and Mockabee, besides Romby of course, were all accounted for and eager to begin. Her first words—an apology for being late—produced a round of laughter.

"What a lovely, feminine boy!" said Mockabee. "Are you come to play at cards, or to sing to us?"

She scowled at him. "I thought it prudent to disguise myself thus, since if the servants recognize me, I am lost."

"My dear, unless you have a man's head to suit those man's shoes, you are lost already," Mockabee replied.

"I beg your pardon?"

"I say you may find yourself outwitted; this is not a ladies' game of Speculation, you know."

"There is nothing deficient in my wit," said she, already

seething with fury; "and if there were, I trust the problem could not be a consequence of my gender. Unless you would care to explain how you suppose it might be—?"

Mockabee declined this invitation and indicated instead his eagerness to proceed with the game. He was not above half pleased with the prospect of playing against a woman, and would have refused if Wolfus (whose lot it had been to ask him) had not made it a point of honour that he accept.

Lord Deatherage dealt first, staking £10 on his own hand. At £10 a fish this was a modest beginning, but the game soon grew more stimulating. Romby, who sat just to his old friend's left, placed his cards face down on the table, folded his hands atop them, leaned forward, bragged, and staked £100 on the issue. "This is something!" Deatherage exclaimed, while Caroline thought the same thing.

"It is just like you, Romby," Mockabee growled. "Staking the limit on the first hand is the sort of thing to intimidate beginners—perhaps our little friend here [indicating Caro]—but I know a bluff when I see one."

"Do you now?" asked Romby coolly.

"Certainly," he answered, and wagered £100 himself, even as Deatherage withdrew his cards and forfeited his stake.

"This is no round for me, gentlemen," Wolfus said, returning his hand. "Lady Caroline?"

She, whose turn was last, followed the lead of Lord Wolfus. "This is richer than I care to go," she murmured, and was about to restore her cards to Deatherage when the baron addressed her.

"Come, come," said he, "will you leave me to stand alone on the field of battle?"

"Lord Romby is with you, sir," she reminded him.

"But he is the opposition."

"So am I."

"Not if you yield so easily!" he prodded. "Not if you do not oppose. Fine examples you are to her," he scolded the others. "One windy bluffer and two jelly-fishes!"

Wolfus and Deatherage grumbled at the epithet, but Romby said nothing. Lady Caroline completed her

unfinished action—which is to say, restored her cards to
the dealer—saying, "I am afraid you two must lock horns
with one another; and if I am a jelly-fish, so much the
worse for me."

It was time to show cards. Romby, with the utmost
dignity, turned over a pair-royal of nines. Pleasant as the
moment must have been to him, he did not even smile.
Baron Mockabee, it appeared, had not the same ability of
keeping his countenance. He let out an oath, scowled, and
showed a pair of tens. Lord Romby drew in his
twenty-one fish and shuffled the cards.

The game continued for six hours till three o'clock,
during which time Lord Mockabee lost some five
hundred pounds. None of the others came out remarkably ahead, which was precisely as Caroline had planned
it. She was a little distressed when Mockabee, failing to be
taken in by one of Deatherage's bluffs, collected five
counters from three of the other players; but this
happened only once, and its effect was fleeting. Lord
Deatherage, she reflected, must be told not to bluff so
outrageously during the next game (he had gambled on
nothing more than a three, a four, and a ten), which was to
take place a fortnight later.

"Nonsense, gal," Romby snapped, however, when she
asked him to keep his old friend's bluffs in check. The
others had left some minutes before, in a body. "He was
perfectly right to do what he did. Do you suppose
Mockabee would never notice if we lost no money?"

"Losing money is one thing, but bluffing on a whim is
another," she objected.

"Phoo," said he, eloquently. "You are the one who
behaved most suspiciously of all, for you would not
pretend to challenge him. We cannot always act on the
knowledge we have of one another's cards; now and
again, someone must risk more than is wise, and the rest
of us must take our chances with him."

Caro continued dubious, but her companion chose to
ignore her.

"Were you not pleased with this first step in your
scheme?" he inquired. "I should imagine you would be,
for it went off mighty well."

"Do you think so?" she asked, with renewed interest.

She yawned after she spoke, and began to loosen the knot of her cravat. "I had no idea these were so uncomfortable," she added by way of an aside. "It will teach me not to mind stays so much."

Romby smiled. "It was quite a triumph," he observed, answering her first remark. "Mockabee cannot wait to return—to win his money back, as he supposes. That is just as it should be."

"And you really think he suspects nothing?" she pursued, releasing her chestnut hair from the tight knot in which it had been constrained all night. She shook it loose and it streamed over her back and shoulders.

"Nothing at all," he confirmed. "Besides, from his prattle to you I gather he deems you too missish and stupid to participate in such a business as this."

Caro smiled sleepily. "That is exactly what makes it so satisfying to do so."

"It is pretty pleasant to Wolfus too, I expect."

"And you?"

"I am happy so long as there are cards in my hand and money on the table," he said simply.

"I suppose your son wishes it were the other way round," she mused; "that you would leave the cards on the table, and keep the money in your hand."

The earl grunted.

"I was very much afraid he would look in on us when they returned from the Opera," she continued. "I do not know how I should have kept my countenance if he had."

"Seabury seldom meddles with me when I am closeted with my friends. He never cared for Deatherage much, anyhow; you may depend upon their avoiding one another when they can."

Struggling against another yawn, Lady Caroline rose at last to declare her intention of retiring. It felt odd to wear pantaloons, and her shoes fit her ill. She would have liked to go to Hoby to have a better pair made, but she could not risk patronizing any fashionable boot-maker, since her purchasing gentlemen's garb must be kept secret. Promising herself a good long sleep in her heavenly bed upstairs, she made her way wearily to the door, bowed her good-night to Romby, and ascended the oaken staircase. At the top she walked straight into Seabury.

Chapter V

Lady Caroline started, stepped back instinctively, and would certainly have tumbled down the long wooden stairs if Seabury had not caught her. Catch her he did, however, with two firm hands round her shoulders. He caught, inevitably, some of her thick hair as well, and its silken texture did not escape his notice even as he released it, and Caroline, safely on the landing. Caro had let out a small Oh! and a gasp, in rapid succession, upon seeing him; but now she did not know what to say. It was left, then, to his lordship to speak first.

"You are not hurt?" was his first inquiry.

"No my lord." She hung her head somewhat, and in doing so became conscious again of her pantaloons. This had the effect of making her blush to her eyes: it was only the deeply entrenched habit of civility that prevented her from running away at once.

"I did not intend to startle you, Lady Caroline. In fact, I was under the impression you were abed with the headache," said he.

"So I was," she lied, "but I—I came downstairs."

"So I see." There was a very uncomfortable silence between them for some moments; then, "Lady Caroline," Seabury continued in a low, gentle voice, "I trust you are not engaged in any activity that may discredit my family, or yours. It is extremely disagreeable to me to be obliged to mention such a possibility," he hurried to say, before she could interrupt him, "but after all, you are here under my protection. Any misfortune to befall you must be held to my account by the world—and moreover, I may add, by my own conscience."

"My lord," Caro said, dreadfully embarrassed and ashamed, "I beg you will be easy on that head. I am indeed sensible of the kindness you do in maintaining me at Rucke House, and should be most unhappy were any disgrace of mine to cast its shadow on your name." Beyond this she could say nothing; she felt suddenly as if she must cry or burst.

"It is not, you understand, my intention to censure you, or to pass judgement upon you in any way," Seabury continued, with a gradual return of his recent coldness to her. "You are entirely at liberty, of course, to conduct yourself as you see fit. I think only of Miss Meredith, whose prospects must suffer were anything to—" he hesitated, resuming, "were anything to happen amiss."

This last sentence had the unlucky effect of pushing Caroline's brimming sentiments over the edge. "I pray you will excuse me," she choked out, turning her head away so that Seabury could not see her tears. "I am very tired." On these words she did run away at last. Though she had kept her tears from his lordship's view, she could not prevent them from creeping into her voice, and she left behind her a very puzzled young man. Ahead of her were Mary and bed, and she welcomed the comforts of each whole-heartedly. When she slept that night her dreaming head lay on a damp pillow.

Hampstead. Friday May 9th.

Dearest Angela,

We are arrived here at last, as you see by my note above, and I must say I am happier to be out of London for the moment (we return on Monday) then I had supposed possible. What a din is there! One remains unaware of it while in its midst, but in the quiet of the country it is remembered as a roar. The Hampstead House (so it is styled by my London relatives; it had no better name) is very lovely, though simple. Its furnishings are nothing so grand or elegant as those of Rucke House, but they are most of them a good deal more comfortable, and I for one am glad for the change. As I think you know, Lady Susan and her parents, Lord and Lady Safford, have accompanied us here; Sir Sidney Pettingill did his best to win an invitation too, and succeeded in being asked to join us tomorrow. My Lord Romby stopped in town, for he has no love of rusticating; all in all we are rather a small party, at least by the standards of the *ton*.

Windle, as you may imagine, is in constant raptures regarding the beauty of the countryside, the sweetness of the air, the freshness of the scenery, et cetera, et cetera. I myself have already joined her for a ramble on the Heath, which we are near, and which I found excessively invigorating.

Oh! Did I say Lady Beatrice was with us? Mr. Walfish too—her invariable companion. I am pleased with that: not only do I enjoy her ladyship's discourse, but Mr. Walfish is generally extremely obliging about amusing Amy Meredith. Now that is a valuable gentleman!

I ought to pity Amy, I suppose. Poor thing, she has attracted not a single serious suitor as yet. The gentlemen buzz about her inquisitively, you understand, but only as bees do round an empty dish of tea: there is nothing for them there, they soon discover, and fly away. Both Mr. Arthur and Mr. John Lanham do, it is true, show her diligent attentions; but it is my feeling that if either cared deeply for her the other would bow out—or if both, that they would oppose each other more effectively. As it is, their banter about which stands highest in Amy's favour is quite tame; it does not impress me as denoting any profound attachment.

What can be worse for a young lady just out than a lack of suitors? Some would say, nothing; but I daresay Amy's own sentiments will bring her more misery than anything else could do. I have endeavoured, believe me, to pretend it was not so, but I am now come to the inescapable conclusion that Miss Meredith has conceived a *tendre* for Baron Mockabee, and intrigues with him when she can. Can you believe it? No grown woman but Amy could fancy him a suitable object for admiration! When I first suspected this circumstance I questioned her closely about it, and I think I did more harm than good that day, for she now imagines their liaison (to whatever extent it may exist) just that much more romantic and starcrossed. I ought to have realized that would be the result before I began; it was stupid of me not to. Now she will take my word for nothing about Mockabee: whatever I say, she adopts the opposite position. Tuesday night at the Opera we saw him sitting in Lady Embrey's box, obviously flirting heavily with her, and since she is rather a gay, lovely woman, I pointed them out to Amy in hopes the sight would alienate her.

"What is that to do with me?" she inquired, shrugging her pretty shoulders. "There is nothing to disturb me in that scene."

"I do not seek to disturb you," said I, "but does it not interest you to find a man you hold in high esteem flirting openly with a married woman?"

She frowned. "If she is married, so much the less for me to fret over."

I was distressed, but persisted. "Even so, you must surely own his conduct to be in questionable taste. Think of Lord Embrey!"

"Oh, as for that," said she, cool as clay, "I suppose I shall flirt when I marry too, so I cannot object to it in them!"

All her shrugs and coolness notwithstanding, I saw her start to cry as soon as the curtain rose and she fancied she was unobserved. All in all she made a very sorry sight.

Dear Angela, sometimes I imagine Lord Seabury would almost marry her himself if he knew what was afoot. His sense of duty is so particularly strong. Of course, it has not obliged him to marry Lady Susan Manning yet, and so perhaps I am wrong.

Forgive me for giving so imbalanced an account of myself and Hampstead, but the bell rings to dress for dinner and I must fly. Tell Edgar I desired my best wishes to him—the Mockabee Revenge Scheme goes on very well, by the way—and kiss your dear mother for me.

Ever yours,
C.W.

Lady Caroline was already heartily sick of wearing rose, and would almost certainly have donned another colour if she had not been sure of meeting Lady Beatrice at the dinner table. Knowing herself to be under surveillance, however, she wearily slipped into a gown of light Indian muslin, deep rose in hue, and made her way to the drawing-room. Lady Susan and her parents were already there, Lord Safford discussing what had become of the Manchester Blanketeers with Lord Seabury. Susan and her mother stood by the window in quiet conference, the younger woman's blond hair glinting dully in the fading light. Neither pair perceived Caro's entrance into the room, nor did she feel sufficiently comfortable to announce her presence to them. She took a chair near the doorway and sat there quietly until Lady Beatrice arrived and joined her.

"Dear girl, this is a bad business, depend upon it," were the marchioness' first words to her protégée.

"I beg your pardon, ma'am?"

"Why, Baron Mockabee's arrival!" said the other, much surprised. "I thought you had known!"

"But I did not, I assure you. What is this?" she questioned eagerly. "Mockabee here?"

"Indeed," said her ladyship, nodding her grey head emphatically. "Arrived not half an hour ago, declaring Amy Meredith invited him, and no more sensible of the impropriety than a cat."

"Or so he pretends," Caro murmured.

"Precisely," agreed Lady Beatrice.

"Oh dear," was all Caro could think to add. Then, "I must confess, madam, I have sometimes thought of hinting to Lord Seabury that Mockabee's attentions to Amy were not quite what one could wish for; but I must say this latest effrontery surpasses even what I suspected him capable of. Is he to be received as a guest, then?"

"Naturally," she said. "What else could Seabury do,

after all? Poor boy, he is the very soul of civility. It must have turned his stomach to be put in such a situation."

Lady Caroline was silent.

"By the by, my dear, what did you do to displease him? I am really vexed with you."

"I do not know what you mean," Caro murmured.

"Oh, phoo! Certainly you do. My nephew took you out driving twice—or thrice, was it—and then, of a sudden, ceased to do so. Now, will you tell me why?"

"I am sure I do not know," she said stubbornly.

"Provoking creature! It is all very well for you to simper and sulk, but in the meantime Seabury draws nearer every moment to offering for Susan."

"Not really!" Caro said in spite of herself.

"Yes indeed," said the marchioness, nodding her head wisely. "Depend upon it, Safford has finally reached the edge of his patience, and will begin to put the screws in this very night. I have seen more matches made, young lady, than you will ever do, and I smell one right now not ten feet from here."

They had been speaking almost in whispers, and Lady Caroline was startled, when she looked up, to find Seabury himself bearing down upon them hastily. He bowed slightly and launched at once in a low-voiced, intense explanation of his mission. "I am sorry to bring disturbing news, dear ma'ams, but I think I must warn you that Baron Mockabee—I believe you are both acquainted with him?—will be joining us here. I am somewhat disturbed myself as to the manner of its coming about—"

"We know," Lady Beatrice interrupted him bluntly. "My dresser heard it from a footman, who had it from the butler who admitted him."

Lord Seabury frowned briefly at such a chain of rumour-mongers. "How can such a thing have happened?" he asked after a moment. "I cannot believe Amy Meredith really invited him."

"I am certain she did—" Caroline began, and blushed. It was strangely pleasurable to her to be included in this little consultation; still, she was not yet entirely at ease with Seabury.

"Are you?" he prompted, as she prolonged her pause. "How? Why?"

"My lord, I have sometimes wondered if you were aware—" she faltered. "I see now you were not ... In any case, Amy is mad for Mockabee. There it is in so many words."

"Mad for—you do not mean she is in love with him?" he exclaimed, forgetting for an instant to keep his voice low.

"Oh, as to that sir, no," she answered. "Love, after all, is a sentiment requiring a certain ripeness of—well, anyhow, that is not quite what I mean. I believe she fancies herself in love with him; that is my interpretation."

"And does he encourage this whim?" the viscount asked in growing consternation.

"I am afraid she requires very little encouragement, my lord."

His lordship was quiet a moment, his brow deeply furrowed. "This is a bad business," he said finally, unconsciously parroting his aunt's assessment. "I am sorry I was not told sooner."

"I did not like to distress you," said Caro.

Lady Beatrice, who had been watching this exchange in thoughtful silence, chose this moment to speak. "Well, Seabury, now that you have been told—and now that Caroline has revealed her awareness—it looks very much to me as if the two of you ought to be able to think of a solution together. Surely two young persons of your parts can find a means to divide a baby from a rascal!"

Caroline, seeing at once that this proposal was made not so much to divide Amy from Mockabee as to throw Lord Seabury and herself together, blushed crimson and then grew a little angry. "I have no doubt but that Lord Seabury is well accustomed to dealing with such difficulties alone; though I should be honoured to give it, I suspect he stands in no need of my aid."

Seabury, to everyone's surprise (his included) suddenly blurted out a contradiction, however. "I should be extremely grateful for Lady Caroline's assistance," he said bluntly, "provided she is not unwilling to give it."

Her fading colour making a rapid return, Caroline assured him she was his obedient servant. "Although I have not the least idea how to proceed," she added.

It was now Lord Seabury's turn to be diffident. "Of course, we must meditate upon the problem," he offered stiffly. "I see Miss Meredith and the others coming now; possibly you and I may speak of this again later in the evening." He then bowed, and went off to perform his devoirs as host of the party. He and Caro had no opportunity to meet privately, despite his hopes, until the following morning.

In the interim an unusual colloquy took place between Lady Safford and her daughter. Indeed, in order to know how very unusual it was, one must know first how excessively ordinary the conversation between these two women generally was. Customarily, it is true, the discourse between a mother and her daughter is not of any particularly original nature; on the contrary, it tends to follow quite predictable patterns. One may expect a good deal of chatter about matters of taste and fashion; not a little advice, and not a few instructions, are handed down from progenitrix to offspring; there may be a good deal of commiseration on the topic of grumpy papas, or thick-headed cooks; and after a certain age, one may be sure of hearing rather too much about gentlemen and marriage. Granting, then, that no mother and daughter can fairly be expected to grip the casual eavesdropper with compelling, riveting intercourse—granting this even before we begin, it must be recorded that the conversations normally shared between Lady Safford and Lady Susan were of a perfectly extraordinary and quite impressive dulness.

Still, on this occasion, the tedious tradition was, as I say, suffered to be interrupted for a moment. Lady Safford had something of interest to tell her daughter, something she had long considered, and frequently discussed with her husband. She began by bringing Susan into a quiet parlour some few hours before supper, pouring her a dish of tea (procured through the obliging Hedgepeth, who had come down with the party to Hampstead), and taking one herself.

"It is time you were married," she pronounced, to begin with, and stopped.

In vain did Susan wait for an enlargement upon this

theme. At the end of a full minute, she said, perplexed, "I should very much like to *be* married, Mamma, if it will please you; but I do not find the means of achieving that state."

"Ah, the means!" cried her mother. "The very thing we must discuss tonight."

"I am sorry, *maman*, but I do not quite perceive how our discussing such a subject can possibly advance the case."

"Well, well, poor girl, it is no wonder you do not perceive it. Indeed, I should be ashamed of you if matters stood otherwise. Still, desperate straits call for desperate measures, and I fear your most becoming naïveté must be sacrificed upon the wide and blood-stained altar of necessity."

Susan, who had not the least idea what Lady Safford meant, found this image rather alarming and requested some illuminating details.

"I mean, my dear, that you must go after Seabury in a more active way. I little thought to see the day when I would recommend such a thing, but here it is, and here am I, and—" Lady Safford faltered, really discomfited by what she was obliged to suggest. "Well we are none of us any younger than we used to be," she finally brought out, "and you particularly have passed through quite a number of your child-bearing years, and since Lord Seabury will need an heir, something must be done at once." Having said this much, her ladyship again made a long pause, during which she sipped her tea and felt exhausted.

"Dear ma'am," Susan took up slowly, "you know, I trust, that I shall do my possible to serve you, whatever the occasion. Never have I refused or disobeyed you: I should think myself a monster of ingratitude if I had. However, I am a little apprehensive of my ability to pursue, as you put it, a more active course with regard to Lord Seabury. It is not, as you must be aware, in my nature to be forward—and I must add, what I hope you will not interpret as argument, that I do not imagine his lordship would care for it if I were."

"I am afraid," Lady Safford said as delicately as she

could, "I am afraid you must be a trifle more than simply forward, dear Susan."

The lady so applied to looked at her mother inquiringly.

"I am afraid, my dear, that we must make Lord Seabury the victim of a small, er, hoax."

"A hoax?" exclaimed she, all uncomprehending astonishment.

"Exactly."

"A hoax!" was repeated, this time incredulously.

"My pet, do not stare so. It is dreadfully rude."

"Yes, but mamma, a hoax? A hoax, mamma?" she went on echoing the same tone one might employ when objecting to the addition of mustard to a bowl of milk punch.

"Dear love, it is not as if I were suggesting something criminal, you know. You are taking this rather harder than I had anticipated. Many young women secure husbands in just such a way; it is scarcely—"

"Did you secure my father in just such a way?" she demanded.

"Well, no; but I might have had I needed to!"

Suddenly Susan did what was for her an extraordinary thing. Susan looked dubious; she looked unhappy. This freak display of emotion did not long endure, however, and a moment later she had reconciled herself completely to doing her parents' will. Her countenance resuming its habitual piscine serenity (marred only by that troublesome squint), she apologized very prettily for having appeared to question her mother's judgement, and announced her utter willingness to participate in any scheme deemed advisable.

"Well then! This is my dear Susan again," cried Lady Safford, greatly relieved. "Really, it is not much of a hoax after all, and you will be far from the first young lady who has employed it. I shall contrive for you to walk out alone tomorrow with Lord Seabury—perhaps on the Heath, if you like—and you will pretend to turn your ankle. You must confess, upon his solicitous inquiry, that it feels too poorly to support you; whereupon he will doubtless insist on carrying you home. Shyly, you submit to this inevitable procedure. Now we arrive at the one segment of the plan which you must devise as you see fit. Somehow, my pet, you must charm his lordship while he holds you in his arms—charm him past resisting. If you cannot, we shall be obliged to resort to even . . . cruder methods . . . so *do* try."

Lady Susan engaged, once more, to do her possible.

"Good, then," said her mother, rising to collect the young woman's empty teacup. "It is all settled. Your father will be very happy to hear you are the same docile, sweet girl we have always known you to be. I am glad too," she added, imprinting a dry salute on Lady Susan's fair, unfurrowed forehead.

The interesting interview at a close, mother and daughter made their way back to the drawing-room, where they formed a whist party with Lady Beatrice and Mr. Walfish. Amy Meredith was engaged in a game of piquet with the baron (supervised, from a sense of duty, by Caroline) at the other end of the Saloon; Seabury had been cornered by Lord Safford, and shepherded by him down to the billiards room. Mrs. Henry and Miss Windle passed the chief part of the evening in a sort of competition to see who could appear the more industrious, Mrs. Henry working furiously with a netting-needle, Miss Windle equally zealous at her embroidery. These two ladies sat facing one another at either side of the drawing-room fireplace; though in their case the term "facing each other" is no more than a figure of speech, for it was a point of honour with each to look up as little as possible, and then only when certain of not being observed. To do otherwise would suggest a neglect of the work in their laps, and was therefore to be avoided. When their glances, as happened several times, met in spite of all precautions, four faded cheeks might have been seen to colour up at once, and four eyes to drop precipitately.

A light supper was all that interrupted these several pursuits, and after that most of the company chose to go early to bed. Seabury was an exception, for he had much to think over and could not rest at first: not only was there the problem of Amy Meredith, but Lord Safford (as Lady Beatrice had precisely divined) had made some not terribly subtle references while playing at billiards to the possibility of Seabury's becoming his son-in-law someday soon, and had also mentioned pointedly how very many years it had been since Lady Susan's come-out. Seabury could understand Safford's concern: even if Susan had not been his only child, her marriage was a matter that ought to have been settled long before. After this piece of brilliance, however, poor Seabury's thinking grew cloudy and muddled, and he could come to no sort of conclusion.

Lady Caroline and Windle were two who sat up later than the others as well. The latter was of more open habits with regard to her thoughts and sentiments, and so it was principally her affairs which were discussed as they chatted in a cosy sitting-room on the second storey of the still house. After the exertions of the evening, it was pleasant to Miss Windle to sit with her hands idle for a time; Lady Caro worked some filagree she had begun in Berkshire. Their colloquy began on a rather excited note, for Mrs. Henry and Miss Windle had fallen to cuffs again just before leaving the drawing-room. Mrs. Henry had begun it (or so said Windle) by remarking heavily, quite a propos of nothing, "And so you never married, Miss Windle?"

"'No indeed,' said I, thinking privately, what a foolish question!

"'And I suppose this was by choice?' continued Mrs. Henry.

"'Choice!' cried I. 'I should say so. The worst woman in the world, as my own mother was wont to say, it too good for the best man.'

"'And yet I suppose your dear mother was married?' said Mrs. Henry, slily.

"I must own, dear Lady Caroline, that this last remark discomposed me not a little. I may even say it angered me, for surely something inspired me to say to her, after a silence, 'And so you never bore children, Mrs. Henry?'

"'No,' said she, very snappishly.

"'And I suppose this was by choice?' I said, quoting her.

"'Indeed it was,' she hissed out; Oh, she was in a fury! She stalked out of the drawing-room as quick as that, and never said a word all during supper; did you notice?"

Caroline said she had not.

"Well, I was very glad for the respite," Windle said emphatically. "Can you fancy so much impertinence? I am delighted to have put her in a passion."

"Let us hope, however," Caro said mildly, "that it is not a blind passion, for she will have much to keep an eye on with Mockabee here. I wish she could be trusted a little more; it was not very pleasant, I may tell you, watching Amy and the baron play at piquet. In fact, it was extremely dull." She kept to herself, naturally, the additional annoyance the baron gave her by making oblique allusions to herself and games of chance.

Upon inquiry, Miss Windle was informed of all Caroline's suspicions regarding Miss Meredith's unhealthy attachment to Lord Mockabee. "I shall take it upon myself to watch her," she declared zealously at the end of this account, "for Mrs. Henry is no more use than a scarecrow."

Lady Caroline thanked her.

"Are we not melancholy, after all, without Lord Romby?" Miss Windle suddenly cried out, when a brief pause had laid to rest the topic of Mrs. Henry.

Caro looked up in surprise, and dropped a bead as well. "I am sure we none of us rejoice in his absence," said she carefully, "but I had not thought of the party as melancholy without him."

"Had you not?" asked Windle, nearly as surprised.

Caro shook her head.

"I wonder if you will marry Edgar Gilchrist after all," mused Windle aloud a moment later, supremely oblivious of the hop her discourse had taken.

"My dear ma'am, what makes you imagine such a thing?"

"Oh, dear! Very often young ladies *do* marry the squire of the neighbourhood—local gentry—that sort of thing, you know. I suppose they find old friends the most comfortable."

"I do not expect to marry for comfort," Lady Caro pointed out.

"Still..." said Miss Windle; and was, in fact, still.

For a short time nothing more was heard in the quiet sitting-room than the ticking of the grandfather clock in the corner.

"Do you suppose his lordship will ever marry again?" Windle demanded suddenly.

"Whose lordship?"

"Why, Lord Romby!"

"I do not know. It is a little hard to believe he ever was married, I find."

"Do you?"

"Yes, rather," said Caro, puzzled. She hoped very deeply that her chaperone was not foolish enough to fancy that Romby, if he ever did take another wife, would take her.

"What a dashing figure is his!" Miss Windle ejaculated, and sighed. After this she stared a little longer into space, gave another, deeper sigh, and finally opened her work-basket. What she found inside so astonished and distressed her that she gave a great cry and immediately set to weeping noisily. In the few words and shrieks that pierced her sobs, and by means of suspending Lady Lillian's ill-fated handkerchief in the air, Lady Caroline was given to understand that the same mischief performed a few weeks before on that scrap of fabric had been repeated.

"What can it mean, what can it mean?" wailed the aggrieved lady, while Caro pondered the same question in somwhat calmer style.

"Shall I ring for some wine?" she suggested at length. Miss Windle's humour improved at once.

"If you please," she sniffled, suppressing a smile.

The wine was fetched and drunk as before, and as before Miss Windle's nose was seen to gain variety of hue; and, as before, no solution could be found to the puzzle of the unlucky embroidery.

"Unless," Windle offered timidly, after two glasses of claret, "unless it were possible ... Mrs. Henry—?"

"The same thought occurs to me, but it seems improbable even she could stoop to so small a revenge."

There ensued a brief discussion as to exactly how low Mrs. Henry might be imagined to stoop; this speculation ended only when Miss Windle, half-way though her third glass, suddenly felt sleep overtaking her, and retired abruptly. Lady Caroline was left to muse alone on Mrs. Henry's character, the question of Amy and Mockabee, Lady Susan and Seabury. She went to bed at last nearly as much in confusion as the viscount himself.

"Dear sir," said Lady Safford the next morning, addressing herself to the same Lord Seabury, "dear sir, I wish you will walk out with Susan on the Heath today. She has never walked there with anyone who knows the place at all, and she is so curious about it. I protest, the last time she and I strolled there I almost drowned in questions, and scarely knew an answer!"

The reader may suppose from Lady Safford's words that her daughter was not present while she spoke, but this was not the case. On the contrary, most of the party was there, gathered about the sunny table in the breakfast room, sipping chocolate and coffee and wishing, in general, they had not consumed so much ham. Lady Susan was much accustomed to being talked of in the third person, whether she was in attendance or not, for her parents had begun the habit when she was a little girl, and had never seen any reason to terminate it. "Susan must have a new frock," and "Susan must have a new tutor," passed easily into "Susan must be presented this season," and "Susan must have a new carriage next year," without a word of objection from the young lady in question. Moreover, Lord Seabury was so used to receive this kind of application from her mother or father that he heard nothing odd in this one, and readily promised the favour asked.

Lady Beatrice heard something odd, however, and was all attention when Miss Meredith (at liberty to listen to the others, for once, since Mockabee took his chocolate in bed) begged to be allowed to join them.

"Oh no, my dear," cried Lady Safford at once. "I hoped you would stop here with me! There is a sort of coiffure I saw in the *Journal des Dames et des Modes*, that I am simply aching to attempt. Susan's hair is far too fine for it, and I am well past the age when exotic styles may be worn. I was hoping—I pray you will not think me presumptuous—but I was hoping you might permit me to have my dresser try it on you."

If she had said she had taken the liberty of hoping Amy would accept a large legacy from her she could not have been more certain of gaining her end—as she prefectly well knew. Lady Beatrice watched in deepening dudgeon as Miss Meredith gleefully engaged to oblige her. The marchioness next turned her attention toward Lady Caroline, across from her at the long table, at whom she stared very hard. Caroline said nothing. "Should not you care to join them my dear?" Lady Beatrice inquired, in a tone very similar to that of a command. "You are partial to walking, I think?"

"I am, indeed; but Miss Windle and I have already visited the Heath. Besides, Sir Sidney will be arriving this morning, and I should like to meet him when he comes." While a solid two-thirds of this excuse was true (everything but the desire to meet Pettingill, that is) Lady Caro's real motive in declining was something like pride. She was by now just as alert to the situation between Susan and Seabury as Lady Beatrice herself, but she refused instinctively to interfere in it. If Seabury meant to offer for a dry fish, so be it. She would wish them happy quite as heartily as anybody else; more heartily, perhaps.

Lady Beatrice, to Caro's surprise, went so far as to give her a kick under the table, but the manoeuver accomplished nothing. If Caroline had a fault (and she had, truth to tell, several) it was that she was headstrong. On this issue, certainly, nothing could sway her now.

The consequence of this pleasant domestic scene was that Amy Meredith passed the morning with Lady Safford, her dresser, and a quantity of brushes and pins; Lady Caroline endured a lecture from her benefactor the marchioness that lasted well over half an hour; and Lady Susan Manning walked out, to her parents' great satisfaction, on the arm of Lord Seabury to Hampstead Heath.

The first part of this excursion generated no conversation that might be described as remarkable. Indeed, scarcely anything but commonplaces were exchanged. Lady Susan (to make an honest woman of her mother, mainly) took care to interrogate her escort as to the identity of this tree, and that bush, and those blossoms, and anything else she could conveniently point out. When Seabury was obliged to inform her that those pretty white flowers were known as daisies he thought perhaps he smelled a rat; but then, Susan had asked some mighty simple questions during the years of their acquaintance, so that he also thought, perhaps not.

It was when she stumbled that he really began to suspect a plot. If any fall may be said to be graceful, or natural, Susan's distinctly was not. It was extremely unconvincing. Susan was not a gifted dancer, and she carried her lack of ability intact into this new field of endeavour. She sat on the ground and bit her lip, however, in a very good imitation of authentic pain. Seabury of course knelt beside her, and asked if she were hurt.

"No," said Susan, wincing; and "Yes, I fear I am," a moment later. "Could you—?" She leaned heavily on his arm and attempted to rise, but failed to support herself more than an instant. "If only I had seen that vine!" she exclaimed, squinting up at him even more markedly than usual.

There was, in fact, a vine across the path, but it did not look as if it could have offered serious resistance to a colt, let alone a well-formed, healthy young woman. His lordship naturally was silent on this point, restricting his comments solely to the sort traditionally reserved for young ladies who have recently taken a tumble. When he came round to the one about insisting on carrying her home, Lady Susan brightened considerably, then remembered herself and frowned. She finished by accepting, and was dutifully hoisted up into the viscount's arms.

The experience must have been reviving, for the injured woman was soon chattering away animatedly. "I do hope," she said, several times, "that no one of our acquaintance sees us!"

"And why is that?" asked Seabury, rising warily to the bait.

"Oh, dear! This is, I fear, rather a compromising situation for me. After all, it might be misinterpreted—"

"I am sure no one, seeing us, could fail to divine what has occurred," his lordship interrupted gently. "Even a perfect stanger must guess. Why else, after all, should I be carrying you?"

Lady Susan essayed a giggle, the first and last (so mournful did it sound, even in her own ears) of her adult life. "I believe that the villains of fairy tales carry off young maidens in just such a manner," she suggested.

"Is that so? Well, then, if anyone is gallant enough to try to rescue you, I shall be sure to be lenient with him, on the assumption he read the same fairy tales as you." Lady Susan, though not an heavy woman, was not a slight one either, and Lord Seabury was beginning to feel the strain of bearing her along. His words came out with increasing difficulty, and he tried to walk a little faster. The house was now within view, as both lady and gentleman noticed, with differing sentiments. The sight inspired Susan to new heights of brazen intimation.

"Do you know, it is so pleasant being a young maiden, I sometimes think I shall always go on just so. Papa and Mama fret, now and then, and remind me I ought to be giving them—a grandchild," she brought out with some difficulty; "but I tell them if they feel that way they ought not to let me lead such a gay life, already so full of happy occasions and worthwhile events. Are you not of my opinion, my lord?"

Seabury, distracted by the necessity of carrying her yet another quarter mile at least, had little attention to spare for his answer. "I am sure if there is anyone capable of continuing young forever," he said rather mechanically, "that person is you."

"But do you feel a young woman ought to marry?" she persisted. "Is she obliged to do so, merely because she has no brother or sister?"

"Many young people do marry," he equivocated, "and from their reports, one must believe the greater part of them happy. From my own singleness, you may observe that I for one have not yet taken their example to heart, however."

This was hardly encouraging, but she thought of her parents and persevered. "You say, sir, that you have not *yet* taken their example to heart," she began, with quite a heroic stab at archness. "Am I to draw from that that you expect you will someday?"

The boldness of this made her cheeks burn, while its bluntness struck fear into Seabury's heart. "I am my father's heir," he reminded her in what amounted to a mutter. "I am therefore as vulnerable as yourself to the accusation that my continuing single is selfish."

To Lady Susan's unutterable chagrin, they were now on the gravel drive that led to the viscount's house. Spurred on by the near exhaustion of the muscles in his arms, as well as by dread of hearing Susan's next sally, Lord Seabury practically ran the remaining distance. When Hedgepeth opened the door his master thought he had never been so glad to see anybody in his whole life. He flew, burdened though he was, to the nearest sofa (it chanced to be in the drawing-room) and deposited Lady Susan upon it. She, poor soul, fought back tears as she listened to his orders: call Lady Safford, fetch a physician, prepare a restorative cordial, find some feathers or a vinaigrette. Glancing back at the patient, Seabury thought somewhat dimly that for the first time that morning she looked really distressed. Poor creature! What hurt her was something worse than a turned ankle, he reflected, though how much worse he could not guess. No matter! A strong impulse, as strong as any he had ever experienced, swept the observation from his mind, forbidding him to concern himself with her case any more than long familiarity and the duty of host to guest dictated. The moment Lady Safford arrived he quit the room, a wave of relief rushing through him.

"Lord Seabury!" He heard his name whispered loudly behind him just as he was entering the only library—a quite inadequate one—the Hampstead house afforded. It was Caroline who called him: she stood at the other end of the corridor beckoning frantically. As he approached her she explained, "Mockabee is in there, waiting for Amy. I thought you would not like to encounter him alone just yet."

She was correct in this hypothesis. In fact he had been in search of a little solitude; but now that Lady Caroline had happened along, he discovered himself just as pleased. He thanked her, hesitated, then said quickly, "Lady Susan had turned her ankle, I am afraid. Should you like to walk on the Heath with me, so we may discuss—him?" he concluded, glancing at the library door.

Caro, fresh from the sermon read to her by Lady Beatrice, assented promptly. Something in Seabury's demeanour informed her at once that the walk on the Heath had failed of its mission, and that Susan had not extracted an offer from him.

"I daresay," Seabury continued in a lower tone, "that it will be best if we depart without fanfare. Lady Susan is still in the drawing-room, awaiting the doctor. Will you think it dreadfully strange of me if I suggest we—ah, sneak out?" It had occurred to him that to return to the scene of the accident with another young lady just minutes after fetching the first one home was not the most gentlemanlike behaviour one could imagine, or even the wisest; still, Lady Caroline looked charming, and seemed disposed to be agreeable, and his desire to be out with her in the fresh air was almost beyond control.

Fortunately for that desire, Caroline answered at once, "On the contrary, I think it delicious. Let us steal away directly, without a word to anyone."

The two made a swift, unheralded escape to the Heath.

Chapter VI

"Dear ma'am, I could not think of it," Sir Sidney
Pettingill said fussily half an hour later. The words that
issued from his glistening lips were addressed to Lady
Susan, who still lay upon her sofa in the long
drawing-room, professedly nursing her twisted ankle.
The physician who had come to look at her had been sent
away directly by Lady Safford, who explained that her
daughter's injury was now discovered to be of no
moment; and Lady Safford herself was engaged in an
intense conference with her husband in the small suite of
rooms allotted to them. Lady Susan consequently lay
alone in the drawing-room, too discouraged and disappointed to care to move; besides, she supposed she ought
to maintain the pretense of having hurt her foot for a little
while at least—even if Lord Seabury, as she had by now
concluded, did not intend to look in upon her until later.
She had thought it was he whose light tap on the half-shut
doors she had answered with a listless, "Pray come in;"
but in fact it had been Sir Sidney. She had sat up upon the
couch, peeping over the back towards the doorway, and
had been more than a trifle startled at the sight of
Pettingill. Ever polite, he had at once offered to remove
himself from her temporary quarters; she had assured him

his coming was most welcome, and that she was not sorry for the company. It was in answer to this assurance that the courteous remark recorded above was made, and Pettingill followed it with the information that Lady Susan "must be odiously fatigued, and doubtless cursed the intruder inwardly even as she so kindly welcomed him aloud."

"But on the contrary, sir," Susan said; then, reflecting that perhaps it was he who did not desire her company, added, "Of course, if *you* had rather be solitary—"

"Never, dear ma'am!" he broke in at once. Lady Susan had been crying just a bit—mainly for shame that she could not do her parents' bidding—and was, strangely, the prettier for it. A few tears seemed to alleviate the squint that marred her beauty, as if it were the relief of crying those cramped muscles round her eyes had been wanting all along. It was a warm day, too, and the strong sunshine pouring into the saloon fell brightly on her blond head, lighting up her features. All in all, Pettingill was struck with the idea that she was good-looking—an idea that had evaded him during their occasional encounters in London society. As was his habit, he immediately began to calculate what sort of a wife she might make him—how much they could expect to have a year, whether or not she was sturdy and healthy enough to bear him many children, what consequence her family held and whether it would outshine him too much—all manner of consideration. It ought to be pointed out that Sir Sidney had not the least notion of presumptuousness in this: to him marriage was something of a mathematical equation, wherein one factor (himself) and the solution (a happy life) were known, and the second factor (the woman who was to marry him) had yet to be discovered. The poor man had no head for algebra, and was therefore obliged to apply the ancient schoolboy's method: try everything, one thing at a time. If it would not answer for him to wed Lady A, he must consider Lady B, and if Lady B proved inappropriate, there was always Miss C, or her sister D. Thus, in his automatic appraisal of Lady Susan Manning there was nothing either to offend her (if she did not care for the idea) or to please her (if she did). It was the

purely mechanical operation of an eminently orderly
mind. The machine was so well-oiled, in fact, that
Pettingill could continue to speak smoothly and pleasantly even while it ran. He did so in this case. "I perceive
you have sustained some injury, madam," he said
solicitously, sitting down opposite to her after a slight
bow. "I hope it is nothing grave."

She assured him it was not. "And you, Sir Sidney; are
you only just arrived in Hampstead? What a pity you
could not have joined us for breakfast; it was delicious."
Her conversation was not, perhaps, brilliant, but she was
in fact glad to be talking to someone after the disgrace and
embarrassment of the morning. It was not until Lady
Safford returned to the drawing-room and found the two
together, however, that Susan talked to Sir Sidney with
any object in mind. Her instinct, upon her mother's
entrance, was to fall into her habitual quietness while her
parent spoke for her; to her surprise, Lady Safford sat
with them only a few moments, and said almost nothing.
When she rose to depart, she leaned down as if to kiss
Susan's cheek; what she actually did during this moment
was to whisper two words: "Encourage him." With this
injunction to spur her along, Lady Susan did a good deal
worse in thinking of things to say to Pettingill—the
luckless girl was quite nervous after her defeat of the
morning—though the gentleman scarcely noticed the
change. In addition to her nervousness, Lady Susan could
not guess why her mother should suggest such a course of
action; it was not until hours afterwards, when the
mystery had been frankly explained to her in the privacy
of Lady Safford's chamber, that she understood her
supposed partiality to Pettingill was meant to make
Seabury jealous. If she had doubts as to the likelihood of
such a scheme succeeding, she kept them to herself. All
she said to her mother was, "Certainly, mamma."

The object of this interesting scheme was, while Susan
sat about encouraging his appointed rival, absorbed in a
conversation of his own with Lady Caroline Wythe. They
spoke, as they were meant to, mainly of Amy and
Mockabee, but many little glances between them, shy and
brief but perfectly recognizable, voiced the pleasure each

felt in the company of the other. They had never, as Caro noted silently, been out together in open country: it was a pity, for they kept the same pace naturally, seemed to chuse without discussion the same paths; in short, agreed in every particular. As to their audible exchanges, these were more complex. Lord Seabury was of the opinion that Miss Meredith ought to be separated from the baron at once, possibly returned to the home of her Aunt Meredith; Caro was of a different mind. "I beg you will believe me, sir," she said. "I thought just as you do, at first, but reflection persuaded me it would defeat our purpose rather than serve it. I hesitate to speak ill of your cousin, but the truth is—well, after all, the truth is that her nature is a little contrary. On the first occasion, for example, of my discovering her sentiments towards Mockabee, I endeavoured to open her eyes to his true character. So far from trusting me, she thought I was trying to spite her. She even supposed me jealous!"

The viscount considered this while they climbed a gentle slope. "It may be that her mind is turned against you," he said at last, "but that she will listen to me. At all events, I think it is my duty to try at least to address her directly on the subject. If she scoffs, so much the worse for me; but perhaps she will not."

"I understand your thinking, but I must insist you are too sanguine," Caro replied. She described to him the incident at the Opera, when they had observed the baron with Lady Embrey. She appended this caution: "It is well to remember, moreover, that once you admonish her on this head she is likely to include you on her list of adversaries. Your first move, whatever it is, ought to be your strongest; for afterwards you will be impeded by her mistrust."

"This is wise," Seabury said simply. They had gained the crest of the small hill and stood for a moment, side by side, feeling a mild warm breeze brush their faces. The trees were too thick with leaves to stir in the wind; they were as still as trees in a painted landscape, heavy with the fulness of ripening summer: tender, fresh, and green. "Look at the sky," his lordship murmured, and Caro surveyed that empty blue dome with as much appreciation as if she had never seen it before. This moment sank deep into both their memories; it was to be recalled by each under more trying circumstances, and remembered with a sensation of peaceful gratitude. Like all such moments, it struck neither of them, while it lasted, as being in any way extraordinary. It endured, none the less, much longer than the memory of any joyful meeting, any parting word or glance ever begged or wrested or contrived at great pains; such is the capricious nature of the mind.

Lord Seabury resumed his train of thought while they descended the incline and pressed on through a tangle of spiky undergrowth. "I suppose the other logical move, since it may be foolish to attempt to sway Amy, is to approcah Lord Mockabee. You will appreciate my unwillingness to do so, however; there is hardly any correct or pleasant way to accomplish such an errand. The very idea of it is an insult, as Mockabee would be quick to recognize."

"True—and yet, suppose I were to speak to him?"

"I am sorry, but I do not see the advantage—" he began.

She interrupted eagerly, "Lord Mockabee and I are neighbours in Berkshire, you know; we were acquainted at—" she faltered as the precise circumstances returned to her—"at quite a young age. If I made no mention of you, it is not impossible he would oblige me willingly. All I need do is dwell upon my concern for Amy's happiness, point out how impressionable a young girl may be, perhaps flatter him a little regarding his attractiveness . . . I shall not do so without your approval, of course, but I think it may answer."

"You are generous to make such an offer," he answered slowly, "for I know no reason why you should be at pains to protect Miss Meredith. Still, I feel somehow as if I were casting you into a lion's pit. May not Lord Mockabee misunderstand?"

Caro, whose growing desire to be of use to Seabury was all that made her so hopeful regarding the baron's supposed cooperation, did not quite take her companion's meaning at first; her zeal caused her to reject automatically any protest on his part, whether she comprehended it or not. "I shall be very clear, I promise you. Besides, what other alternative have we?"

He paused before responding. "There is one solution, though it is rather drastic, which cannot fail."

"To wit?"

"I might offer for Amy myself."

Caroline was silent. "I seem to be scarcely able to speak today without a risk of offending you," she brought out at length, "but does it not occur to you that your cousin might—for whatever extraordinary reason, dear sir— refuse you?"

Seabury, who had very little of vanity, was not in the least offended. On the contrary, Caroline's phrase "for whatever extraordinary reason," interested him far more than any uncomplimentary aspect of her objection. He had no leisure to contemplate it at the moment, however, for they had by now been walking quite a long time, and it was dawning on him that they really ought to return to the house. He could not, indeed, remember in retrospect what precisely had induced him to leave it in such a harum-scarum manner; it was not at all like him. He might even have imperilled Lady Caroline's good name by whisking her away so indecorously; and certainly it did not look well in him to have quitted Susan's vicinity before the physician had made a pronouncement on her ankle. The more he considered it, the more reprehensible his behaviour appeared. For this reason he ceased to amble on as the whim took him and instead bent his steps (and Caroline's) directly towards home. In answer to Caro's last remark, he merely said, rather absently, "Perhaps." Lady Caroline mistook his absent tone for a return of his customary reserve and aloofness, however, and this impression was strengthened by his sudden turn homewards. Distressed, she sought at once to repair her error, before it caused (as had another rash remark of hers) a prolonged uneasiness between them.

"I did not intend, dear sir, to suggest Miss Meredith would be likely to refuse you," she began. "I am miserable if I did so; I beg you will forgive me! If Amy were not infatuated with Mockabee—if she manifested more

prudence in her attachments, and less girlish wilfullness—
the idea would be unthinkable."

This interested Seabury even more deeply than her
earlier qualifiaction, but he hardly knew what to say to it.
He assured her he had not felt slighted (though in terms so
formal that Caro was not convinced), then added, "In any
case, it has ever seemed to me that even more important
than the virtues of the wife, or the attributes of the
husband, is their suitability to one another. It signifies no
disrespect—"

Caroline jumped in to answer him before he could end
his sentence. "This is precisely my feeling, my lord!" said
she. "How should you and Amy ever be happy together?
It would be a shame, a dreadful shame!"

"To say truth, I never imagined we should suit, Lady
Caroline. Were I to offer, it would be purely from a sense
of responsibility to her. As for happiness—we should be
obliged to rely on time and habit to bring it."

"I am afraid time and habit have a false reputation,"
she replied. "for instead of bringing happiness, I have
never observed them to do anything but remove it.
Naturally, a gentleman's principles are his own," she
continued, "but I find it hard to credit that it may ever be
anyone's duty to enter permanently into an unhappy
union. In the case of Amy Meredith—" and here she knew
perfectly well she was going too far; but she could not
seem to stop the habit of hasty speech in spite of that
"—so many other acceptable solutions may be reached
that it would be absolutely barbarous in you to make a
human sacrifice of yourself. Besides," she concluded,
desiring somehow to lessen the intensity of her argument,
"there is Lady Susan."

They were in sight of the house now, and it would be
difficult to say who was the more dismayed by the
impending termination of their discourse. Determined to
satisfy as much of his curiosity as should be possible in the
remaining yards, Lord Seabury demanded rather sharply,
"And what has Lady Susan to say to it?"

The question confused her. Did Seabury mean to deny
his long-standing intimacy with Susan? Perhaps he had
really made up his mind not to marry her after all! Or,

more likely, he was piqued at Caro's continued interference into his privacy and code of conduct, and only sought to silence her. Whatever the case, she eluded the necessity of replying pretty well, for they were now so near to the door that she could say with good reason. "Oh, dear! Before we go in, pray tell me if I may speak to Lord Mockabee as we discussed. Soonest is best, I think, so if you approve I shall do so this afternoon."

Seabury's handsome mouth tightened before he spoke, but in the end he assented. It went against the grain with him to yield the burden of such a responsibility to anyone else, and particularly to a woman. Still, Caroline had presented her logic forcefully, and in the case of so unscrupulous a gentleman as the baron, unconventional methods might be justified—or even necessary. Lady Caroline thanked him for his permission as if he had granted her a great favour; it was indeed an unusual speech for her, who was so little accustomed to asking permission from anyone at all, still less to being grateful for it.

They were greeted, upon their return, by a scolding from Lady Beatrice, who had perceived their approach to the house from a window in a front sitting-room upstairs. She had slipped out alone, she said, upon seeing them; but the two hours previous to this had been taken up by the annoying business of keeping Miss Meredith and Lord Mockabee from being *tête-à-tête*. Mrs. Henry and Miss Windle, it seemed, were engaged in another of their needlework competitions, and could not be bothered with such minor details as tending to their charges. "And you two!" Lady Beatrice continued, warming to her subject, "I cannot decide which of you surprises me more! Did I not expressly desire you, only last night, to devise some means of separating Amy from Mockabee?"

Both parties owned that she had.

"Then what has kept you from it?" she demanded, her wide face reddening with indignant anger. "When I request a thing to be done, I expect someone to do it, and no shilly-shallying. Do you know what I have been obliged to do today?"

They owned they did not.

"I have been obliged to ride out on horseback," she pronounced majestically. "At my age! With my figure! Do you know how long it had been since I last rode out in such a fashion?"

Still trying hard to look ashamed, Caro and Seabury said they could not guess, looked at one another and burst out laughing.

"All very well for you to laugh," said Lady Beatrice, looking (in spite of her words) pretty near to giggling with them. "You two are the cause of my undergoing such a humiliation. Lord Mockabee invited Miss Amy to ride; and she, you may be sure, was very willing. What was I to do but insist upon accompanying them? I declare I thought my legs would fall off, and the poor horse—!"

Seabury, who cared as much for horseflesh as the next man, was a little alarmed at this, though he could not help but laugh again anyhow. "Is it really two hours though, since we quitted the house?" he asked a moment later.

"Quite," Lady Beatrice informed him. She did not, as he had expected her to do, follow this with a harangue regarding how remiss he had been in the business of Lady Susan's ankle; he could not imagine how or why he escaped this. Caroline knew very well the answer to that puzzle, and her consciousness made her blush. "Anyhow, I trust by now you have hit upon an ingenious scheme for thwarting this incipient disaster." Lady Beatrice prompted after a pause.

"Not exactly," said Caro, acquainting her with pertinent points of their discussion on this head. It was agreed among them that Lord Seabury ought to go and greet the newly arrived Sir Sidney, and to look in upon Lady Susan; while Lady Beatrice and Caro returned to the front sitting-room. Once there, Lady Beatrice very firmly requested Miss Meredith's assistance in responding to a letter she had just received—Lady Beatrice was so fatigued she could barely hold pen to paper, whereas Amy was so young such an effort was nothing to her, etc. Amy left with misgivings, for she had been alone with her adored baron no more than fifteen minutes; but even in that short interval their conversation had achieved (in her estimation) a tone of intimacy hitherto unprecedented.

She did not like to leave Mockabee when so warm a note had finally been established—particularly not if it were Caroline who would remain in her absence.

In truth there was not so much in that conversation to please Miss Meredith as her youth and inexperience caused her to imagine. Lord Mockabee was not a man to play with fire unless the prize for doing so were great; what he had been trying to do, in fact, was to make certain Amy was really as plump a chicken as she appeared to be. To do this he had turned the topic to her family. He supposed, he had said, they gave her all the ribands and baubles she desired?

"Oh, dear," she had cried. "My cousin Seabury attends to that; he is very generous with me it is true—although," she added pettishly, "he insists I am not to have a fur-lined cloak until next winter, which I must say I think very small of him."

Fortunately for Mockabee, his prey was so innocent as to require very little in the way of dissimulation about his object. He pursued his inquiry into her financial standing in pretty much the most direct way possible, troubling with delicacy only to prevent her blurting out at dinner that she and Lord Mockabee had had the most interesting discussion imaginable about her money. "Lord Seabury controls your fortune?" he asked. "How vexatious that must be for you!"

"Dear me, Lord Mockabee! I have not got a fortune! Papa died quite destitute, poor thing. He had no head for affairs, my Aunt Meredith says. What made you suppose I had such a thing as a fortune, you silly creature?" the lamb continued coyly.

"Now that you ask, I cannot remember!" said he, as if very much amazed. "I am curious to know, then, why it is your cousin Seabury undertakes to maintain you, dear ma'am."

"But he acts as my guardian," she replied at once.

"Yes indeed, but if he holds no funds in your name, how is he to pay for that lovely muslin shawl, and those pretty slippers?"

She smiled at the compliments and said, "But since he acts as my guardian, must he not pay for those things?"

Miss Meredith was really so absurd as never to have asked herself, hitherto, why indeed Seabury should maintain her, or how much the undertaking cost.

"I fear the revelation will shock so nice a sensibility as yours, but in fact there are many young ladies in your position who are premitted by their relations to starve."

"Permitted to—angels defend us!" cried Amy. "How can such things be?"

Lord Mockabee shrugged his narrow shoulders; it was well, he considered, that he had had this interview with Miss Meredith. It appeared she was practically a pauper after all, though it might be supposed that Seabury would continue her support as long as need be—perhaps he even meant to give her a dowry.

Amy interrupted these thoughts. "I am glad to know," she observed, "in view of such things, that I shall always have Lady Beatrice to depend upon as well."

"Ah, is it she, then, who—who is so generous?"

"Not yet," Amy exclaimed, her brown eyes sparkling; "but when . . . that is, if she were to die, I should probably come into all she has."

"How pleasant for you," Mockabee observed. "Who, after all, could spend it to more advantage—I mean, the way you carry off that rich gown, for example, is utterly splendid. So it is all decided between good Lady Beatrice and yourself?"

"Oh no, not yet. I should never dare to broach the subject myself, sir! And she never mentions it either."

"Then what has put it into your head—?"

"That I shall inherit? My aunt, of course. She has often expressed her conviction that I am to be the chief beneficiary. She says Lady Beatrice was very fond of my mother—her sister, you know—and that when it comes time for such matters to be decided, she will never leave the money to Seabury. Why he has a ton of it already! What should he do with more?"

"Well asked," murmured his lordship, his dark glance resting intently upon her face. Amy blushed under this searching gaze, which she supposed to be a loving one, but which was actually full of calculation and contempt. A remnant of that expression had still lurked in his black eyes a moment later, when Caro's light tap and quick entrance caused them to turn towards the door. She had found the effect, diminished though it was, rather chilling. Lady Beatrice propelled her swiftly forward, however, so she had little time to contemplate its significance. A minute afterwards Amy had been whisked away to attend to her aunt Beatrice's correspondence, and Caro was left with Mockabee alone.

"Lady Caroline," he addressed her, before she had thought of anything to say, "I have never seen such high colour in your cheeks. It is most becoming!"

"I thank you; but it is not of myself I wish to speak, sir," said she, the uncomfortable sensation she invariably felt in Mockabee's presence returning to her now.

"There is some particular person of whom you do wish to speak?" asked he sharply.

"There is," she said, and paused. "Lord Mockabee, I must beg you to forget, in so far as such a thing is possible, whatever association you and I may have had save one."

The baron was far too crafty to imagine that Caroline referred to her early, childish passion for him, but he chose to pretend otherwise. "Let bygones be bygones," he answered promptly; "I should never be so foolish now as to meet your favour with indifference, my lady."

"Dear sir, that is not what I mean at all," she said, openly annoyed. "I allude to the circumstance of our being neighbours in the country—acquaintances in the way that all neighbouring landowners are acquaintances. I pray you will attempt to consider me in that light for a moment; nothing more and nothing less."

"I shall do my possible," said he, curious to hear her out. "But may I say first, that I am really delighted to be private with you for once. I regret that we must play at cards among so many others; if not for that, next Saturday should beckon to me like a perfect paradise. You make such a pretty boy!"

"Please, Lord Mockabee, this is a miserable start at forgetting our associations. I must speak with you about Miss Meredith. I am concerned for her happiness."

"If there is anything I can do to ensure the happiness of a friend of yours, dear ma'am, I beg you will name it!"

"Then cease to tease Amy with your attentions," said she flatly. "She does not know the difference between lighthearted banter and a sincere regard, and I am afraid she will someday learn it most distressingly."

"My dear Lady Caroline," he replied after a pause, "I should like to know what exactly leads you to suppose my attachment to Miss Meredith is insincere." He leaned forward upon this and showed his teeth in a not very agreeable grin.

But Caro waved all this away with an impatient sweep of her hand. "Good Lord," she ejaculated, "I hope you do not take me for such a fool as to suppose otherwise."

"Your concern for Miss Meredith, madam," Mockabee observed drily, "seems hardly borne out of your opinion of her attractions."

Exasperated, Caroline clicked her tongue against the roof of her mouth. "Naturally my interest in Amy's welfare is mostly of a general nature. She is young, and therefore requires protection no matter who she may be. She is connected to my family, and therefore has a demand upon me particularly."

Mockabee took this in. "And you do not believe," he persisted, "that I am seriously attached to her?"

"Not for a moment," said she, fixing him boldly with her large green eyes.

He was silent for a full minute. "Well, you are correct," he brought out finally. "Miss Meredith is very pretty, and very sweet, but she is scarcely a match for me. You, Lady Caroline, are more in my line, for example." With this he stopped and eyed her carefully with that bright beady glance Miss Meredith found so fascinating.

"Dear sir, I hope you are joking," she said slowly.

Suspiciously undaunted, he assured her he was not.

"Then it is my unpleasant task to inform you that you, for example, are not at all in mine." She had not quite given up on securing a promise from him that he would leave Amy Meredith alone, but she had to admit to herself it looked more doubtful every moment. Her judgement, moreover, was clouded by an increasing disgust with Mockabee. Apparently there was no length to which he would not go to irritate her.

Lord Mockabee answered her rebuff with nothing more than an incredulous sneer, as if to say, inclination bows to nesessity, and if it were convenient you would find me attractive enough.

"In any case," Caro resumed, at last despairing of a reply, "you admit that you have no serious attachment to Amy. Will you then be so good as not to encourage her admiration of you? I beg you will," she forced herself to add. "She is extremely silly, and wilful, and may easily be hurt."

"You require me to be unkind to her?"

"I request you simply to leave her alone."

The sitting-room was quiet for some moments.

"I came to Hampstead only to see you," Mockabee brought out suddenly. "You are all that drew me here."

Caro jumped from her chair, all the growing fury in her overflowing at once. "Impertinent!" she cried out vehemently. "Even if he had such a motive, no gentleman could ever say so."

"You beg a favour strangely, dear ma'am," Mockabee said icily. He still sat, though she stood, watching her with a wary, dangerous-looking expression. "I could swear that so far from imploring, you are actually angry with me."

"I *am* angry with you, but that is not a reason for you to neglect your duty as a gentleman—towards Miss Meredith or me."

"My duty as a gentleman?" he echoed mockingly. "Is this the Lady Caroline Wythe so widely famed for her unconventionality? So mannish in her pursuits? So free in her demeanour? The champion of liberality? The season's loveliest eccentric?"

With each phrase Caroline's wrath increased. The worst of it was that Mockabee was right, after a fashion. She had created and cultivated what really amounted to quite a wild character for herself. Her tobacco smoking, her solitary drives, her snuff taking, her calculated bluntness at London gatherings—all these, coupled particularly with Mockabee's experience of her as a card-player, distinguished her from other gentlewomen, set her apart as a person to be dealt with not under the

normal habits and laws of society but in some more
original, less accepted manner. It was not fair in her to
break the rules of social intercourse only to invoke them
later, when they became convenient. Lord Mockabee was
(in outward behaviour at least) no more ungentlemanly
than she had been unladylike. He did not know that she
gambled with him only to teach him a lesson, that all his
losses would be returned to him intact; he did not know
that she already regretted the scheme profoundly. Only
she and Lady Beatrice—and Angela—were aware how
calmly her eccentricities had been contrived, how little
they reflected her true nature.

It was not until hours later, however, that these
significant facts became clear and coherent in Caro's
thoughts; at this moment, they were no more than dim
blurs. The only point she was acutely conscious of was
that she had been misunderstood: the idea that she herself
had engendered and fostered the misunderstanding had
little reality. She spoke out of a deep, stinging sense of
injustice to herself and snapped out, "If I were in fact a
man I should challenge you to a duel. As it is I cannot do
so; but you shall answer for this, depend upon it.
Somehow you shall." With these words she turned on her
heel and left. She did not even see Sir Sidney Pettingill in
the corridor, but walked directly past him on her way to
her chamber. Poor Pettingill stood for five minutes
rooted to the spot, wondering vainly if her failure to
return his greeting had been meant for a snub, and if so
why; and if not, how she could possibly have overlooked
him. It made him feel very small indeed, and it was a
comfort to him to find Lord Safford in the library shortly
afterwards, and to engage with him in a stimulating
discussion of the enforcement of the game laws.

Caroline meanwhile was shut into her bedchamber,
pacing about in a fury, then flinging herself on the bed to
cry. She was incensed by the memory of Mockabee's
words to her; but the recollection of hers to him brought
painful frustration and remorse. What a dolt she had been
to hurl that last threat at him! She had no means of
carrying it out. It only made her appear an imbecile. Of

course she could appeal to some gentleman who might champion her cause—Edgar Gilchrist would jump at such a chance to serve her, for example, or even Seabury... But what sort of a cause was it? As her passion tired itself out, leaving reflection in its wake, she began to realize it was a very muddy one at best, if indeed it could be called a cause at all. What had the baron done to her? Been forward; that was all. He had not attempted to touch her, had not accused her of anything he might not reasonably believe to be true. He had not insulted her. The more she examined their interview, the more she felt she had erred—not only on that day, but in all her dealings with Mockabee. If he had played a stupid trick, she ought to have ignored it. If he had declined to apologize for it, once she had been fool enough to bring it up, she ought either to have insisted on an explanation or declined to know him. Having failed to do either, but instead chusing some confused middle course, she ought never to have contemplated revenge on him. Having contemplated it, she ought never to have started to carry it out—and having started, ought not to finish. This was where reflection caught up with the present. Was it possible to reverse herself? she wondered dubiously. Lord Romby would be furious if she cried craven and deprived him of his games of brag. They had counted on at least three more before the fleecing could really be considered successful. Besides, it was Caro herself who had started the whole affair; to oblige her, in part at least, Romby had invited both Deatherage and Wolfus to become embroiled in a scheme that was far from wholesome. The mere planning of how to signal to one another—memorizing that folded hands meant a pair-royal, and leaning forward a high one, and leaning back a low one, and so many other details—all this had been extremely tedious. The old earl was certain to squawk if she bowed out prematurely—particularly since he had been playing with *her* money; and how much more so if she tried to persuade him not to find a replacement, but rather to curtail the games altogether?

No matter, she decided suddenly: it must be done. But

immediately she came to this conclusion she felt it was not
enough. Lord Mockabee's losses from the first game must
be restored to him, and—he really ought to be told what
had happened. She reached the second half of this
resolution with much more reluctance than the first. The
money was nothing; no one had ever intended to keep it.
But the confession of an aborted revenge was very
different from the victorious unveiling she had formerly
envisioned. Perhaps, she reconsidered, it would be
enough simply to return his five hundred pounds; but how
to achieve this was another question almost as puzzling as
the morality of the first.

Dinner ended this solitary interlude, but before she
rejoined the others Caroline had determined that the
properest course of action was to take the whole business
and lay it before Lady Beatrice. Caro had never taken
counsel of anyone before save her brother, Lord Inlowe,
since early childhood; this was consequently a quite
revolutionary plan for her. Even Angela had never been
asked to advise her, so thoroughly was her ladyship
accustomed to independence. Lady Lillian Inlowe had
felt positively slighted by her sister-in-law's refusal to
consult her, even in matters where the merest common
sense dictated that Lillian must know more. What put it
into Caroline's head, at this late date, to bare her soul to
Lady Beatrice was her extreme contrition—that and the
knowledge that the marchioness was the very essence of
practicality, and was certain to suggest a reasonable
solution with a minimum of shocked outcry.

She could never have anticipated the response Lady
Beatrice actually gave her though, for (when at last, just
after mass on Sunday, she secured a private interview
with her) the good old lady absolutely screamed with
laughter. It began with a reddening of the already red
face, grew gradually into a huge shaking of those
well-cushioned sides, and ended in shrieks and tears.
After a most frustrating interval, when Lady Beatrice
could finally speak, Caroline was told that Lord Romby
and Beatrice had perpetrated the exact same trick on a
gentleman of their acquaintance some forty years before.

"Can this be true?" asked Caro, astonished. "Lord Romby never breathed a word of it!"

"It is gospel, my dear; believe me. My brother is too much a rascal to tell you, no doubt; he adores to make things difficult, you know. But we most certainly did fleece Lord James Barstone—may he rest in peace—forty years ago and more. Did it very well too, I may say," she added, wiping her eyes with a corner of her handkerchief. "Took him for ten thousand pounds."

"Ten thousand pounds! I assure you, I had in mind no ambitions to match that. My goal was two thousand, or less if need be."

Lady Beatrice resoundingly pshawed this trifling sum.

"But why did you and Lord Romby do it? Did you give the money back?" Caro pursued, all curiosity.

"Dear me, I hardly recall why, though it seems to me it was something to do with a cock-fight. As for giving the money back, certainly not. He owed it to one of us anyway; Romby, I guess."

Lady Caroline felt somewhat vertiginous at the sudden revelation of this ancient crime. Though musty, it was still scandalous, and took a little getting used to. "I feel very silly now," she said after a moment, "with my paltry five hundred pounds. You must think me a perfect ninnyhammer."

"Oh phoo; in this thin-blooded day and age it is a wonder you attempted any scheme at all, gal. Why our little trick was nothing compared to Barstone's revenge!"

"What did he do, ma'am?"

To her surprise, Lady Beatrice seemed suddenly agitated. She even stuttered a bit when she answered, "Well, now that I think of it I do not suppose I had best tell you my dear. Of course it is a very long time ago, but—allow me to assure you, in any case, that he succeeded very well in putting me in my place."

Caroline would have liked to press, but she felt the discourtesy of it and refrained. Instead she brought the conversation back to her present situation *vis-à-vis* Mockabee, soliciting Lady Beatrice's opinion of how she must act.

"First of all, it is ridiculous to consider revealing the plot to him," said the old lady briskly. "When you have seen as much of the world as I have you will know the value of keeping your mouth closed as much as possible. Certainly one ought never to open it to incriminate oneself!"

"But I feel I ought to do some kind of penance—" Caroline began weakly.

"Fustian," was the reply. "Even if it were wise, or good, a confession is hardly practical in this case. How could you confess without implicating my brother, and Deatherage, and Wolfus?"

This difficulty had not yet presented itself to Caroline. Its introduction now made her realize how selfish her desire to own her sins before the baron really was. She murmured her acquiesence and reverted to the question of the money.

"If Mockabee were a bit more well heeled, I should say you ought to forget it; but I have heard that he has suffered some losses recently—his holdings in the West Indies, or some such—and I suppose he may need the cash." Her ladyship paused to think, wrinkling her broad brow with the effort. "I would tell you to play at brag with him again and make sure he wins it back, but I doubt if Romby and the others would cooperate. Who has the money, anyhow?"

"Do you mean, who actually holds it?"

"Just so."

"Lord Romby. He insisted upon it."

Lady Beatrice smiled oddly and made a clicking sound with her tongue. "Told you you would lose it no doubt, eh?"

"Yes, exactly." Caroline's large green eyes surveyed her companion anxiously. "Was I foolish?" she asked finally.

"Rather. I am afraid you may be obliged to pay the five hundred pounds out of your own pocket."

"Surely his lordship would not take advantage—"

"Oh, nonsense; no such thing is sure with Romby. Quite the contrary in fact! Why do you suppose Seabury was obliged to allowance him?"

"*Was* he obliged to?" she asked, with a sinking sensation.

"Why of course, my dear," said the other, in a matter-of-fact tone. "You do not suppose he would have done so capriciously, I hope! My nephew never does anything capriciously."

"Then you—" she faltered, "you approved of Lord Seabury's actions?"

"Absolutely," said Beatrice at once. "I only wish he had done so sooner; as it is it will take five or six more years to unravel the tangle my brother made of his fortune. You never saw such a pile of notes of hand! He had scarcely a shilling in ready money, and was drawing against the most indispensable securities . . . I myself was frequently in the habit, before Seabury took over, of blessing the gods for allowing me to keep my money separate from Romby's. As it was he borrowed a considerable sum from me; never paid it back, naturally."

Caroline's mind had flown back to the first *tête-à-tête* she had had with Lord Romby—ages ago, it seemed. What a different colour his complaints took on, in the light of this information! Caro began to feel, not very pleasantly, that she had done nothing since her arrival in London save make mistakes. She had leapt from conclusion to conclusion as easily as a frog hopping lily pads, and embraced each wrong-headed point of view with increasing vigour. This inward volley of strictures was interrupted by Lady Beatrice, who had been struck by a new thought.

"My dear girl, I should not be the least bit astonished to learn that Romby has been playing you for a fool all along! Indeed, the more I consider it, the more I am convinced he was. He never meant to give a penny of the money back, not to Mockabee and not to you! It is spent already, I can feel it in my bones. Oh what a scoundrel!"

"Dear ma'am, can this indeed be true?"

"We have only to ask him to be certain, but I would wager any amount that it is." Lady Beatrice was at first too absorbed in her realization to feel anything about it, but after a moment she started to laugh, ending up in just such a tearful roar as she had displayed earlier in the interview. "I am sorry, my dear, for I know you will be the one to pay in the end," she gasped out between whoops, "but the thought of his impudence makes me laugh; I cannot pretend otherwise."

"Frankly, my lady, I am just as pleased to be obliged to pay the money myself. It is the penance I was looking for," Caro said, even as, in the back of her mind, a scheme to avenge herself on Romby was brewing. With a start she recognized this for the very sort of high-spirited error that had brought her so much trouble already. She forced her mind to drop the notion, therefore, and returned to the question of how she ought to restore Mockabee's money to him.

"Well you might simply leave it where he will find it," the marchioness said, when again applied to. "It is a trifle crude, I admit, but it will answer."

"I had thought of losing a wager to him—laying a monkey on something occuring that I knew very well would not."

Beatrice consideered this. "Sticky," she concluded aloud. "Too sticky. The less to-do the better: that is my advice. Wrap it up and send it to him in the post."

"In a blank cover?"

Lady Beatrice nodded.

"Perhaps I might write, 'From a friend.'"

"It would be neither true nor illuminating."

Caroline thought again. "But if I write nothing, what will he think?"

"It hardly matters, dear girl," Lady Beatrice replied, smiling. "I promise you he will keep and use it; possibly it will even make a religious man of him, if he can find no explanation."

Caro was not deeply satisfied with this plan, but as she could propose no other she assented to it. She still felt uncomfortably guilty about it when, having obtained on Monday morning the needed sum in cash, she directed the packet to Lord Mockabee. It seemed cowardly to her, even if it was wisest. Her guilt and all traces of remorse were effectively removed, however, for better or for worse, by a poem in *The Times* on Tuesday. Indeed, the opening of that newspaper had, for Lady Caroline Wythe, nearly as many consequences as the opening of Pandora's box itself.

Chapter VII

It was Amy Meredith, in the event, who first set eyes on the extraordinary poem that fateful Tuesday morning. She sat at the breakfast table, flanked by Mrs. Henry and Miss Windle, and opposite to her cousin. Lady Caroline was at the end of the table, for it had become her habit to do the honours of the tea-tray at Rucke House each morning, and also in the drawing-room at night. Lord Romby's place lay undisturbed amid the clutter of cups half-full of tepid tea, dishes smeared with butter and dusted with crumbs, and salvers still laden with superfluous delicacies. Though it was not uncommon for the earl to breakfast in bed, the cause of his absence this particular morning was that Caroline's informing him of her withdrawal from the brag scheme had sent him into a passion, and he had been awake all night drinking and swearing and abusing the servants. Lady Beatrice had been quite correct, as Caro discovered during her colloquy with Romby: the old man had already lost the money entrusted to him by wagering the whole sum on the wrong side of a cock-fight. It consoled Caro a good deal to think of this betrayal, since it justified her abandonment of the proposed revenge on Mockabee. She was sorry, though, for the servants.

Seabury, who of course knew nothing of all this, had pushed his chair back from the table and sat frowning over a letter just delivered to him. In spite of his evident absorption in this document, it was chiefly to her cousin that Amy addressed herself when she said mildly over the open *Times*, "What a curious poem!"

Seabury answered nothing at first, but soon looked up for courtesy's sake and asked her to repeat herself. "I say, what a curious poem in *The Times!* Listen to it," she added, and she read aloud:

> First of all the chariot she drives in t'other Park;
> Next the naught she cares for airs, sith candour is her
> mark.
>
> Last of first, the ancestry, quite clear of any taint:
> Where birth is high, behaviour low admits of no
> complaint.
>
> We may remark, ere we proceed, that last may be
> suppressed;
> Not so the girl, nor yet the hue in which she still is dressed.
>
> First of last, the question on the tongues of great and
> small;
> Last of last, sith commonest, is like her most of all.

"It's got Lord M. below it. I suppose a Lord M. wrote it," Amy went on when she had finished reading. "How awfully strange!"

"Actually, my dear," Seabury told her kindly, "such poems are very commonly printed in London newspapers. It is a riddle, you see: each line refers to part of a name, and the whole is the subject of the verse. Have you never seen one before?"

"Indeed I have," Amy cried, stung at being supposed ignorant. "It is not the form which intrigues me, but the matter. It sounds just like Caroline!"

The lady mentioned, who had come to this same conclusion some time before, was seen by all the eyes now turned upon her to be excessively rosy-cheeked. In fact, the flush was visible all over her face, and even on her neck; but she only said, "What a silly notion, dear Amy; how could it be?"

"Well it certainly is," Amy averred, setting about to prove her surmise. "Look—a chariot. He must mean car, an ancient chariot. The Romans had them," she appended, for Caroline did not look convinced. "Anyhow, who else wears only one colour—'the hue in which she still is dressed?'"

"The Green Man," Caro said rather weakly.

"I never saw such a stubborn girl!" exclaimed Miss Meredith. "What do you make of the next line, then? A naught is an O. That makes Car-O. That is you, Caro." She paused to stare rather spitefully at her ladyship.

"There are other Carolines in London," Caroline pointed out, with scarcely even a semblance of conviction.

"Oh faugh," Amy ejaculated, full of disgust. "If I must I shall go through it completely. Last of first is the last of the first name, the Christian name that is. Surely it signifies line. Line is another word for ancestry. Besides which, it goes on to say that the 'line' may be suppressed. That means that one may say Caro instead of Caroline."

"Many," Miss Windle murmured suddenly, though very faintly, "many many Carolines in London."

"Oh, dear, this is most vexatious. You are doing this on purpose, are you not? Both of you, I am persuaded you are! Seabury, you see it must be Caro, do you not? Who else is frank and drives in the Green Park? That is the other one, of course, since everybody in the world drives in Hyde Park, except Caro."

Lord Seabury not answering, save by a long, interrogative look at Lady Caroline, Amy Meredith continued her argument alone. "Here is the second name, the surname. The question must be why; you see that, I hope. Why does she wear rose all the time, and drive in the Green Park? You see? And the last line, the last of the last name, is—what is it?" she checked herself all at once, a little puzzled.

"I hardly think it matters," Windle announced in a loud voice, "since it is beyond imagining that our Caro could be named in a poem in a public newspaper.

Absolutely beyond imag—" she was repeating when Amy abruptly shouted out.

"Oh! It is the! The last word is the! Caroline Wythe, there you have it," she said triumphantly. "Now I wonder who Lord M. can be."

Mrs. Henry was distinctly heard to murmur, "I do not," at this juncture, but no one paid her any attention.

"I am sure I have no notion how you arrive at your conclusion," Miss Windle fairly shrieked. "I am sure you are very rash, Miss Meredith. There must be an hundred solutions to the puzzle. For example, chariot might be coach, or wagon. Then naught—that is nothing, or . . . or nil! There, you see? Wagonilla! The last is A, not The. Wagonilla must be her name; now let me see, that sounds so very familiar!"

"Miss Windle, I appreciate your loyalty—" Caro began to say, but Windle cut her off.

"Now as to the question on the tongues of great and small, that is just as easily read as How. Probably her name is Howe, Wagonilla Howe," she persisted. "A shocking girl, Wagonilla Howe; I remember her very clearly. No wonder her name appears in such a context!"

This time it was Amy Meredith who prevented Miss Windle's continuing. "Lord Mockabee!" she exclaimed suddenly. "Caro, is it Lord Mockabee?"

But Caroline could no longer sit still. She jumped up from the table and began stalking the length of the breakfast-room, too furious to take any heed of Amy or the others, muttering all the while in an edgy undertone. "The dolt! The scoundrel! How dare he, after all—" She stopped, came to the end of the room, turned on her heel and continued, "He could not even make proper verses. The idea of such long dangling things! All different sizes too; most impossible, most ridiculous . . . Well, I will not sit still for it, I will not, I will not! Do you hear me?" she demanded savagely of the firescreen.

"The child is not in her right mind," Miss Windle said desperately. "She responds dreadfully to heat; it is the heat which agitates her. Really, my lord, you ought to send her back to Hampstead, the poor girl!" With these

words she rushed over to Caroline and attempted to lend
her an arm to lean on. Since Caroline was travelling up
and down the room at breakneck speed however, Miss
Windle found herself unable not only to assist her, but
even to keep up with her.

"Lady Caroline, I should very much appreciate the
honour of a word with you this morning," Lord Seabury
said, his letter now quite forgot. "Perhaps in the Gilt
Saloon?"

Caro gave a sharp nod of assent. Even as she did so,
Miss Meredith cried out vehemently, "What have you
done to Lord Mockabee? You monster! Can you not let
him be? He is my friend, mine! Henry, support me; I feel I
shall faint," she added in the dramatical manner she
assumed whenever she fancied herself wronged.

"Amy, this is not becoming behaviour," Lord Seabury
said, quietly and firmly. In the same breath he dismissed
the servants from the room.

"You side with Caro all the time," Amy accused him. "*I*
am your cousin; she is nothing to us! Why do you
persecute me?" she demanded, more hysterical every
moment. Mrs. Henry did nothing all this while but
encourage her by looking anxious and standing back, as if
to leave more space for the tantrum.

"Amy, I beg you will sit down [for she had jumped up
the better to stamp her foot] and make yourself tranquil,"
said the helpless viscount, pinched uncomfortably
between his duty as a gentleman and his chosen role as
Amy's guardian.

"Why do you not beg Caro to sit down?" she shrilled.
"Why do you torture me? You are in love with her!" she
brought out suddenly, quite in a scream. "Admit it, admit
it! I shall tell Lady Susan about this, see if I do not!"

Seabury, who had also risen to his feet, sank back into
his chair without a word.

"Amy, sit down or I shall strangle you," Caroline
finally told her, having first come sufficiently near to do
so. Caro's tone was so fierce, though carefully controlled,
that Miss Meredith obeyed her at once, meekly falling
into silence as well. Through all this Miss Windle had

stood by the door, watching closely but poised as if for flight; indeed, she had been planning to summon Lord Romby if nothing else availed. Lord Romby, she had persuaded herself, was omnipotent. Mrs. Henry had shrunk back into a corner; she came forward only as Amy seated herself, full of solicitude and offers of hartshorn. Disgusted though she was with Miss Meredith's ridiculous display of temper, Lady Caroline could not help reflecting that it was hardly the girl's fault that she was still so childish. She had been hideously spoiled, it seemed, accustomed always to be felt sorry for, cosseted and petted. Mrs. Henry, solid and dignified as she appeared, Lady Caroline now perceived to be actually frightened of her charge. The whole business was pitiful, Caroline thought; however, it was a more comfortable subject to reflect upon than the one which really concerned her: Amy Meredith had just screamed that Seabury was in love with Caro, and Seabury had said nothing in answer. In fact, save for Henry's murmurs to Amy (now weeping copiously), the breakfast-parlour was silent as a tomb.

The meeting in the Gilt Saloon that Seabury had applied for took place in due course after Amy, still shaken by her own fit, had been returned to bed to rest. Lord Seabury was excruciatingly conscious of her last words in the breakfast-parlour, nor was Lady Caroline less so. Neither, as might have been expected, said a word about it however; they merely allowed it to hang very awkwardly over them, and colour all their words to one another. "I am desolate," were Caro's first words to the viscount, "to find that despite your warning to me, and my assurances to you, and my real and honest efforts to avert this calamity—I hope you will believe me—that despite all that I have made my name, and therefore yours, an object of ridicule and censure by the public." His lordship fancied he saw tears in her eyes, or something very much like them, as she continued, "I can only beg you to forgive me, and accept a truly abject apology—" here her voice broke, and she swallowed hard, "from a person who was too foolish to see the value of your cautions from the first, and take them to heart then. If you think I ought to leave London I shall abide by your decision willingly."

"Good Heavens, no!" he exclaimed at once, with an absence of deliberation not at all like him. "I am certain you have done nothing to merit such an attack as this poem—I am certain you *could* not," he went on, while Caroline fairly squirmed at the thought, impossible to mention, of how easily indeed she had been able to earn it, "and I pray you will not suppose I asked you to meet me here in order to exact an apology from you. On the contrary, I should like quite simply to hear what you know of the poem, and its origins, so that I may consider what ought to be done. It was written by Mockabee, was it not? There can be no other Lord M?"

"I am sure it was he," she answered, too full of tears—from gratitude now at his last speech—to say more.

"Well, you told me your interview with him in Hampstead had not succeeded," Seabury returned, turning his eyes away from her face with instinctive gallantry, since she could not, momentarily, prevent her features from expressing the grateful, tearful sensations she experienced, "but I had no idea it went off this poorly."

"I had no idea of it myself, my lord," she returned, still struggling against her unruly emotions. "Indeed, I considered it was I who was insulted during that encounter; I am astonished to find the baron retaliating, since I considered myself the loser already."

This interested his lordship very much. "How did he insult you, dear ma'am? I may remind you that it is not mere curiousity that provokes the question, but also my obligation to you as a guest in my house. Therefore I beg you will answer me fully."

Caroline felt remarkably foolish and regretted her rash mention of an insult. "Since you ask..." she faltered; "since I think of it, I suppose there was no insult to me after all. I merely—I referred to the fact that Lord Mockabee did not chuse to honour my request. That is all."

Her companion knew perfectly well she was concealing something, but found himself unable to think of words to express the conviction that would yet not constitute an insult themselves. "In any case," he returned after a pause, "this piece of doggerel is an insult, and I shall respond to it as such."

"You will not—" she exclaimed at once, her alarm finally banishing her tears; then checked herself abruptly. "I hope you will do me the favour of ignoring it, my lord, as I intend to do."

"Ignore it? Dear Lady Caroline, I am afraid you do not know me very well. However, the matter need concern you no longer," he concluded, for if it came to a duel between himself and Mockabee he had no desire to embroil Caroline in it any more than was necessary.

Her ladyship entirely divined his meaning, and was apprehensive. "Lord Seabury," she said carefully, "the thought of your . . . taking any action whatever in defence of me, I find extremely . . . repellent. Lord Mockabee is a vicious and unprincipled man." She thought, as she said this, of how probable it was that the baron would take advantage of a challenge from Seabury to wound or even to try to kill him. He had probably done as much before, to persons who had irritated him less. Had not Lord Embrey once appeared in society with a badly injured leg? He blamed it on a fall from his horse, but all London rumoured it to have been the result of a meeting with his wife's impudent lover. The injury to his leg had been so severe as to have prevented him from repeating the challenge since then, though the liaison had continued just as openly and strongly. Indeed, Lady Caroline had thought of mentioning this to Amy that evening at the Opera when she had pointed out Mockabee and sought to dissuade Miss Meredith from pursuing him; but intuition told her such a scandalous *on-dit* would merely have made the baron that much more intriguing to the foolish chit. Neither did she mention it now, to Seabury, though it was much on her mind; instead she merely continued, "He will soon enough be brought down by his own behaviour; there is no point to your sullying your hands by dealing with him more than need be."

Seabury could not guess her motive, but the idea that Caroline did not desire him to champion her came through with oppressive clarity. The extreme boldness she herself frequently displayed prevented his supposing that she could possibly be frightened for him. Rather her words suggested a certain fastidiousness at the thought of his acting as her representative, an unwillingness to link her name in that fashion with his. It did not influence his decision, but it certainly caused him a great deal of pain to be rebuffed in this special way. Conscious of an aching he could not examine just then, he suppressed it and turned the topic from Caro and Mockabee to Amy and Mockabee. "I am no longer fool enough to suppose," he said, not addressing himself otherwise to Caroline's last remark, "that Amy would accept me were I to offer for her. Indeed, I am amazed I should ever have been persuaded of it. That alternative barred, then, I begin to wonder again if she ought not to be returned to her Aunt Meredith for a time, so that her—ah, passion for Mockabee may subside. Do you suppose she will go? How does the idea strike you now? I rely upon your perspicacity to enlighten me."

Pleased at being consulted in this matter, and delighted to leave the other topic behind, Caroline could not help but smile. However, she said dubiously, "At the height of the season? I am sure Amy is devoted to her aunt, but I do not believe I have ever heard her say so. Certainly she does not appear to pine for home . . . I rather doubt, I must own, if she will go voluntarily."

"Setting that aside for a moment, do you think it a useful course of action?" His handsome, expressive features, stong and pronounced as they were, nevertheless showed much faith in her, and much uncertainty of his own judgement. Caroline, returning his dark glance, thought she saw something almost of timidity in his eyes.

"At first I did not," she said, "but now I do think it wise. Mockabee has proved quite intractable, and Amy is not less so. Perhaps you ought to ask her if she will go home for a fortnight, no longer. Once she is there, she may chuse to extend her visit. I even—this is a bit devious—but I even think we might do well to enlist the support of her aunt. Could she not pretend to be invalidish, and require the presence of her niece? Is she a woman who could do such a thing?"

Seabury laughed outright. "No, alas, she is not. Agatha Meredith is the kindest, roundest, dearest creature in the world, but she is also the silliest. She could no more maintain a pretense than the man in the moon. Hers is a weak character too, I fear; all the Merediths are weak of character, unfortunately. I suppose you have seen enough of Amy to guess that by now."

"It does not astonish me," she conceded.

"If you will permit, I shall summon Amy immediately, and propose to her this temporary retirement into Kent—that is where her aunt resides, you know. I hope—I pray you will remain with me during the interview," he added gravely. "I have never seen anyone quell Amy as you did this morning; I am sure I could not. Will you help me just this little bit more?" His handsome eyes trained on her, he awaited her response.

"I shall be delighted," she said simply. This softening trend in the viscount she found most intriguing, not to say disquieting. The stiff, cold gentleman whose acquaintance she remembered to have made on first arriving in London—the man who bore so close a resemblance to the disagreeable Lady Lillian—where had he gone? Her misadventures with the baron and Lord Romby had done more than cause her to rescind her initial harsh opinion of Seabury: they had made her admire him. How well he had dealt with the folly and malice around him! In a sudden rush of confidence, she informed him, while they waited for Miss Meredith, in what high esteem she had learned to regard him. "As for your consulting my judgement, I am as amazed as pleased to be so applied to by you," she continued, speaking now not only with candour but also with deliberate precision. It was a happy union; Lord Seabury was aware of a delicious sensation when she added, "Except for my brother, I know no gentleman with qualities to equal yours—or even to approach them."

Amy Meredith's graceless entrance into the saloon prevented his lordship from replying. "I am wanted, I understand," she remarked sullenly, looking at neither of them so much as at the floor. "I suppose it is a matter of some significance, or I should not be called from my bed."

"My dear Amy," her cousin said very gently, taking her arm and leading her to a comfortable settee, "I have a proposal for you which I hope you will like."

Amy looked up at him mutinously.

"I wish you will return to your Aunt Meredith for a fortnight," he went on mildly. "Your—your indisposition this morning convinces me that London is unhealthy for you. You are vapourish, and I am concerned for your happiness."

"Do not be, I beg," said she, with heavy sarcasm. "If my friend Lady Caroline would but leave me in peace I should do very well, thank you."

He hesitated a moment, then said quietly, "It pains me that you should feel such things."

"I suppose you desire me to take her tenderly to my bosom?" she inquired, eyeing Caro warily.

"A simple polite tolerance would content me," said he.

"She does not tolerate me."

"On the contrary; I am sure Lady Caroline is very fond of you."

"She loathes me," said Amy. "And I do her."

"Please be so kind as to apologize," Seabury directed abruptly, with a sudden return of that inflexibility which had for so long been his refuge in times of strain.

"I shall not! It is true," Amy cried, quite glaring at Caroline.

"If I may be allowed to speak?" Caro said slowly. "It occurs to me that it is no more than honest to admit to Miss Meredith that I am not, as indeed she charges, overly fond of her. I take no great pleasure in her society; no more does she in mine. This does not alter the fact, however, that I bear no ill-will towards her whatever, or that all my behaviour to her is dictated by her best interests. Let us dispense with the formality, therefore, of pretending to love one another, Miss Meredith, and see if we do not breathe more easily."

"You see, she hates me," muttered the stubborn young lady.

"I beg you will attend me," said Caroline, with

surprising patience. "I do not hate you, nor do I love you. It is my opinion that you frequently act contrary to your own interests, and certainly, quite wilfully, contrary to those of your cousin and his family. This is not behaviour calculated to endear you to anybody. I should like, for your sake and that of your family, to see your conduct improve. As for you hating me, you are entirely at liberty to do so. It does not disturb me in the least."

Amy was silent for a moment. "She persuaded you to send me away, did she not my lord?"

"Not at all. It was my thought entirely."

"Well I will not go," Amy declared, flinging a defiant glance at Caroline.

"You are asked to go, and go you shall," said that lady energetically. "I shall not stand by while you bully your cousin, merely because he is too good and too gentlemanly to exercise his power. You must behave as his ward while he acts as your guardian. You will do as he says, and you will do it cheerfully. You may return to your chamber if you like," she concluded, seating herself and taking a large album into her lap to signify that the interview was at an end.

Amy stood, still looking dangerously rebellious. "When?" was all she asked.

"In a week. Monday, perhaps," said Caro, looking to Seabury for corroboration.

"Monday," he repeated, nodding.

Amy turned and trudged towards the door.

"I am very glad you have decided to cooperate," Caroline told her. "Your Aunt Meredith will doubtless be delighted to see you, too."

Amy said nothing. She should have liked to say that she would see Caroline at the devil first, but this was too shocking a retort even for her. Her initial instinct, on arriving again at her bed-chamber, was to throw herself on the bed and repeat this morning's tantrum, only with fresh ruffles and flourishes. Her next instinct was unhappier still, and of course it was the one she followed. She flew for her desk, scribbled out a note, sealed and directed it. Next, she handed it surreptitiously to a footman, along with the promise of a coin if he were swift, and told him to wait for an answer. Three hours later the footman returned, bearing the eagerly awaited reply. After that no complaint was heard from Miss Meredith on the subject of her visit to Kent.

While this clandestine exchange was going forward, Lady Caroline was faced with yet another vexation: Miss Windle had discovered a new case of mischief in her work-box. "I daresay there is some perfectly simple explanation," said the poor lady, tears standing in her eyes and choking her voice, "and that it is nothing to do with Satanic intervention or any such thing, but I assure you I cannot divine it if there is! It looks like Lucifer himself to me; how else is one to understand it?"

Caroline offering neither a solution nor a glass of wine, Miss Windle boldly requested the latter as a consolation. Caro bespoke it of a servant while Windle expanded her lament.

"This time it was not the handkerchief," she sniffed, "for I keep that locked up—can you imagine, locking up a handkerchief?—but a cap I was working for your niece, little Delphina. How sweet she might have looked in it! Fancy a lavender ground with green and yellow stitches—oh, and a little red—representing a lettuce patch! With little brown bits for earth, and a blue sky...my heart fairly breaks when I think of it," she ended on a sob, accepting the comforting claret Caro now proffered. It sounded to Caroline as if the cap were much better off in tatters, but to say as much was unthinkable, and so she merely murmured what solace her conscience would allow.

"Delphina adores to run about bare-headed of course," said she, "so perhaps it is all the same to her. I am certain she would love to receive a reticule, however; though I doubt Lady Lillian deems her sufficiently grown up to carry one."

"Ah, little Delphina!" said Windle, relaxing into a pensive mode, as she frequently did over claret. "How much a mother is blessed, who has children!"

Caroline silently wondered what sort of mother, blessed or unblessed, has no children. Miss Windle, however, was already giving voice to further reflections.

"I have often observed, that a primary joy of the married state is the introduction into the household of children. What pleasure, what interest is taken in the little ones! What pride does the proud father experience! What love the loving mother! Oh dear, there is the last drop of claret," she said, swallowing. "Might I trouble you for another glass?"

Caroline poured again from the decanter. They sat in the snug parlour situated between their bed-chambers. Caro kept her work-basket there, so it was not much trouble for her to take out her filagree and keep herself occupied with it while she listened to her chaperone's verbal meanderings. She even took some amusement in them.

"I never married, as I think you know," Windle resumed rather loudly, "But I might have, I might have. Yes, I say to you without fear of its going farther, I might have married twice, had I desired it. My papa two times informed me of the tender emotions harboured in the breast of a young man in our village—emotions, I may say, gathered like little boats in the cove of my admirer's bosom, and bobbing there like tiny buoys on the ripples of the sea—yes, twice did my dear papa inform me gravely of this fine young person's love for me (I do not shrink from calling it love, as you see; I name it freely) and twice did I refuse him. Why, you will inquire; why did I refuse him? Was I an icy maiden, my frost-bitten ears deaf to his bootless pleas? Was I a stone, over which the warm flood of his sentiments ran as over a rock? Was I pitiless, merciless, cruel in the face of that love, so heated by the fires of his passion, so sharp with the keenness of his desire, so deep with the depths of his profundities?" Miss Windle paused to take a long swig of her claret. "Yes! Yes, I was! I tell you baldly and truthfully—yes! I was utterly without compassion for him of any sort. I may even say—yes, I do say—that I did not like him. Not a bit. A slobbering hulk, with his shoulders hanging over his sinking chest like bushes over a cliff, and soiled linen round his red neck, that smelt of garlic, and a great purple nose like a turnip. Why, you ask? Why!" she demanded, draining the second glass and rising to pour a third for

herself. "Because . . . I despised the brute! A monster! The
blacksmith's son, that is who he was, and my father would
have thrown me to the dog and a dowry besides—would
gladly have tossed me away to live in a smithy and stitch
eternally at a lot of garlicky collars—" Miss Windle
stopped talking as abruptly as if someone had smashed
her over the head with a club. "Oh dear! I hope . . . I do
hope, my dear Lady Caroline, I have not been saying what
I think I have in fact been saying. Have I?"

"Have you what?" Caro asked.

"Been saying what I think I have been saying. Oh my, I
hope not!"

Charitably, Caro assured her she had not.

"Thank Heaven," breathed the good lady. "I expect I
have been talking about Lord Romby then, have I? It was
Lord Romby I meant to speak of all along."

Caroline hesitated. "Yes, rather, though you have not
said much just yet. What exactly was it you wished to
mention?"

"Oh my, only what a fine man he is!" said the other, as
if this were self-evident. "You do think he is a fine man, do
not you?"

She debated within herself. "Certainly he is not a bad
man," she said finally, "though he cannot be said to be
without vices."

"Who among us can?" inquired Windle dolefully; then,
"What are they, my dear?"

"Romby's vices? Why, intemperance, and wrath, and
prodigality, and an addiction to games of chance; and
then he is blasphemous, and refuses to go to church,"
Caroline answered, surprised to be able to hit upon so
many so easily. Really, his lordship was not a very fine old
man at all!

"Oh, that," Windle replied after a moment, as if
Caroline had made note of some tiny flaw. She made a
large gesture with a pale hand as if to sweep the objections
away, and pointed out generously that she herself drank a
glass of claret or two on occasion.

"Yes, but my dear ma'am." Caroline answered, putting
down her filagree the better to fix Miss Windle with her
gaze, "that is quite a different matter. I am sure you have

never taken an oath in your life stronger than 'Angels defend us.' I know for a fact you have seen the priest every Sunday for the last five years. You are patient, and resigned, and frugal, and if you ever play at anything deeper than Speculation, you make an excellent secret of it. Lord Romby, by comparison, is practically a devil."

Miss Windle, who on this particular occasion had drunk a glass of claret or four already, promptly and spiritedly denied this accusation. "Lady Caroline, I think you are the best young lady in the world—I often have said so to Mrs. Henry, if you do not believe me—and compared to that disaster of a Miss Meredith, *you* are a seraph. However! To say that Lord Romby, a good, long-suffering, sweet, though much maligned old gentle-man (and he is not all that old, by the bye) is 'practically a devil' shows a singular lapse of judgement, an hideous and most disappointing want of insight and charity, which is excessively painful to me—as your chaperone and relative no matter how distant—to be obliged to mention. I ascribe it—no no, let me proceed," she insisted, as Caro attempted to interrupt, "—I ascribe it to youth, to the lack of ripeness of your soul which, like a green cherry on a tree, hangs awkwardly from the yet springy bough of your meagre experience. When the sap," she continued, ever gaining in volubility, "when the sap that shoots madly through your childish veins, like arrows shooting wildly through a verdant wood, shall cease to boil and froth as the foam on a brewing posset; when the sap shall subside, I say, you will see things in a different light. Different, did I say? Nay, better. Truer. Brighter. A brighter light, dear young miss, beams on us in maturity, than ever shines on any golden-headed child—not, you know, that you are golden-headed, or ever were—and shows us where to walk, and how to walk, with a precision, and clarity, a cloudlessness of vision such as you can never fancy. Mr. Wordsworth notwithstanding!" she shouted trium-phantly, adding a second resounding, "Mr. Wordsworth NOT withstanding!"

After this Miss Windle crumpled up into a heap, exhausted by her oratory, and more than a trifle bosky. Caroline, as she assisted her to rise and bundled her slowly back into her bed-chamber, assured her no gentleman had ever been so well defended as Lord Romby had just had the honour to be.

"I endeavour," the collapsed lady said faintly, "to be a friend to my friends."

Lady Caroline made soothing noises and rang the bell for Mary, into whose care she shortly afterwards entrusted her chaperone. This gave her time to shut herself gratefully into her own chamber and lose herself in her thoughts. She had a good deal to think about, and her reflections were not entirely pleasant. It was cheerful to remember that Seabury had turned to her for counsel; cheerful too to recall the mild, trusting glance of his dark eyes. Even the sudden confession she had made, regarding her esteem for him, was not altogether disagreeable to consider, though it did make her a trifle giddy to remember how boldly she had made her avowal. This was a subtle vertigo indeed for Lady Caroline! The melancholy, even frustrating theme of her meditation was that in spite of all she had done to disentangle herself from mischief and Mockabee, she had none the less exposed Seabury and his family to public scrutiny and ridicule— for it was beyond hoping that anyone should fail to recognize her is the subject of the poem in *The Times*. In fact, Lady Beatrice had already sent over a note (Mr. Walfish had discovered the verse and interpreted it to her) informing her that half London was in a hum over it, that at least half of those who read it guessed correctly the identity of Lord M, and that this was *not* what she had meant by developing an eccentric character. Caro thought it a little hard that Lady Beatrice should chuse not to acknowledge her share in developing that character— for whether or not Caro had ultimately misused it, there was no doubt of its being in large part what made the doggerel so delicious an *on-dit*—and yet she was obliged to own, very mournfully, that she had really brought it on herself. She regretted it infinitely more for Seabury's sake than for her own; otherwise she should not have been sorry, but rather merely furious. Retaliation, which would once have been her first concern, was out of the question on the same grounds.

She must bear it as she could, she told herself grimly; after her first excursion back into the world the worst of the humiliation would be behind her.

Baron Mockabee received two communications from Rucke House that thirteenth day of May. The tenor of the first the reader may guess. The second, no less interesting, arrived towards the close of day, when his lordship was just on the point of retiring to dress for dinner and the Opera. With a sigh the baron sank into an armchair to examine the missive; with a gasp, almost, he read its contents:

> This present writing comes to you in consequence of a poem appearing this morning in The Times, which I perceive to have been written by you on the subject of my kinswoman Lady C.W. She being under my protection, it falls to me to act for her when I discover her the topic of a sly, unflattering piece of verse in a public newspaper. Sir Matthew Winterborn does me the honour of acting for me in this matter. If you will be so good as to appoint a time convenient to you, and a place also convenient, I will be pleased to meet you there.
>
> > I have the honour to remain
> > Your obdt. etc,
> > Seabury.

Mockabee's first thought was that the challenge had nothing to do at all with Lady Caroline, but rather that she, and the poem, were being used as a pretext to mask the more alarming issue—Amy. But could the chit keep a secret no longer than a few hours? How had she made the viscount suspicious enough to question her, and how much had she told? If she were really so unaccomplished in the arts of duplicity, might he not do better to drop the whole scheme at once, before it even began? Her part in the business, it was true, was very slight; he would do most of the work. Still, some little deception would be required of her... The baron next considered that perhaps Seabury was indeed concerned only with Caroline— though now that he had vented his spleen against her,

Lord Mockabee could not imagine why anybody should
trouble with the ridiculous creature. If that were the case,
then Amy had governed herself adequately. Moreover,
Seabury would not be shooting to wound over a mere
poem; it was a simple matter of the honour of a
kinswoman, nothing deep or complex. Maybe, Mockabee even considered, he ought to offer an apology and let
it go at that. But the memory of the graceless rebuff
Caroline had dealt him, and her nasty parting threat,
immediately made this alternative too distasteful to
pursue.

He must meet Lord Seabury as his lordship requested;
if he could first discover from Amy Meredith what exactly
was at issue, so much the better. With a fresh sigh he wrote
out a terse note to the Honble. George Blount, a young
hussar who was not, for reasons both obscure and
compelling, in a position to refuse Lord Mockabee a
favour. The baron would have preferred an older man,
but the gentleman he generally chose for his second had
been greatly affected by the bloodshed resulting from the
Embrey affair, and was, upon the whole, better left to cool
for a while. It was troublesome, these challenges. They
seemed to appear with a startling regularity, at least one a
month. At least, the baron imagined with some
satisfaction, Lord Seabury passed too many hours in
Parliament to be a very good shot.

Chapter VIII

"My dear man," Sir Sidney Pettingill kept sputtering, "My dear sir . . . My dear man," he repeated, while a fresh burst of perspiration appeared on his brow, forming a thin bright mist in the morning sun, "My dear man, I am at a loss for what to say." On these words he exhaled mightily, as if much relieved to have ended his sentence (as indeed he was) and sank, a plumpish mass, into a fatly cushioned chair. His dear man, always gazing at him curiously, seated himself too and waited patiently to hear what mission aroused such inarticulateness in the glib Pettingill.

Lord Seabury (for he it was whom Sir Sidney addressed) thought it appropriate at this moment to offer his caller a dish of tea, or perhaps some orgeat since it was so warm.

"Sherry, if you please," came the hoarse reply. "I should die, I sometimes think," he further remarked, with a glistening half-smile, "were it not for a glass of sherry. Ghastly heat, I protest."

"Abominable," the viscount agreed politely, though he did not appear at all oppressed by the weather. He rose again, crossed the Gilt Saloon, and poured from a crystal decanter into a silver cup.

"This is a sticky business, I assure you, my dear man,"
Pettingill went on, "or else I should not be so long about
it. It is about Lady—Lady Caroline I am come, you know.
Dear fellow, bless you for this," he injected gratefully as
he accepted the cup from his companion. "It is a matter
of—I dareswear you do not win quite so often at brag as
you once did, sir!" he suddenly exclaimed, with a sly wink
Lord Seabury found almost as surprising as the words it
underscored.

"I am afraid I do not entirely understand you," he said.
"Though what you say is true, it is equally true that I no
longer lose quite so often at brag either. In short, Sir
Sidney, I no longer play quite so often. Indeed, I have not
played this age."

"Gave it up out of frustration did you? You ought not
to have let her discourage you so easily, dear fellow! I
could have educated you, had you but asked, just as I did
her. What a minx she is!"

This was all much gibberish to Seabury, and he did not
disguise his confusion.

"You do not understand me yet?" asked Pettingill.

"I am sorry to say I do not."

"I refer very simply to—but maybe I had best not
pursue it after all," he amended in a rush, for it struck him
that perhaps this was a sore point with the viscount. "In
any case, that was mere conversation, you know. My true
goal—my real—" after much hesitation, Pettingill took a
handkerchief from a pocket in his waistcoat and mopped
his damp brow with it. The moisture there was really
remarkable; it had even seeped up into his (somewhat)
carroty hair, which it was causing to curl still more
profusely than was usual. He regretted deeply, though
silently, having worn such a high collar; of course he had
wished to cut a fine figure before Lord Seabury, but this
was nonsense. Casting a voiceless curse at the day, he
attempted to resume his thought. "My real aim in coming
here is to ask—no, first I must remind you that I am,
though not of so high a rank as yours, still not bereft of
gentility. I suppose you know—in any case, I inform you
now—there have been Pettingills in Dorset an hundred
years or more, nor has one left any legacy but honour to

the name. Oh dear!" he corrected himself an instant later, "what have I said? I do not intend to state that one Pettingill has left nothing but honour to the next, for indeed, on the contrary—as I was about to say, dear sir, my ancestors have left a good deal more, of property and such, naturally. I only wish to note, that no scandal has ever attached to the name of Pettingill. No scandal," he repeated for emphasis. "That is my meaning."

His lordship had not misconstrued the initial statement for a moment, but he attempted to look enlightened now in order to soothe Sir Sidney. The phrase, "Pettingills in Dorset," fell oddly upon his ear, and reminded him for some reason of Mrs. Wickware complaining that there were mice in the pantry, but he did not allow his handsome mouth even to hint at a smile. Sir Sidney looked too earnest to be calm under such an indignity.

"I have got, to put it bluntly, twenty thousand a year in income, you know," the visitor now went on. "My estate in Dorset is considerable, as I suppose you are aware. In brief, if you can tolerate a baronet for a kinsman, I should like to offer for Lady Caroline. If she will have me. That is to say, I shall offer and see if she will have me."

Lord Seabury had formed several conjectures as to what Sir Sidney had on his mind, but none was so extraordinary as the one he had just revealed. The effect upon Seabury was that of a sudden piece of very bad news. He sat almost staring, and said nothing.

"Dear sir, my dear man!" cried Pettingill, immediately putting a woeful interpretation upon his host's silence. "I hope you do not consider I am too young for her ladyship! Indeed, I thought of it long and hard, and though it is true she is no green girl, I am not quite an infant either. It is a fact, sir," he went on somewhat more reflectively, "that her ladyship has passed through a large number of child-bearing years already—six or seven at least, I am well aware of it—but she has more than a few ahead of her, and I need only one heir after all." On these last words Sir Sidney gave a little chuckle, and tossed a knowing look at Seabury, who did not return it.

"This is a surprise, sir," he finally said, very gravely and slowly. "I must think for a moment."

The baronet apparently considered that no one ought to be obliged to think in peace, for he at once began to speak again, babbling on quite maniacally. "I could have gone to her brother, Inlowe; and indeed I almost did write to him, my dear man. But then, thought I to myself, why she is under Lord Seabury's protection now! Perhaps it will be enough to apply to him. Besides, Lady Caroline is no baby; if it came to that, she could marry as she chose. So I am come to you, my dear fellow, as a sort of compromise. Perhaps you are not the properest person to ask, but you are more proper than no one. Hey, old man?" he concluded, feeling quite cheerful now that he had managed to say what was necessary to be said.

Seabury, who had scarcely attended him, finally brought out carefully, "I am the more surprised that you should chuse this particular morning to apply to me since it was but yesterday that all London read that unfortunate poem about her ladyship in *The Times*. I suppose it does not distress you overmuch?" he asked, with a peculiar intonation.

"Poem about Lady Caroline?" Sir Sidney echoed, obviously hearing of it for the first time. "What poem is that, my dear man?"

"Why—this," Seabury said, rising again and returning with the unhappy newspaper. Pettingill stared at it, frowning, for a minute; then raised his head and looked, amazed, at Seabury.

"This is about Lady Caroline?" he asked incredulously.

"Assuredly," Seabury returned, equally incredulous that Pettingill should doubt it.

"I read it yesterday, but I assure you I had no notion—! I thought it a most curious little rhyme!"

"In that case, though it is not pleasant, I must suggest you read it again. As you see, it is far from kind."

Sir Sidney read and reread the poem. "I am sorry," he confessed at last, "but I do not understand this—this last of first bit. What the devil does it mean?"

Lord Seabury explained that it referred to the word Line.

"Oh my! So it does indeed," said Pettingill, looking at it once more. "Deuced clever. Who wrote it?"

As Pettingill appeared only to be mildly interested—not the least bit dismayed or outraged—Seabury saw no point in answering his question truthfully, and only said, "I do not know. It will be some time, however, before the *ton* stops prattling about it, so you may wish to take that into account when you consider offering for Caroline."

"You do not mean to say that other people knew it to be she as well?" Sir Sidney asked in wonderment.

"Everybody, I fear; or so it seems."

"Extraordinary!" opined Pettingill, while his host thought, very uncharitably, that he had never seen such a clunch as this Sir Sidney. He murmured an indistinct reply, so vague that Pettingill supposed he must be thinking about the proposal again, and again set out to provide a background of aimless chatter. "It will be pleasant for Lady Caroline, I believe, that she need not be too very far from her home. It is not a morning's walk, that is so; but it will not be too much for her to travel into Berkshire, if she cares to, as many as two times a year, I should think." He was silent, briefly. "I suppose you can tell me, my dear man, what sort of a dowry Lady Caroline might receive?" He paused, peering from under carroty brows at the viscount.

"I am, indeed, privy to those details of her ladyship's affairs," Seabury replied cautiously, "and can tell you at once that she will have a generous portion. I am informed that Lord Inlowe is very much attached to his sister, and since he is a man of some means, he will see to it she is always comfortable. As to the exact sum, I must consult my papers to ascertain it."

"Not at all necessary, not the least needful," Pettingill protested at once, waving a hand as if to dismiss the question altogether. "I was merely curious, nothing more. But does this—am I to understand you will permit me to address her ladyship?"

Seabury fixed him with his steady blue regard and said, "Indeed, if you desire to do so, I am sure Inlowe can have no objection, nor can I. Lady Caroline, as you observe, is pretty much her own mistress in any case. If she accepts you, her brother and my sister will embrace you as their own; I believe I can assure you of that."

"Ah, Seabury! I am a very happy man," said he, his tongue recovering its customary knack for finding smooth, if only because well-worn, phrases.

The reply, "Well, I am not," flashed through Seabury's brain and was rejected in an instant, to be replaced by, "You will chuse your moment to address Lady Caroline as you like, naturally; but I am afraid you cannot do so today. She visits my aunt, Lady Beatrice, this morning."

"Good Lord, my dear man, you do not suppose I could speak to her today!" exclaimed the other. "I feel as if I could sleep for a week after all this." The poor man really did look exhausted, not to mention damp. He was a little intimidated, if the truth were known, by the magnificence of Rucke House, and the urbanity of its inmates. His twenty thousand a year notwithstanding, Sir Sidney was a simple country squire at heart, and knew it. If not for his wealth, and his willingness to part with it through gaming, he must have had a hard time gaining an entrée into society, for those and his facile speeches were all that distinguished him from the keeper of the Old Crown Inn. It was certainly, as Lord Seabury could not help thinking, no inborn delicacy which marked him out from his countrymen. Perhaps he was prejudiced against the fellow—for some reason he pushed from his head at once—and could not judge fairly, but it seemed to him most applications of the order just made by Sir Sidney must somehow achieve a greater degree of elegance than this one. Never having received one before, or having made one for that matter, it was difficult to say. Still, Seabury suspected this one to have been rather blunt than otherwise.

Whatever it had been, it was over, and Pettingill took his leave pretty quickly to go home and recuperate. No sooner had Lord Seabury resumed his chair, after the departure, with the intention of devoting a few minutes to reviewing the scene, than he was interrupted by Hedgepeth, who knocked with some urgency. "It is a caller, sir," said the discreet butler, proffering a tray with a card upon it. "I hope I do well in bringing this to you, my lord, for the caller desires to see Miss Meredith, and not yourself."

Hedgepeth was soon told he had done very well indeed,

since the card belonged to Baron Mockabee. "Impudent scoundrel!" Seabury could not help but exclaim aloud—quite an outburst from so reserved a gentleman, as Hedgepeth later remarked to Mrs. Wickware. "Tell him Miss Meredith is not at home."

Hedgepeth bowed and disappeared upon this errand. A very few minutes later, Amy Meredith burst into the Gilt Saloon, an indignant reproach upon her lips. "How dare you deny me to a caller?" she demanded shrilly, tears of frustration already standing in her eyes. "I insist you turn off Hedgepeth at once! What business had he to run to you with Lord Mockabee's card?"

"How, if I may inquire, do you come to be aware of Lord Mockabee's having asked for you?" Seabury asked calmly, offering her a chair.

She preferred to stand. "I saw him from my window," she said, omitting to add that she had been watching for him there all morning. "He was obliged to behave so indecorously as to call up to me from the street with an account of his reception here. Of course he thought *I* refused him, which I told him could not be farther from the truth. He is furious with you, and so am I."

"Well," Seabury observed quietly, "and so am I furious with him."

"Why?" she countered. "Because of that silly poem in *The Times?*"

"Yes, cousin; because of that silly poem."

"If it had been about me you would not care so much," she charged.

"That is perfectly untrue," said he.

"You mean it is perfectly true," she retorted, continuing with a new tone of sullenness. "In any case she has had her vengeance. She drove up to our door just as Mockabee was leaving, and gave him the cut direct."

"Did she?" he murmured, catching at this detail.

"Yes she did, and I thought it abominably low. Why is she so certain he wrote that poem anyway? There are crowds of Lord M's in London, I trust. And even if she knew it to be him," she went on, pulling her pretty mouth into a terrific pout, "it is hardly sporting to take it in such bad part."

"My dear Amy," said he, suddenly softened, "what do

you know of sporting behaviour? Even if you were thoroughly versed in it, you would be wrong to think this situation calls for it. Lord Mockabee's poem constitutes a public attack on Lady Caroline's name. It is a very grave offence, and has not been easy for Caroline to bear."

"She looks careless enough," Amy interjected sulkily.

"Indeed she does," said he, smiling strangely. "It is our obligation to assist her in maintaining that mask of indifference. She has elected not to go out for the next few days, except among family; but when she feels ready to venture forth, I think we must all go with her. Yes, we must; I propose we walk in Kensington Gardens that evening, all of us. It will be a pleasant, simple return into society for her, and open enough so that no one gossip can start all the others humming."

"Obligation," Amy spat out disgustedly. "Protect Caroline, that is your byword these days. What became of 'Walk Alone?' I thought that was the motto on the Romby crest."

"So it is, my dear," said he, losing his patience again. "I suggest, therefore, that you walk alone to your bedchamber, or somewhere, for I feel the need of solitude myself."

This unusually abrupt dismissal had its desired result: Amy, silenced, quit the room and left her cousin in peace. The events of the morning had stimulated his thoughts greatly. Most of all, the idea of Sir Sidney Pettingill offering for Caroline caught hold of his imagination. It was not impossible, he incorrectly supposed, that her ladyship would accept him. Seabury saw in him no special charm, but he was so much cried up by the match-making mammas that the viscount concluded he must have qualities visible only to the fairer sex. If she did accept him—but this was too disagreeable to contemplate. If she refused him—could Seabury offer himself? Would she have him? Her initial response to him had been dreadful; of that he was sure. One had only to remember the speech he overheard her making to Romby that day, so soon after her arrival, to know it beyond a doubt. And yet, as time went by, he had seemed to perceive a warming of her sentiments towards him. On those occasions when he had invited her to drive with him in the Green Park, she had never refused; but then, he reminded himself, there had of course been the unpleasant scene which had caused the curtailment of those drives. She was harsh in her judgements, as he knew through observation and through experience. She was rash too, and stubborn. He had felt the disadvantage of all three of these faults more than once; but were they not, perhaps, compensated for by her candour, her sincerity? He had been interested to hear Amy's account of Caro's meeting that morning with Mockabee: it seemed to him a manifestation of restraint, of an ability to govern her feelings which he had sometimes feared she lacked. Moreover, he had seen her only yesterday a very picture of contrition. Her insistence upon making an humble apology—was that not behaviour graceful enough to erase the memory of her errors in judgement?

With a start, he remembered Lady Susan. Horrible to recognize how wholly he had forgot her! He could no longer pretend, even to himself, that she was anything to him except an object, by long habit and mild inclination, of friendly solicitude. Nonetheless, Lord Safford had stood by him unfailingly for years, in Parliament and out, and Seabury had pretty much given him to understand that Susan and he would marry someday. True, he had not said it in so many words—not an easy achievement of late, either, since Safford had begun to grow impatient. It gave Seabury a queer feeling, a feeling almost like a repugnance against himself, to admit that he might actually be capable of leaving Susan on the shelf. After all, besides her father's kindness to him, Susan herself had been unobjectionable all these years (barring perhaps the recent incident in Hampstead), never giving him the slightest cause to complain of her or regret his association with her family. He liked to think what he could no longer comfortably think: that he was a man who paid his debts, who would fail in no explicit or implicit promise, who struck out upon the road of honour and never faltered, though sentiment might fall behind. Must he offer for Susan then? How had his desires drifted so many miles away from his conscience? To offer for her was to win her; of that there was no question. The idea of winning Susan had an heavy irony in this context, yet she was a gem in her own way; his lordship could not dissuade himself of that early conviction. She was docile, well-intentioned, pretty and agreeable. Why should he long for a bold, high-spirited, impetuous woman, when Susan was his for the asking?

If the reader feels at once that such a question answers itself, it is perhaps well to point out that Lord Seabury had never set eyes upon Caroline until six weeks before, whereas Lady Susan had been his chosen companion upwards of seven years. Furthermore, Seabury was a man universally acknowledged to be firm of resolve, a man whose political ambitions meant a great deal to him, who was noted for his sense of honour, his dignity, and his gravity. It was not long before his well-disciplined mind had forced the thought of marrying Caroline into a narrow and dark recess, and brought the idea of Lady Susan out into air and sunlight again. Of course he would marry Susan, he said to himself calmly. He must offer for her soon, in fact. He would do very well with her for a wife; they had been compatible these seven years—not a single quarrel, he observed brightly—and they would be compatible ten times that long. He would be at peace, thank God, with both the world and his own conscience; and through that peace should find strength to pursue his career in government. He emerged from the Gilt Saloon a moment later with a sensation of tranquillity that had been eluding him for some time. Of course there was a duel to be fought at dawn next day; but that was a case where his duty was clear, and soon dispensed with. He slept better that night than many a man with a similar appointment ahead of him.

May the fifteenth was not a fine day that year. Even before light began to gild the edges of the dark sky there was an oppressive humidity, a lingering sultriness that night had been unable to overthrow, which recalled the heat of the previous evening and promised a renewal of dull, enervating weather. It had been unseasonably warm, indeed, for weeks; and though the sky seemed continually to threaten rain, it never went so far as actually to produce any. Oliver, Lord Seabury made his toilet by candle-light that morning, assisted by his valet, and conscious more than anything of the necessity of making no sound that might arouse the guests at Rucke House. As the ladies were quartered at the opposite end of the house, his task was not difficult; but his anxious conviction that Lady Caroline would be highly displeased if she knew what he was about to do aggravated his fears and caused him to hush his servant several times. "See to the door," he finally hissed, for though he had instructed Hedgepeth to watch for Sir Matthew Winterborn's arrival, he had a sudden fancy that that competent gentleman would forget to do so, and that Winterborn's knock at the door would awaken the household.

His man gone, Lord Seabury drank coffee at his dressing-table and sleepily pondered the approaching encounter. If Mockabee offered anything like an apology, his opponent was disposed to accept it, for a duel—besides being dangerous in the obvious sense—was not the sort of affair a politically ambitious young peer wished to be frequently involved in. The fact was, that it was illegal; and Seabury, more punctilious than most in matters of the law, found the very idea of this distasteful. Certainly duels were still common among the *ton*, and the courts showed a deep tolerance for them in most cases—but even if this morning's encounter were kept an utter secret, Seabury did not like the thought of it. His scruples notwithstanding, he had twice before sent such a challenge as Lord Mockabee had received of him; one had resulted in an apology, the other in a grazed shoulder and a misfire. The injured shoulder had been his, but it had been nothing great, and was soon mended and forgot. Never once had he received a cartel: he was too circumspect, too politic. He could only guess, therefore, at Baron Mockabee's feelings, and the probability of his offering an apology at the duelling-ground.

Sir Matthew arrived before ten minutes had passed, full of bracing remarks and yawns to belie them. He was a fresh, round-cheeked young man, with a bright pair of brown eyes and an endless supply of enthusiasm. "Had a

chat with Embrey yesterday, my dear fellow," he said
jauntily, pouring himself some coffee. "Upon my soul,
you look fit this morning! Anyhow—this is in strictest
confidence you know—Embrey says Mockabee shoots to
his left. Fancies himself an excellent shot, but never fails
to pull to the left, that is what Embrey says. Of course it
could be his pistol—he would not budge on the business
of the pistols. Each his own, he absolutely insisted—I
think I told you so?"

Lord Seabury nodded.

"At all events, he shall have no advantage over you in
the way of fire-arms," Winterborn continued. "Yours
from Manton's are lovely, lovely." As if to demonstrate
his sincerity in this opinion, the good young gentleman
gently stroked the top of the leathern pistol-case he had
brought with him. "And besides, this Mr. George Blount
who acts as his second is a perfect idiot, I assure you.
Nothing more likely than that he will foul up the pistol
when he loads it. Actually, Seabury, I am not at all
satisfied with the man myself: a second is meant to be a
gentleman of equal rank to the principal, or at least
something approaching it! This Blount is no one, that I
can discover, though he claims an Honourable to his
name. Very young too," he added, shaking his head
disapprovingly. "Not but what I am young, naturally, and
hardly close to you in station—but still, my dear fellow, if
it came to your having to face this little hussar, the
situation would be most ridiculous."

"It is not a situation likely to arise," the viscount
remarked mildly.

"Nonetheless," Winterborn objected vaguely, "it don't
speak well for Mockabee." He was silent a moment,
sipping coffee. "How the devil did Lady Caroline get on
the wrong side of such a fellow anyway? Not that it
matters," he hastily added, seeing Seabury scowl. "You
will be calling me out next, hey?"

"They grew up in the same country," his lordship
replied, somewhat obscurely. "I daresay we had best be
off soon. We will need time to get to Putney Heath."

"No cause to look so grim!" Winterborn remonstrated
gently. "By all means, let us be gone. Mr. Ellis will be

happy to see us, in any case; he has been waiting all this while in the post-chaise."

"Mr. Ellis—?"

"The surgeon, dear fellow. A very able gentleman, I assure you, though a trifle—ah—eccentric."

"I do not care for this business of the post-chaise," Seabury murmured as, a light cloak thrown over his shoulders, he prepared to quit the room. "I had much rather take my own carriage."

"Impossible, dear sir," Winterborn replied firmly, who had expected such a protest. "You cannot take such a risk as that with the good gentlemen of Bow Street swarming all over London. I suppose you would think it only right, but in fact it would be nothing more than absurd."

Seabury would have objected again, but as they were by now descending the great oaken staircase he preferred to keep silent. His last thoughts, as he stepped outside the massive doors of Rucke House, were of Caroline; but since this struck him at once as being quite improper, he sought diligently, while entering the post-chaise, to summon up the image of Lady Susan Manning. Ah, there she was! But no, her blond hair darkened inexorably until it was chestnut brown, like . . . somebody else's. There were her eyes, however, squinting slightly just as they did—alas, they widened slowly and revealed themselves to be the eyes of . . . somebody else. Poor Seabury put the thought of women out of his mind altogether, to concentrate on the business of the day.

The surgeon, Mr. Ellis, was a pasty-faced, corpulent man, whose fat little hands were adorned with fat little fingers that squirmed, like curious sea-creatures, atop his broad, plump thighs. His nose was very red, though evidently not as a result of drinking, for a more phlegmatic gentleman would be hard to find. "I like a duel," he was saying ponderously, when the viscount began to listen to him. "Even if there is some risk to it, in terms of laws and licences and such, I mean; and even if one must arise in the middle of the night; still, I like a duel. No one ever forgets to pay my bill, for a duel. Too much honour at stake! And besides that advantage, if one of the participants is wounded, why I have only to bind him up

for an hour or two, and then he is off home as quick as can
be to his favourite family surgeon. No one ever badgers
me to help him once he is safely home! No indeed, I am
abed and nice and cosy all over again, no later than nine in
the morning. A gentleman likes to be attended by his own
physician. I am sure you would, my lord."

"I suppose I should, come to that," said Seabury.

"There, you see? Now another fine thing about a duel,
is no moaning if a man is wounded. No groaning, no
grumbling—because it would not be gentlemanly! I tell
you to your head, sir, there is nothing that annoys a
surgeon more than a nasty, groaning patient." After this
Mr. Ellis was quiet for some minutes, during which time
he turned his lack-lustre gaze first on Winterborn, then on
Seabury, and then on Winterborn again, looking all the
while (except for the smooth movement of his short, fat
neck) as if he were stuffed.

The carriage rattled through the sleeping streets with a
noise like thunder, for Sir Matthew had promised the
coachman a guinea if he made haste. Seabury had been
looking forward to some fresh air, for the atmosphere in
his bedchamber that morning had been quite stuffy; but it
seemed there was no fresh air to be had anywhere near
London that day. Even as they gained the edge of the
great Metropolis, no country breeze sprang up to revive
him. If he had been a man of nervous temperament, it is
certain he would have arrived at Putney Heath gasping
and faint—but he was not of nervous temperament. He
forced himself to focus on the dim outlines of the trees and
cottages they rolled past, and to ignore the monotonous
rumble of the wheels and the steady, soporific swaying of
the coach. When this became difficult, he initiated
another conversation, though he little desired to talk, in
the expectation that it would help him to remain alert.

"I suppose you do a great deal of this sort of thing, Mr.
Ellis?" he inquired.

"Indeed I *do*! I *like* a duel, as I often say. Although," he
added thoughtfully, "they are monstrous awkward when
one of the gentlemen is killed."

"Do you find that happens frequently?" his lordship
politely pursued.

"Seabury, really," Sir Matthew interrupted. "What a question! It is sufficiently unpleasant to hear about wounds and groans and such, but death! Let me tell you rather about...about Charles Stickney's new curricle. It *is* a dasher! Have you seen it?"

"Please, Winterborn; I should like to hear about Mr. Ellis's experiences."

The surgeon, evidently flattered at being preferred in this wise, drew up the corners of his bloodless mouth into an approximation of a smile. "I dislike to interrupt the gentleman—" he hinted, with a pointed glance at Sir Matthew.

"Oh, tell him you do not mind, dear fellow," Lord Seabury said a little testily.

Sir Matthew unwillingly consented to be cut off.

"I thank you sir," Ellis replied, smoothly ducking his great head several times in acknowledgement of the courtesy. "In answer to your question then, my lord, indeed I have not seen many gentlemen killed, I am happy to say. I should think no more than one gentleman in ten duels."

"Dutch comfort!" murmured good Sir Matthew.

"Oh, but then—this is not a mortal issue, my lord, I think?" Mr. Ellis suggested. "I had understood, if I remember correctly, that this particular duel is to be of the milder sort," the surgeon went on, faltering a little as he groped for the proper words. "What I mean, to say it bluntly, is there is no, er, infidelity in the case. Is there? Not that it signifies to *me*, gentlemen! Not in the least!"

"If you mean, how many shots will be fired, indeed there will be but one on each side," Sir Matthew told him, a bit coldly. "And there is the possibility of a reconciliation even before that."

Mr. Ellis looked uncomfortable at once, and stared balefully at Seabury until that perceptive gentleman inquired if something were the matter.

"Dear me, my lord! Only that... I wonder if I ought to point out... I wonder if you know, that my fee is the same regardless of how the affair goes off." His fat fingers crawling about wildly on his thighs, he continued with the severest unease, "No matter if no shots are fired, or one, or two. No matter if you are killed—alas, my lord, it is the nature of my business to exact a fee, even if a gentleman is killed—"

"Devil take the man!" Sir Matthew finally burst out. "Close your mouth sir; close it, I say! What do you mean by talking such drivel?"

"He has got a right to secure his fee," Seabury interrupted mildly, amused at his even-tempered friend's outrage.

"Of course he will have his fee," cried the agitated Winterborn. "on condition he keeps his peace, that is. Mum, Mr. Ellis, mum! If you are not scaring his lordship, you are certainly scaring me!"

Lord Seabury, who always lost much of his reserve when threatened with a personal disaster, could no longer contain himself, and simply roared with laughter. Mr. Ellis watched him impassively, concluding (silently, since his fee was at stake) that Sir Matthew had, after all, been offended by his continuing to speak when the younger gentleman had desired to describe Charles Stickney's curricle. What the viscount found so hilarious Mr. Ellis could not have said; he only hoped the man was not cracking under the strain of the coming encounter. If he were he would probably fail to defend himself, and any wound he might receive in consequence of such inattention would be an inconvenience, at best, to his surgeon.

Seabury was still wiping tears of laughter from his handsome blue eyes when the carriage arrived at the appointed meeting-place some few minutes before five o'clock. "Upon my honour, Seabury," Sir Matthew hissed as they crossed the heath to where the other little party was already gathered, "if you do not control yourself better Mockabee will suppose you have been crying."

"If I thought he supposed such a thing I should shoot to kill him," his lordship returned, sobered at once by Winterborn's warning. Now that he could see the baron again, he recovered his grimness. The man looked so sinister, so wolf-like! Not only his pale lips and his strange, glittering eyes, but his whole carriage and all his traits expressed a malign distrust of everyone around him. It would be a positive pleasure, Seabury suddenly felt, to take a shot at him. He would almost regret an apology.

Sir Matthew had gone over to confer with Mr. Blount, to determine if the baron had undergone a change of heart. Evidently he had not, for Winterborn returned to Seabury—who stood, with Mr. Ellis, a short ways off from the others, and exchanged no more than a nod across the open field with Mockabee—with the news that the seconds were now to load the pistols, and that afterwards Seabury would be at liberty to take his ground as he chose. "You will fire at pleasure," he added, "at whatever distance you like. Only tell me, and I shall tell Blount."

The viscount shrugged to signify that the matter was indifferent to him.

"I suggest ten yards, then."

"Very well. A reconciliation is out of the question now, I gather?" Seabury added quietly.

"Quite, I fear. That Blount is a fool," Winterborn muttered, his patience obviously strained. "In fact, I think I had best go and keep a watch on him while he loads. No idiocy is beyond him."

Seabury nodded and allowed his friend to depart. Mr. Ellis was keeping very still, and his lordship had leisure to look about him. The air was still sultry, but the sun had risen to the extent that the sky, though dull, at least gave that impression of infinite expanse that encourages one to breathe deeply regardless of the dampness or insalubrity of the air. The rough grass beneath his heavy boots was full of moisture; it made a springy carpet as he paced a little distance away from Mr. Ellis. Seabury was glad to find himself still so angry at Mockabee. Without that it must have been difficult indeed to rouse all his faculties on such a leaden morning. When at last Sir Matthew returned to him, and handed to him one of the fine pistols from Manton's, his lordship felt nothing so much as relief that the waiting was over. Mockabee watched him with those distrustful eyes as he took his place at one end of a long, flat strip of turf. He turned his back to the rising sun, so that its rays would fall on his right cheek, and the baron's left, as they turned to aim at one another. He was too fair-minded, though it was his prerogative not to be in this particular, to cause Mockabee to look into the sun while he looked away. If Mockabee noted this fine piece of justice, he did not allow his gratitude to appear on his countenance, for all that showed there was a long, pale sneer and the suspicious gaze.

Sir Matthew and Mr. Blount retired the prescribed eight yards behind the line of fire, while Mockabee took his place at the other end of it. The baron's surgeon hung back a little behind Mr. Blount. Mr. Ellis stood back so far as almost to be out of earshot, even behind the coachmen. The principals turned their sides to one another and presented their weapons. From an oak tree a bird sent up a burst of song.

Oliver, Lord Seabury aimed and fired. An instant later a second shot rang out. Mockabee dropped to the ground.

Chapter IX

My Dearest Angela,

I am forcefully reminded of my failure to answer your last letter by an arrival this morning which will not surprise you, I am sure, but which surprised me very much. How absurd your brother was to come down to London with so silly a purpose—and yet, how very sweet as well! That is like him, as I am certain you agree.

I was as astonished to find him standing in the Gilt Saloon as if I had not seen or heard from him in a decade. I do not know why, but I feel as if I have aged years since my arrival in London. According to Edgar, I do not look as if I had done so, but rather as if I had grown younger—but then Edgar never does leave off flattering me. He has gone back out to find lodgings for the moment, since he rushed directly here this morning without pausing to settle himself. I should have asked him to stop on here, but I could not take the liberty without consulting Seabury, and he is absent for some reason. Indeed, Edgar was calling on *him*, officially at least; I was summoned as a second choice. He tells me he left home within an hour of his deciding to make the journey, and, moreover, that he rode at least half the way. Impetuous Edgar! I wonder Lady Trantham permitted it!

I am expected shortly at the breakfast table, but I think it only fair that you receive some account of our conversation, poor thing. It must have vexed you dreadfully that you were not invited to accompany him; it certainly does me. It is just as well Seabury is not at home this morning, by the way, for my first thought on being told a gentleman was waiting, was, "Who can be so oafish as to call upon us at this hour? Or else, what catastrophe has occurred?"

My astonishment on seeing Edgar I have already mentioned, and this was for some time the topic of our speech. After the ordinary inquiries were made, though, I at last asked why he had come. "Because of this," announced he, producing with a flourish that ill-fated number of *The Times* with which I think you are already familiar. Frankly, I am a little annoyed with Humphrey for bringing it to you with such haste; at least he did not feel it necessary, however, to tear up to London and defend his helpless sister.

"But my dear Edgar, how can that concern you?" I asked.

"How can it fail to concern me?" he countered, straining his delicate features in an effort to appear serious and dignified.

"But it is nothing to do with you," I said.

"It is something to do with you, I think. Is not the solution to this puzzle, Caroline Wythe?"

I agreed that it was.

"Then it is something to do with me; for whatever pertains to you touches me as well."

"My dear," said I, as kindly as I could be, "you speak as if we were betrothed, or married."

Edgar gave it as his opinion that we were betrothed, or as good as betrothed.

I am afraid I lost my temper at this juncture. I believe (I am embarrassed to mention it) I even struck a table with my fist as I exclaimed, "Fond as I am of you, Edgar, we are not betrothed, nor anything like betrothed, nor ever shall be betrothed." I saw how this hurt him, and endeavoured to soften my tone as I added, "I am sorry it cannot be otherwise, but we really should not suit."

He turned his back to me and averted his face. It makes *me* almost cry to think of how I disappointed him, but at the time I was miffed, and heedless. *You* know, if anybody knows, how frequently this scene has been enacted between Edgar and myself, on any pretext at all. Presently he turned round again and said in a low voice, "Be that as it may, if nothing else we are as brother and sister to one another. At least, I feel as much concern for your happiness as a brother might do," he went on quickly, seeing me about to object, "and I cannot sit idly by while your name is held up to public ridicule."

I had quite recovered control of my tongue by this time, and expostulated with him calmly. "If it was your object, in coming to London, to serve me as a champion, I regret to say that your visit is—whatever else it may be— superfluous in that aspect. I have already received a very kind, exactly similar offer, and have already refused it. The fact is, that I was in the wrong with regard to . . . to Lord M—"

"Ah! Who is the villain?" demanded your gallant brother.

"It is not necessary that you should know, my dear, and I prefer that you do not. The significant point is that I was in the wrong, at least sufficiently so to make the case unclear. It is best, therefore, that nobody champion me at all. Besides, Edgar, it is stale news already, for two more editions have appeared since that one, and a perfectly devastating attack on Lady Halsworthy was printed yesterday. I am sure no one talks of anything else."

"Nonetheless," stormed the mighty Edgar, "someone must defend you. Who is this white-livered knight, who stops at a word from you?"

"It is not necessary," said I, "that you know his identity either."

"Who is it?" he raged, immediately answering himself. "It is that rascal of a Seabury, is it not?" I must have coloured, for he went on, "It is! I see it is. A fine gentleman, answering an insult to you with silence. A fine protector! I knew a brother of Lady Lillian could not be much to speak of."

Here, I am sorry to say, I lost my temper again. "Lord Seabury is an excellent man, a man of honour and ability. How dare you disparage a connexion of mine, a man whose acquaintance you have never even made? What Lord Seabury does, no man is in a position to censure, least of all a country squire's son who never set eyes on him!"

"Dear me, Caroline," said your brother, with an amazement both touching and comical to behold, "how old is this man? Is he well-looking?"

At this juncture I know very well I coloured. "About thirty-two," I said, "and yes, quite well-looking."

"You are in love with him!" gasped Edgar.

You will observe, my dear Angela, that all editorial comment ceases here.

"That is not your concern," said I, resuming my losing battle. "All that you need be assured of, is that if there were a time for valiant action, Lord Seabury would have taken it; and if there were an issue to be settled, Lord Seabury would have seen to it. He is a very careful man, and feels his obligation to protect me most keenly."

"He is no man if he suffers you to be made the subject of insinuating verses in *The Times*," muttered young Sir Lancelot.

Alas, it seemed as if I could not exchange more than two remarks with poor Edgar this morning, without flying into a rage. I was so much disturbed by his denigration of Lord Seabury that I sent him out with an invitation to return later and argue the point with his lordship himself. I hope my good kinsman will not think I have gone mad.

Ah! The hour for breakfast is upon me. I must go, for it is I who pour the tea you know. *Quel honneur!* I shall give you the sequel to this interesting visit in another letter, lest Edgar's account be prejudiced against me, or against Seabury. Adio my dear, and believe me,

Most affectionately yours,
C. Wythe

Lord Seabury took his place at the breakfast table at Rucke House some twenty minutes after his guests had seated themselves. He entered to discover his father deeply embroiled in a vicious quarrel with Amy Meredith, a quarrel apparently having something to do with the dropping of a certain spoonful of sugar into a certain cup of tea. "It was my cup," Amy was saying spitefully, as her cousin entered and sat down, "as you perfectly well knew. Henry, did he not deliberately reach over and take my cup? Oh, good morning, Seabury. Your esteemed father is trying to poison me this morning."

"Good Heavens, I trust not," said the newcomer, attempting to look something fresher and more composed than he felt.

Evidently he failed, for Lady Caroline's first words to him were, "Did you sleep last night, sir? You do look fagged."

He was prevented from replying by Romby's crying out roughly, "I am sorry I did not try to poison you, my fine young lady! Damme but you are a monster!"

"I believe I asked you to sit by me, Amy," Caro said, calmly entering the fray. "This would not have happened if you had. What a scene!"

"What is this about poison?" Miss Windle suddenly demanded, for she walked about of late in a private fog, and rarely heard anything until it had been repeated three times.

"Nothing, dear Windle," Caro said soothingly.

"A nothing! A fiddlestick," shrilled Amy. "How do you think I like it to pick up my tea and find it positively saturated with sugar? I might have choked! I might have suffocated, and died!"

"Drowned in a cup of tea!" shrieked Romby. "There is a fitting end for a bloodless chit, by God! Yes, yes," he continued to shout, more and more pleased with this image, "drowned in a cup of tea!"

"Merciful powers, my lord," Mrs. Henry at last addressed him. "You have distressed my poor girl quite enough this morning, have you not? I beg you will excuse us." On these words she pushed back her chair and went to her charge, whom she then tenderly exhorted to come

along and breakfast in peace, upstairs. She fixed Lord
Romby with an awful look before quitting the room,
which rather than quelling him seemed only to excite him
more.

"Driven away by a tempest in a teapot!" he screamed.
"Yes, by God, yes! A fitting end indeed, a very fitting
end!"

"My lord, I should like to get on with my breakfast in
something like tranquillity," Caroline interrupted him
rather fiercely. She was ashamed to have Lord Seabury
discover his breakfast-room in such an uproar, and felt it
to be her fault that matters had reached such a pitch.
Judging by his appearance, Seabury was not in perfect
spirits this morning; and knowing that an encounter—
possibly full of histrionics—with Edgar Gilchrist was in
his immediate future, she doubly regretted the *contretemps*.

His lordship did not appear at all displeased with her,
however; in fact, she could not help noticing, quite the
opposite: he several times glanced at her as if fearing that
she might be displeased with him. Perhaps he felt
responsible for his father's bad behaviour, or even his
young cousin's. At all events she was reassured by his
seeming forbearance, and soon found a moment to say
what must be said. "You had a caller this morning,
Seabury, whom I met since you were out." At this he
glanced at her again with a flicker of—something;
apology, or timidity?—in his wonderful eyes, a glance she
was unable to account for. She continued after a brief
pause, "It was Edgar Gilchrist, the brother of my dearest
friend in Berkshire, and a very old acquaintance of mine.
He would like—I, in fact, invited him to wait upon you
again, at about three this afternoon. I hope I did not take
too much of a liberty?"

"Not at all," said Seabury. "I am engaged to drive out
with Lady Susan Manning at four, however, so I cannot
give him more than an hour. Do you think that will
suffice?"

Caroline had found herself quite startled by the
introduction into the conversation of Lady Susan's name.
It was a name, it may be noted, easily forgot in Rucke

House that week; Lady Caroline, for example, had for days lost track of it altogether. She recovered herself at once, and replied in a rather subdued tone of voice, "I am certain it will. I feel obliged to caution you, sir, that Edgar is come with a very specific purpose."

"And that is?" he prompted. He, for his part, had found that he already did not care overmuch for this Edgar to whom Lady Caroline referred so freely and familiarly.

"I am afraid, dear sir," she began, immediately colouring, "it is to do with that unfortunate poem in *The Times*. It appears that Edgar stumbled upon it some few days after its publication, and galloped down here all afire to protect my honour. I endeavoured to convince him it was unnecessary, but I seemed destined to fail. For that reason, you see, I encouraged him to consult with you. Is it dreadfully inconvenient?"

"Not at all. I am delighted you referred him to me," said the viscount who had a good reason for being so delighted, in view of his early adventures that day.

"You are very good."

"Not at all. I am curious to make the acquaintance of this ancient friend of yours in any case. He must feel some—paternal interest in you?" Seabury suggested hopefully.

"Oh, la! No indeed," Miss Windle replied, having recently awakened from a deep meditation concerning the present Earl of Romby. She was very fond of Edgar herself, and laughed with pleasure as she went on, "Mr. Gilchrist is no more than a year or so older than our dear Caroline. In fact, they were sweethearts in childhood, and may someday even—"

"Windle!" Caro cried out.

"Well, my dear, there is no cause to keep secret from his lordship what half of High Bowen knows! Edgar has been in love with Caroline forever," she said confidingly to Seabury, while Caro writhed with frustration, "and has offered for her any number of times. Of course it would not be a brilliant match for Caroline—so few would—but Mr. Gilchrist is a young man of such delicacy and sweetness, and the acquaintance is so very old, that it may be she will accept him one day. At least, I continually

remind her that she may, for Lord Inlowe favours the
suit—"

"Windle!" came again from Lady Caroline.

"Well, he does not discourage it," the elder lady went
on smoothly, "and I am of the opinion that it would be a
very pleasant and reasonable match, especially since
Caroline would not be under the necessity of quitting her
brother's neighbourhood. Moreover, the—"

"Miss Windle," said Caroline through clenched teeth,
"pray be so kind as to leave off this theme and find
another, if you must talk at all. I shall never marry Edgar
Gilchrist, as I told him this very morning—Oh! How
odiously indiscreet," she broke off, clapping a hand to her
mouth and almost crying, for she had taken a vow
recently to maintain a strict government over her words.

Miss Windle looked indulgently upon her, then leaned
over to Lord Seabury and said in a very loud whisper,
"She may marry him, for all that; I, for one, expect that
she will; and so does Lady Trantham, I think."

"Lady Trantham?" he repeated interrogatively, for this
intelligence interested him.

"His mother," Windle hissed, very audibly.

Lord Seabury nodded and was silent a moment,
thinking of the application made to him the day before by
Sir Sidney Pettingill. "I suppose," he said slowly to Caro,
"that it is important to you to reside near to your
brother?"

"Not at all!" she contradicted, with a trifle more vigour
than was absolutely necessary.

"Then you would be just as glad to live at a distance
from him?" At such a time as this, when he had a great
curiosity to know the answer to a question, the viscount
often forgot how that question might strike his interlocu-
tor. With this principle at work he continued, "You would
not mind, for instance, passing much of the year in
Dorset?"

Included among the many properties of the Earl of
Romby was a perfectly enormous estate in Dorsetshire. It
was, in fact, a favourite retreat of Lord Seabury's, a fact
Lade Caroline happened to have in her possession. She
spoke very faintly when she replied, again, "Not at all."

The viscount said "*Hmmm*" in answer to this and appeared to consider the subject closed. Lord Romby, who had been sulking and fuming in majestic isolation at one end of the table all this while, abruptly exclaimed, "Damme! A fine day we have come to when a man cannot sit at his own breakfast table without hearing a lot of rubbish about a lot of romantic sapskulls!" Having said this, and muttered something unintelligible besides, he rose with a great deal of clatter and took his leave, pausing only to inform the footman at the door that he was a shatterheaded clunch.

"Poor Lord Romby!" Miss Windle exclaimed dolefully, immediately following his departure.

"Why on earth should you say so?" asked Caroline.

"Well it is very clear," Windle commenced, then checked herself to look sidelong at Seabury and concluded, "but another time perhaps."

"Pray do not allow me to inhibit you, dear ma'am," Seabury said, rising. "I have some business to attend to in any case, and so if you will excuse me..." He bowed slightly and left the table. Caroline, watching him depart, noticed to her surprise that his boots were stained near the soles, as if he had walked through a puddle. It was not like his lordship to continue to wear the boots if he had; there had not, moreover, been any rain to make any puddles in quite some time. It was odd.

"Lord Romby is lonely," said Windle, when only she and Caro were left in the room, for the older lady had seen fit to dismiss the servants as well. "No wonder it hurts him to hear love discussed frivolously; no wonder it makes him cross."

"Miss Windle, am I correct in believing that you base your remarks on conjecture?" Caro asked, quite out of patience with this obsession with the earl.

"No, my dear, you are not," said Windle, with a peculiar smile.

"Do not tell me he has said as much to you!"

"No my dear, I do not refer to any such open avowal either, when I say I rely on more than conjecture. I rely, my dear, on insight and instinct. A woman has such things."

"Doubtless, Miss Windle. And a woman uses them, furthermore, to embroil herself in all manners of folly. I suggest, dear ma'am, that you turn your back on this instinctual knowledge and give your attention, instead, to facts."

"Facts?" echoed Miss Windle, but with scorn heavy in her voice.

"Facts, dear ma'am. To start with, there is the fact that Lord Romby's wife died, I believe, some fifteen years ago—and yet he has never, since then, shown the least interest in marrying again."

"How," said Windle very slowly and distinctly, "do you know?"

Caro was forced to concede that she could not verify this. "But if he did offer for somebody, she refused him; and that seems unlikely, does it not?" She chose this tack because she suspected Windle was disposed to agree, at least, with this lack of likelihood.

"Perhaps," said the other drily. "But any gentleman may be refused, for any number of reasons which are nothing to do with him in particular. The lady's family, it may be," she suggested grandly, "objected. Lord Romby could not love a lady who ignored her family, I trust!"

"This is most exasperating," Caro burst out. "You have developed a perfect fixation with Romby, which I am at an utter loss to comprehend. What is your object in this, dear Windle? Pray, pray take me into your confidence!"

"I wish to marry him!" Miss Windle exploded, not entirely voluntarily. "I wish to stand by him, be his help-meet, honour and obey him! I wish to comfort and support him. Is that so much?" she demanded tearfully. "Is that so dreadful?"

"My poor Windle!" was Caroline's surprised exclamation.

Miss Windle was lost in sobs for a time, but then she sniffed mightily and drew herself up to say, "I suppose you pity me because you think I can never fulfill my desire, but you need not do so. I do not think the case is so hopeless as that. I have reason to believe it is not."

"Do you mean that Romby has shown you some particular attentions?"

"Yes I do. Or rather . . . Well," she faltered, dabbing at her watery eyes with a lace-edged handkerchief, "he often looks at me in a manner that seems to—to say something."

Caro tried to speak mildly. "Is that all?" she asked.

"No. Even more than the way he looks at me, I notice the way he does not look at me. The way . . . the dear, peculiar way," she continued, beginning to smile shyly, "he avoids my glance, or turns his eyes from mine."

It occurred to Caroline to point out that even a cat must look at a person, or not notice him, or turn away from him; but she successfully suppressed this observation and replied instead, "I only consider your happiness, my dear. The season will not last forever, you know. We must go home someday. How will you feel if we are obliged to leave, and the earl—the earl does not come forward?"

"Ah, now that! That," said Windle, with a very mysterious little smile, "will not happen."

"How can you know?"

But Miss Windle only shook her head, still smiling the enigmatical smile. No amount of teasing could elicit more from her than that nod and that grin. In the end, Caroline was obliged to yield, and to part from her without learning anything else. She went upstairs to wait for Edgar's return to Rucke House, and to wonder how so insipid a person as Lady Susan Manning could possibly have become a serious annoyance to her.

Edgar Gilchrist's eventual arrival afforded Caro nothing more satisfying than the privilege of observing the top of his head as he passed through the great front doors, for otherwise his call concerned Lord Seabury alone. He arrived in much the same excited state as he had been in when he left, for the idea that Caroline was wronged not only by Lord M, but also by Seabury, had taken hold of him powerfully. His brown eyes glittered with a feverish volatility altogether foreign to them under ordinary circumstances; of course the viscount could not know their customary appearance, and he rather wondered if the young man might not be consumptive, or otherwise afflicted with disease. If so he was sorry for him.

If not, he begrudged him every pleasant feature, every gentle, even trait in his young-looking face, not to mention his excellently proportioned figure, and his neat hands and feet.

"I hope you have been able to find some suitable lodgings," Seabury said, with a cordiality not entirely sincere, when the requisite courtesies had been accomplished.

"Quite, I think," replied Edgar. Uncertain as he was of the older man's guilt or innocence, he considered it a point of honour to be somewhat abrupt—though not excessively so, since this was after all his lordship's chair he sat in, and his lordship's sherry he drank. "I am come to London, sir, in order to discover who—"

But Seabury, observing him about to produce the offending poem, interrupted him. "Lady Caroline was so good this morning as to mention to me your reason for coming. I have the happiness to inform you that the matter has been settled already. I regret that you could not have been advised of this sooner, since it might have spared you much trouble—but perhaps you will enjoy your visit here as a holiday."

Eager to express his indignation, and delighted at what he supposed was an opportunity, Mr. Gilchrist retorted, "My dear sir, I am afraid you and I have some difference of opinion as to what constitutes a settled matter." He pronounced the word "settled" with deep sarcasm, and at once continued, "It is my understanding, from my conversation with Caro—ah, Lady Caroline—earlier this morning, that she discouraged your pursuing the affair, and that in consequence it has been allowed to drop. Now that is not, sir, what I call a *settled* matter."

Lord Seabury rose and crossed to Edgar's chair, the better to look down upon him. "Indeed?" said he slowly. "And what would you have done, in my place?"

"Found out the villain and challenged him!" cried he.

"And what," Seabury continued, his arms folded across his considerable chest, and a gleam of amusement in his blue eyes, "do you suppose I have done?"

Edgar, looking up at him, suddenly began to feel a trifle uncomfortable. His suspicion, acquired this morning, that Caroline was in love with the viscount had grown (on seeing how handsome Seabury was) till it approached a positive conviction. Something in his lordship's manner now suggested to him that not only might his supposition have been correct, but also that Seabury loved Caroline. He was certainly behaving towards Edgar as if he were a particularly unwanted intruder. Mr. Gilchrist fidgeted under the weight of the reflections as he said weakly, "Nothing."

"Ah. Indeed," said the viscount. "My dear young man—for you are a young man, I think, and I take that into account—I must ask you if, having met me, you still imagine me to be the sort of man who, in the face of an insult to a lady under his protection, does nothing?"

Gilchrist fidgeted even more. "Not . . . quite," he finally brought out.

"Ah!" said Seabury carefully. "Not—since I put it to you that way—quite. You are a perceptive young man, Mr. Gilchrist."

Edgar Gilchrist twisted the brass button on his blue coat, and knew shame.

"Your concern for Lady Caroline's reputation is, I am sure, laudable," Seabury went on.

Edgar squirmed.

"I wonder how you slept all these nights she has been away, supposing her to be insufficiently protected?"

Edgar writhed. The brass button, twisted beyond its limit, fell off.

"Not well, I fear," the viscount answered himself, picking up the button without the hint of a smile, and returning it to its owner. "A pity," said Seabury. He paused to observe Edgar's mute discomfiture, and the anger he had been, feeling towards him went away. He had been at first, really quite furious; and something of his fury, evidently, had been communicated to his young visitor, in spite of his lordship's quiet speech. Why had he been so angry? he asked himself. Anyone would be whose reliability as a gentleman was doubted, answered another inner voice. But this was not the whole truth, as he could not entirely avoid acknowledging.

"I owe you an apology, sir," Mr. Gilchrist at last said in

a muffled voice. "I regret very much the doubts I have
entertained—however innocently—with regard to your
character. I ought to have thought...I ought to have
asked Inlowe, I suppose. But I was pleased with the idea
of defending Caroline. You must think me a perfect idiot,
my lord."

Though the difference between their ages was but eight
years, both gentlemen felt as if they had been separated by
several decades. This contrite, artless apology on the part
of the younger man made the older feel, almost, benignly
paternal towards him. For this reason, and with the issue
of Lady Caroline herself temporarily forgot, Seabury
answered quickly, "Not at all. I dareswear I should have
done the same thing in your place, at your age. It was very
gallant and brave."

"You are kind, sir," Edgar replied, still dejected but
nonetheless showing a brief smile. "Very stupid and
thoughtless is what you mean; but you are kind."

"Not at all, dear boy," repeated the other. "I beg you
will take another glass of sherry. And come to dinner
tonight, if you like."

Mr. Gilchrist, after a little more coaxing, accepted
both these offers. "May I inquire," he said, when a few
other topics had been touched on, "whether Lord M.
tendered an apology, after all? I ask for mere curiosity, my
lord; I hope you can believe that."

"I do believe it; and to lay your curiosity to rest, he did
not offer any kind of excuse, no. He was very obstinate, in
fact. In short, and not to put too fine a point upon it, the
last time I saw him he had sustained an injury to his right
shoulder. More I cannot wisely, nor honourably, tell you,
Mr. Gilchrist, though I might like to. I hope you
understand."

Edgar, quite awed by this dispassionate (if sketchy)
account, indicated that he understood perfectly. "And
Caro—ah, I see! Caro has no idea of your acting in her
behalf."

"Precisely. And of course we must continue to keep her
as ignorant as she is now, for her own happiness and
security. You will, I hope, leave her in that state?"

Gilchrist swore no power could wrest a whisper from

him on the subject; and indeed, it was not from his lips
that Caroline learned the truth. It was from other lips:
softer and prettier ones.

Amy Meredith was due to quit London on May 18,
three days after the interview recorded above. Though the
18th was a Sunday, it had been decided for a variety of
reasons that she could travel to her Aunt Meredith's most
conveniently on that day. Mrs. Henry might have her
regrets at such an infraction of the rules of piety, but Amy
had none; therefore the date had been selected and
confirmed, and the elder Miss Meredith anxiously
anticipated the younger's arrival then. The younger Miss
Meredith, for that matter, seemed quite content to be
going as well. Her early sense of ill-usage had apparently
vanished, for no complaint was heard from her. Caroline
tried to believe that Amy's new docility indicated a
praiseworthy effort on the girl's part to mend her ways
and show a proper gratitude to her cousin; but she could
not help suspecting some mischief was afoot. Her
misgivings were strengthened by an expression she several
times observed on Amy's face, a secretive and not
altogether pleasant smile, coupled with a peculiar
brightness in her brown eyes. She said nothing to
Seabury, however, for she knew his lordship wished there
were more goodwill between herself and Amy, and she
disliked to vex him.

On the evening prior to Amy's departure, a party
consisting of the two young ladies, their chaperones, Lord
Seabury and another gentleman set out from Rucke
House with the intention of visiting Kensington Gardens,
to stroll there awhile and thus effect a fresh introduction
of Caroline into society. The gentleman accompanying
them was Mr. Edgar Gilchrist, who had elected to remain
in London briefly in spite of his being without a purpose
there. Lord Romby, who had lately become (it seemed to
Caroline) nastier and more dissolute than ever before, did
not join them. Miss Windle affected to have the headache
late in the afternoon, when she first heard of Romby's
projected absence; but when he announced his intention
of passing the whole night at Brooks's her indisposition
miraculously disappeared and she informed Caro that she

could, after all, join the expedition. Sir Sidney Pettingill, who had called at Rucke House the previous day (and had shown himself, at that time, to be strangely inarticulate— almost incoherent, as Windle and Caro agreed between themselves afterwards) was invited to join them as well, and had at first accepted; but he later sent his regrets, along with polite best wishes for a safe and pleasant journey for Miss Meredith.

It has been feared initially that Mr. Gilchrist would be unable to walk with his friends, on account of his not having brought with him the requisite cloth knee-breeches, silk stockings, and shoes. Lord Romby was nearly a foot taller, and Lord Seabury at least six inches wider at the shoulders, than the slight, slender Gilchrist, so it was out of the question for the gentlemen of Rucke House to supply their new acquaintance from their private wardrobes. To purchase the missing items seemed not only silly, it was also beyond Edgar's means, at least on the spur of the moment. The day seemed lost until, Lady Beatrice having heard of the dilemma, Mr. Walfish was pressed into service. There could have been no favour more to Ansel Walfish's liking than to outfit an attractive young gentleman in formal evening attire; indeed, his pleasure at fretting and fussing over the business so outweighed the disagreeableness of having to lend someone his clothes, that he wished he could be set such a task every day for a year. Mr. Walfish was a valet at heart; at least, that is what Lady Beatrice told him.

"I should like very much to adjust my left shoe, for it pinches extremely," Mr. Gilchrist confided in a low tone to Caroline, as they entered Seabury's crested barouche, "but I dare not, for fear of destroying Walfish's masterpiece." The work of art to which he referred, and which he now indicated with one delicately pointed finger, was the *Noeud Gordien* that Mr. Walfish had made of his cravat.

Lady Caroline laughed and encouraged him to place comfort before art in spite of his scruples.

"Oh no! Walfish was an hour and a half creating this, and if he finds me at the Gardens without it just so, I am sure he will stab me."

"Not while you wear his clothes!" Caro smiled. "Think of the bloodstains!"

Miss Windle was the only other occupant of the barouche; Seabury, Amy, and Mrs. Henry were in another carriage. Talk among the three old acquaintances flowed easily until they reached their destination; after that their conversation became fragmented, for a party of six cannot easily walk in a bunch, and tends rather to elongate itself into a line of pairs. Gilchrist contrived to remain, at first, beside Lady Caroline; but the curious, occasionally uncivil glances she found she was receiving from so many passers-by soon caused her to seek the protective wing of Miss Windle instead. She distinctly overheard, to her excessive discomfiture, two persons mention *The Times* as they passed in her vicinity, and one rude young man (whom she did not remember ever to have seen before) actually burst into laughter at the sight of her. She clung a good deal closer to her chaperone than was her habit, but except for this she gave no visible sign of embarrassment, even when their party encountered the Marquis of Safford with his wife and his daughter, and Lady Susan Manning stared at her for full thirty seconds, evidently speechless from fascination.

Caro was delighted when they at last encountered Lady Beatrice and her faithful *cavalier servente*. "Have you seen Lady Halsworthy?" were almost the first words Walfish spoke, in a very excited undertone. "She dares to appear here with no one more respectable that Mrs. Fallerton, and absolutely without other escort! Is it credible?"

Caroline looked pained, however, and answered, "My dear sir, if you were not my friend, would you not refer to me as well in just that tone of scandal?"

Walfish understood the reproach but chose to ignore it. "Oh phoo," he said, "that dull little poem in the newspaper is nothing compared to Lady Halsworthy's behaviour. Who can even recall it? This Halsworthy affair is something else, however! It is a perfect assault on every gentlewoman in society, that is what it is! Can you imagine?" And he went on to recount, in breathless detail, all that was known or supposed to be known of Lady

Halsworthy's recent escapades.

Walfish was often a silly young man, but he was kind too, and much as he enjoyed rumour-mongering, his real object in this outburst was to set Caroline at ease. He succeeded pretty well, for by the time the two parties took leave of one another, Caro was able to relinquish the protective arm of her chaperone and walk beside Lord Seabury instead. They fell into conversation naturally, arguing in a pleasant and passionless manner the advantages, if any, to be gained from a foreign education. Their discourse was punctuated ever and anon by exclamations of wonder and delight as the eye of one or the other fell upon a particularly brilliant bloom, or caught sight of an attractive vista. They went some distance in this wise, turning their steps from one path to the next as seemed agreeable, and assuming that the others of their party followed in their wake.

They were correct for a while. Miss Windle had claimed Edgar's attention, and interrogated him closely on the health and happiness of all their common acquaintances in Berkshire; Amy Meredith, refusing the proffered arm of her chaperone, dawdled along silently behind the rest. But when they had proceeded in this manner for some fifteen minutes, their advance was broke by a sudden cry from Mrs. Henry: "She is gone!"

Chapter X

"Dear, dear Amy," murmured Lord Mockabee, as he swept her thick curls from her forehead and pressed his lips to each temple. "My lovely girl!"

Amy settled herself happily in his embrace and said nothing.

"We have but a moment; any longer and the peril is too great," Mockabee took up. "We must think of your good name."

"I do not care about my name," said Amy, pretending to pout.

"But I do," said the gentleman gallantly. He leaned his back against the wide tree trunk behind him and drew Miss Meredith closer to his breast. They stood in shadow to avoid observation, at the centre of a small clump of trees near a narrow path in Kensington Gardens. The darkness that hid them from the eyes of the crowd also obscured them from one another's view, and they mostly felt and heard each other, seeing only vague shapes. Amy Meredith thought it very daring to steal kisses in the dark and hold the baron's warm hands when she could hardly even make out his features.

"You are so careful of my virtue," said Amy innocently, "you begin to sound like Seabury."

"Seabury!" spat out the other abruptly. "Do not say that name to me, if you please."

"But why?"

Mockabee pushed her away a little and brought out, in a voice full of emotion, "Your fine cousin has put a bullet through my shoulder, my dear. Touch this!" he instructed, placing her hand on the spot where the bandages under his coat caused a bulge over his right shoulder.

"Oh, my dearest!" cried she, withdrawing her hand in horror. "How did it happen? Does it ache dreadfully?"

"The pain is not much," he said, wincing dramatically as he readjusted the sleeve of his coat, "but the frustration is difficult to bear. I might at least have repaid him in kind, except that my imbecile of a second put too little powder in my pistol."

"But why did he do that?"

It was fortunate for him that the shadows prevented her from seeing the extravagant glare he gave her. "I imagine, my sweet," he said after a pause, "that he was trying not to put too much in, and cause it to blow up in my hand."

"But when did this take place? It was a duel, was it not? Over what?"

Amy's questions continued, and Mockabee answered them all patiently, though with an audible straining in his voice—audible, that is, if there had been disinterested ears to hear it. There were not however; Amy Meredith drank in every word, and commiserated volubly with each new outrage or disappointment.

"I could scream when I think how they concealed this from me," was Amy's major concern at the close of the narrative: "I shall throttle Caroline when I see her."

Lord Mockabee merely nodded. "But we must settle some details," he told her after a moment, kissing the top of her head as if to signal the beginning of a new topic. On that new topic they spoke a few minutes longer; then, with many protestations of love on both sides, and distress at being obliged to part, they quitted one another's company. Miss Meredith proceeded, without escort, to the gates through which her party had entered the Gardens, and waited until they should find her.

"This was very naughty of you indeed, Miss," was what Mrs. Henry said when, discovered at length at her chosen post, Amy had been roundly frowned upon and bundled summarily into the crested barouche. "It was all very well for Miss Windle and me, who were sent to the gate to wait for you, but his lordship and Lady Caroline and Mr. Gilchrist have fairly exhausted themselves looking for you. What made you wander off that way, you bad creature?"

"I am sure Caro enjoyed herself thoroughly," Amy muttered, ignoring the question. With a jolt, the barouche began to move.

The viscount, who shared the carriage with them, himself ignored Amy's dark comment and said sternly, "I am not much distressed, Mrs. Henry, at having been obliged to search for your charge. What disturbs me is that Amy has been so foolhardy as to walk about alone at night in an open garden. I hope you will give me a full account, Amy, of what drew you away from our party, without my having to press you for it unduly."

"I lost my way," said she sullenly. "I lost sight of you."

"I beg you will not ask me to believe that," Seabury replied. Mrs. Henry put a protective arm round Miss Meredith's shoulder, as if warning his lordship to proceed carefully.

"I lost my way," Miss Meredith insisted peevishly. "Where else should I have been?"

"Perhaps you had a rendezvous," he suggested, though he was unwilling to consider this possibility himself.

"With whom?" asked she, sarcastically.

"I should not like to guess."

"Well then." She folded her arms stubbornly across her chest, and stared at him through the dimness of the coach.

"Well then, do not oblige me to guess," said he gently.

"Oh my, you are gallant and graceful, are you not?" she suddenly lashed out, her voice heavy with scorn. "You are a fine and righteous gentleman! How dare you bully me this way? How dare you demand accounts from me? How dare you shoot my only friend in the world?" she ended, descending abruptly from high displeasure into a torrent of tears.

"Shoot—what?" inquired Mrs. Henry, bewildered.

"My dear Amy, you have had a tryst with Mockabee," cried the viscount, very much dismayed to be forced to this conclusion.

"Baron Mockabee?" asked the horrified Mrs. Henry.

"My only friend, my one friend!" repeated Amy miserably, while Mrs. Henry, impeded by the slight lurching of the carriage, attempted to put her other arm round the weeping girl.

"Mockabee is hardly your friend!" objected Seabury, but in consternation, not in anger. "Look at what he has exposed you to this very evening! It is not at all prudent for a young girl like yourself to wander without an escort. Remember what Ansel Walfish said of Lady Halsworthy, my dear, and think who may now say the same of you!"

"I do not care, I do not," she sobbed. "What is the use of a good name if the person called by it is unhappy?"

"This is a question we might argue for hours, my dear cousin, probably to no advantage. I am grieved, however, to learn that you do not think of me as your friend. How is that, Amy?"

"You send me away," she accused, "the moment I become an impediment to you. How is that, cousin?"

"An impediment?" he repeated inquiringly.

"I prevent your being alone with Caroline!" she brought out. "Do you suppose I am deaf and dumb?"

"But my dear, why should I wish to be alone with Lady Caroline?"

"You need not play the innocent with me," she flung at him, her rage returning. "I know of your little *affaire d'honneur*, cousin, do not forget. And I know for whose sake you arranged it."

"For yours, my dear. And mine. For all our family."

"For Caroline."

Mrs. Henry, who had been listening to this dialogue with increasing confusion and distress, now besought her young charge to be calm, lest she work herself into full-fledged hysteria. "Tomorrow night this will all be behind you, my dear," she said soothingly, glancing at Seabury with eyes that seemed to convict him of being solely responsible for her darling's upset. "We shall be home again, with dear Miss Meredith, who loves you very much and will cosset and pet you just as much as you like."

Amy sniffed as if she found some comfort in this image, but Seabury could not help murmuring, "Heaven forbid!"

"Yes, just so," exclaimed Amy, shrinking back further into Mrs. Henry's arms. "Just so, no one must be kind to *me*, Seabury! No one must love and cosset *me*! No, we must all bow and scrape to Caroline. She is the ideal woman."

"Amy, I am at a loss to understand this fixation you have regarding Caroline. I assure you my attitude towards you would be exactly the same if she had never come to London," he continued, wondering even as he said the words if they were true, "and I must beg you, at all events, to cease intimating that my relation to her is anything else than what it purports to be." This last phrase having been spoke quite severely, Amy Meredith did not chuse to challenge it, but rather settled down to whimper comfortably in her chaperone's arms. She excused herself from Seabury's company very quietly when they at last arrived at Rucke House, and submitted to be tucked into bed by Mrs. Henry; but the moment that lady had left she jumped from her couch, threw a light pelisse over her night-dress, and stole softly down the corridor to Caroline's room.

"Who is it?" came the inquiring voice.

Amy hissed her reply.

Caroline, who had stopped downstairs a while to say good night to Edgar, had not yet extinguished her candle. She came to the door holding it and admitted Amy to her chamber. "But let us go into the sitting-room," she suggested, referring to the small apartment that divided her bedchamber from Windle's. "It is pleasanter to talk there."

"No, no," said Amy, whispering to ensure that Miss Windle would not hear them. "I have some news for you, perhaps; or maybe a difference to settle before I leave."

Caroline, surprised but not at all delighted with the honour of this visit, invited Amy to sit in an armchair and stationed herself at the end of the enormous bed.

"You know that poem in *The Times*," Amy began, as Caro said nothing.

"Certainly."

"Well Seabury has challenged Mockabee to a duel over it, and they have met, and Mockabee is wounded!"

"Never!" she cried, even as she realized that it would, unlikely though it was, explain where Seabury had been before breakfast Thursday morning.

"But it is true, indeed," the other persisted, quite hugging herself with the joy of being the bearer of such exciting tidings, and moreover at being able, finally, to astonish Caroline. "I saw Mockabee tonight, and he showed me the injury."

"Is that where you were?" she asked, feeling the intelligence as a second shock.

"Oh, yes," Amy returned impatiently, "but was it not worthwhile to learn the truth?"

"The truth," Caroline repeated thoughtfully. "Amy, does it not occur to you that this particular truth is one you have no business knowing?"

"Why not? Mockabee told me perfectly freely."

"Well then, does it not strike you that Mockabee himself had no business telling you? This was an affair between himself and Lord Seabury. A duel is a serious matter."

"Oh, la, why should he not tell me, if he cares to? After all, Mockabee is my—" She stopped dead.

"Is your what?" Caro asked carefully.

"Nothing." Amy stared at the floor and pulled her pelisse more tightly around her.

"Thank Heaven you will be in Bessford tomorrow," cried Caroline, after a pause.

"Yes, everybody is very thankful for that, except me," observed Miss Meredith darkly.

"Everybody must be thankful, who has your welfare at heart."

"If you mean to preach I shall be leaving you, dear

ma'am," said Amy, picking herself up with an extravagant gesture and tripping towards the door.

"No, wait a moment. I do not mean to preach. Tell me if you know for certain why this duel was fought?"

"Ah, now mademoiselle shows some curiosity! This is very interesting."

"Do not tease me, I warn you," said Caro, so threateningly that Amy dropped her sneering tone at once.

"Yes, since you ask," she said sulkily. "Lord Mockabee told me."

'Alas that we have only Lord Mockabee's word to go on!"

"Do you doubt it?"

"Absolutely!"

"Dear me, since you are so monstrous difficult to convince, perhaps you will like to know that I have since discussed the matter with our fine Lord Seabury, and he does not deny it."

Caroline, divided between her fury at Seabury for ignoring her stated desires and her pleasure at knowing he acted according to his scruples—and championed, and vindicated her—had scarcely sensations enough to spare in order to deal with Amy. She was horrified that the younger woman could have been so brazen as to grant the baron a clandestine interview, still more so that she had done so in such a way as to raise an alarm among her friends for her safety. In fact, every step she had taken in order to procure, and then to impart, this knowledge of the duel was steeped in an element so unsavoury that Caroline recoiled from it instinctively. She herself had been mischievous at best, and ought perhaps not to judge; but she could not prevent herself from judging, and she could not but feel that Amy was conducting herself in a manner vastly more reprehensible than ever she had done.

On the other hand, the information itself—no matter how outrageously acquired—interested her so acutely that the thought of trying to sleep, while it was yet new to her, was almost painful. She was immediately obsessed with the idea of confronting the viscount with Amy's story; but before she could contemplate how, when, and whether to do so, she felt compelled to enjoin Amy to be silent on this head in the future.

"Oh, Seabury babbled something about that, too, just before he left me tonight," said Miss Meredith, without embarrassment. She shrugged as she added, "What does it signify anyhow? Mockabee told me; so *he* does not feel any great compulsion to keep quiet on the subject."

With much effort, Caro was able to suppress the quick retort this philosophy naturally provoked in her, and merely repeated her request to Amy.

The younger lady shrugged. "If you insist," she said carelessly. "To whom could I say anything, after all? I shall be stuck away in Kent tomorrow."

"You will not be there forever."

"Ha! I shall if you have anything to say to it, I know."

"Amy, how can you make such an accusation?"

"I see how you smile at my cousin, and how he smiles at you. You want me out of the way," Amy said hotly, "and though you say I am to stop away but a fortnight, I am not idiot enough to believe you."

"And when your cousin says so, do you not believe him?"

"Certainly not," said she, her hand upon the knob of the door. "Shall I take the word of the man I love, or the man who attempts to kill him?"

"Amy, you do not refer to Lord Mockabee?"

"I do."

"But he has not led you to believe—has he?—that Seabury is not a man of honour!"

"Lady Caroline, I pity you. You are so full of my precious cousin Seabury that you do not know A from B, not one from two. You make me sick with your prosing about honour and secrets and my welfare at heart! If there is one thing I shall not regret leaving in London, it is you!" With this she pulled the door open and darted through it. She reached her room still in a fury, and flung herself about the chamber for half an hour, now striking her little fist against her palm, now stamping her foot. Her rage did not subside until, sitting down at her desk, she penned a short note and folded it up. When this had been done, and the direction had been inscribed upon it, she was able to be calm at last, and shortly afterwards climbed into bed to fall asleep.

Miss Windle shed tears when Amy departed next morning, chiefly, she explained in a whisper to Caro, because she pitied "that poor, silly girl, with not a soul to guide her but that nasty, haughty, indulgent woman." The remainder of the party bade farewell happily enough, however; Lord Romby, in fact, was positively gleeful. Nor did Amy look very sorry to be going, a circumstance that rather added to Caroline's misgivings about the child than otherwise. She wished Seabury had given her a better account of the aunt, Miss Meredith; Amy needed a firm hand, and Windle was quite right (though not altogether coherent) in her assessment of Mrs. Henry. The woman was too cold and too fond by turns; she had no idea how to lead her charge, and instead followed her about, despairing and rejoicing as the occasion arose, like a Greek chorus.

Edgar Gilchrist was there to say good-bye to Miss Meredith too, having called at Rucke House unseasonably early (he could not accustom himself to town hours) to beg a private interview with Lady Caroline. This was granted him, though Caro had it in mind herself to seek an interview with Seabury as soon as possible. While the others disbanded—Lord Romby to drink a celebratory glass of sherry—Caro invited Edgar to follow her into the Gilt Saloon. Miss Windle was the last person in the world to prevent their being alone together; she disappeared on a murmured pretext, still wiping the good-hearted tears from her bleared, delicately lidded eyes. "Dear Caroline," commenced Mr. Gilchrist, when the great doors had been shut upon them, and he had seated himself rather stiffly on an intricately carved mahogany chair, "dear Caroline, will your patience suffer me to address you once more upon an old theme?"

Lady Caroline smiled, though not broadly. "This is a mild beginning for you, my old friend, if I guess correctly what is to follow."

Edgar grimaced sheepishly. "I suppose I have offered

for you so many times now, you amuse yourself with cataloguing the different varieties of proposals—by tone, and urgency, and place, no doubt?"

Caro said nothing but shook her head gently.

"The consciousness of my long suit, and my many failures, only prompts me to apply ever more often, dear Caro, for I have no pride to lose now, nor dignity, and must place all my hope on striking, by some lucky chance, at just the right moment."

"But there is no right moment, as I have told you before. There will be none."

"Ah, I cannot believe that!"

"So I observe!"

He glanced reproachfully at her. "Will you be my wife, though, my dearest?" he asked sweetly, an instant later.

"No, my good friend. Though I am, as ever, sensible of the honour you do me, I must repeat, no. May I be dismissed now, Edgar?" she added. "I have some business to attend to."

He hesitated. "No, if you please, I beg you will stop a minute longer. There is something . . . I have no right to ask you, but I wish very much to know."

"And that is—?" she prompted curiously.

"Are you in love with that fellow Seabury?" he demanded flatly.

"Merciful Heavens, whatever makes you fancy such a thing?"

"Caroline, you are absolutely crimson."

"Do not be foolish."

"But you are, dear girl. Oh Caro, this is a blow to me!"

"You are making much out of nothing," she returned, a little severely. "Why should you disquiet yourself with such surmises?"

"Does he know?" asked Gilchrist, rising from his chair and pacing the length of the saloon. He reached the mantelpiece at one end and leaned against it, fixing her with an intense gaze.

"Does who know what?" she asked, looking at the floor and fighting down her colour.

"Seabury, does he know you love him," he explained impatiently. "What makes you suppose you can lie to me, after all these years? I allow I have been a clunch just recently, but I know you a little better than that!"

There was candour in this last speech that she could not help but return. "I do not know," she said quietly. "I do not know, for that matter, if I really love him."

"Well, if it were left to me to guess, I should say you certainly did, my dear," he answered, almost angrily. "Angela told me she fancied as much from your letters, for that matter, but I could not believe her."

"Angela thinks I am in love? I never said so."

"Truly, Caro, you under-estimate the both of us. Since your second letter she has been pretty certain. At first I thought she did it simply to tease me, but after a time she began to frighten me with her seriousness and conviction. She is very concerned lest you love where—where you are not loved in return. That is why I inquire . . . well, that is one reason I inquire whether Seabury knows your sentiments."

Lady Caroline hestitated. Did Seabury know? "I am afraid," she said a moment later, "you must ask him, since you are so curious. I have no idea, though I sometimes wonder; I shall not deny that."

"Well, my dear," said Edgar, grinning rather strangely after a deep breath, "I think we have hit upon a means to discourage me. For I am very discouraged indeed, hearing this."

"I am sorry that it hurts you," she said softly.

Edgar inhaled deeply again. "I leave this afternoon," he said. "I should like to see Lord Seabury once more before I go; could you summon a footman to fetch him?"

"Certainly," she answered, ringing the bell. A servant entered the saloon a moment later and was despatched upon the errand.

"Thank you, my dear," he said, with a slight bow. "I shall take my leave of you now, in that case."

"Do you mean for me to quit the room?" she inquired, when neither of them moved.

He looked embarrassed. "Yes, rather, I suppose I do. Do you mind terribly? It is only because . . . I shall not have another opportunity of seeing his lordship."

"It has not occurred to you, I gather, that you might

achieve that particular aim while I am *in* the room?"

"But I desire to see him alone!" he objected.

"Ah!" cried she. "Apparently I forgot your saying so, for I am sure I cannot recall it. Why, if I may take the liberty of asking, do you desire to see him alone?"

Now Edgar turned red. "I must—put a question to him."

"You could not possibly—it seems so unlikely, yet I must proceed—you could not possibly be going to ask him if he loves me, could you?"

He returned her dangerously sarcastic glare with a sullen one. "Damme, Caro, yes I am. How can I leave London with your happiness in such danger? Angela would kill me if she knew of it."

"Angela will kill you if she learns you interfered, I can promise you that," she said grimly. "Or if she does not, I will."

"It does not signify to me. I must and will do my utmost to ensure your well-being."

"Then do not jeopardize it by exposing to Lord Seabury what I revealed in confidence to you."

"You never warned me it was in confidence."

"For the love of Heaven, Edgar—" she began angrily, but she was interrupted at this point by the arrival of Lord Seabury himself. His lordship greeted each of the old friends, then stood smiling affably, if inquiringly, upon Mr. Gilchrist.

"Good-bye, Lady Caroline," Mr. Gilchrist said pointedly.

"Good-bye, Mr. Gilchrist," she returned, not moving a hair.

"It is you who are leaving, I think?" he suggested.

"Oh no! Not I." She sat politely staring daggers at him, and glancing now and then with a pleasant smile at the viscount.

"I seem to have interrupted a disagreement," he remarked at last.

"Merely a misunderstanding, I assure you," said Caro. "Mr. Gilchrist appears to have mistaken me for a chambermaid, for he seeks to dismiss me with a nod."

"Really, Caro, I should like to speak with his lordship in private—"

"Whatever you have to say may be said, I think, in my presence," she broke in firmly. "Go ahead, dear sir; thank Lord Seabury for his kindness during your visit."

As Edgar said nothing, Seabury stepped in diplomatically and assured him there was no need of thanking him.

"Yes there is," contradicted Edgar roughly, losing his patience all at once. "But that is not why I have come, as Lady Caroline is perfectly aware. I have come to ask you—that is, I have come in behalf of Lady Caroline…"

"As ever," the viscount put in drily, as Gilchrist faltered.

"Yes, as ever, because Lady Caroline's happiness is of great significance to me, and I cannot bear to leave her where it may be shattered at any moment."

"Edgar!" she exclaimed imperiously, but he would not be silent.

"I must ask you, sir," he plunged on, "if you are prepared…if you are aware…if, in short, you are conscious of—"

"Edgar, in the name of all that is reasonable!"

"If you know what honour is done you in the breast of—"

"Edgar, you must not!" she cried, horrified.

Lord Seabury intervened at this point. "If you mean to ascertain, my young friend, whether Lady Caroline is treated in Rucke House with all the respect and admiration due her, I may allay your fears by informing you that she is, unquestionably. I know you are somewhat nervous of her welfare—as her friend, I believe?—and so I do not begrudge repeating to you, what scarcely requires stating at all, to wit, that Lady Caroline is as safe here as she could be anywhere, and will never want for a protector. I hope you can make your journey now with some measure of serenity."

"I appreciate your courtesy, my Lord, in assuring me of this, but quite frankly my concern goes a little beyond—"

Caroline had finally given up, and sat, despairingly, with her head buried in her hands. She was rescued at this juncture, however, from what had seemed inevitable disaster by the viscount himself, who advanced a little ways towards Edgar and broke in upon his sentence. "My young friend," he said, in a low but compelling tone of voice, "once before you came to me, full of good intentions but, as I think we agreed then, somewhat rashly. Your behaviour at that time put me in—if I may say so—a rather awkward position. I hope you will regard this present reminder as nothing more objectionable, than a piece of, ah, avuncular advice, dear sir, and not resent my suggesting that before you proceed you consider once more exactly what you are doing." Seabury spoke these last words most distinctly, and so slowly that each of them seemed a little sentence unto itself. Gilchrist, feeling once again the viscount's steadying influence, was silent and thoughtful above a full minute before he replied.

"Sir, it seems I am to be continually in your debt," he said quietly, while Caro felt as if the weight of the world had been lifted from her shoulders. "One would think your good right hand was manacled to my foot, so surely do you prevent my putting it where it does not belong. I thank you, sir. Thank you, and good-bye." He bowed as he said this and, with another bow to Caroline, hurried from the room despite all they could do to encourage him to remain a little longer.

"He has always been impetuous," Caroline remarked, with an apologetic smile, as the great doors closed behind him. "I hope you do not find it disconcerting?"

"Not at all; he is a fine young man." Lord Seabury had discovered that his opinion of Gilchrist rose immediately upon that gentleman's removing himself from Lady Caroline's vicinity; why he could not have said. "He is very fond of you, I think?" he added, yielding to curiosity.

"No one is fonder, if he is to be believed," said she. "I sometimes feel the inconvenience of it very much."

"Inconvenience?"

"Occasionally one does not know what to do with...so much admiration," she explained inadequately, though with a delightful grimace.

Lord Seabury began to wonder if perhaps he ought not pass too very long a time alone with Lady Caroline. He had begun to excuse himself from her company when she interrupted.

"I must beg a moment more with you, sir," she said, forgetting Edgar as she remembered what Amy had told her last night. Seabury obligingly reseated himself. "My dear sir, whatever possessed you to challenge Mockabee when I expressly desired you not to do so?"

Seabury stared in confusion a moment, then saw the light and cried, or rather groaned, "Oh, Amy!"

"Yes, Amy indeed," said Caro, with a tight smile. "She came to my room last night."

"Oh, Amy!" he repeated. "Thank Heaven she is out of London."

"Just so. I said something similar to her last night, in fact. She took it very ill."

"I am miserable to find you have learned of the duel—still more so in such a manner," Seabury took up. "You are very angry with me?"

"I am," she said, then immediately added, "No, I am not." Suddenly shy of raising her luminescent green eyes to meet his handsome blue ones, she explained, "I seem unable to be angry with you, sir, though I am quite as unable to comprehend the difficulty."

"You relieve me greatly."

"I am glad it is in my power to do so."

"You understand I was obliged to act according to my judgement?" he said a trifle anxiously. "I should have liked to honour your injunction, but I could not."

She nodded. "You sustained no injury, I hope?"

"None at all." For a moment they sat still gazing at one another, in silence. Then Seabury roused himself. "I really must go now. I am engaged to dine with Lord Safford and his family tomorrow, and I promised to prepare some documents for his lordship and deliver them then. They are far from ready—so if you will excuse me—" He took his leave with a few more words; shortly afterwards Lady Caroline also quitted the Gilt Saloon, and sought the privacy of her chambers. She found the thought of Lord Seabury's dining with Lady Susan rather lowering; she could not know Seabury himself contemplated to the occasion with an unaccountable reluctance. Nor could

Seabury, in his turn, know how very disturbing that seemingly innocent engagement was destined to be, still less that his twin cries of "Oh, Amy!" would strike him, a mere twenty-four hours later, as having been darkly prophetic.

Chapter XI

Lord Safford, a large man on the brink of old age, squinted at Seabury with that same squint Lady Susan had unfortunately inherited from him, and repeated his question. "What," he demanded ponderously, shaking a scrap of hot-pressed notepaper with a trembling hand, "can this mean?"

Seabury answered in a strangely faltering tone, "I am afraid, sir, that I hardly know what to make of it myself."

"But is it true?" persisted the older man. "Is there any truth to it, or none? Frankly, my friend, I had expected to hear a flat denial from you by now. What prevents your giving me one? You know I should not question your word."

Lord Seabury continued his silence for some moments. The paper of which Safford spoke so vehemently was a letter headed, "Rucke House, May 18th." It had been addressed to the marquis, and contained this message:

> I cannot leave town in good conscience, dear sir, without apprising you of a situation which ought to have been brought to your attention long ago. My cousin Seabury is head over ears in love with Lady Caroline Wythe. How far matters have advanced between them I

can only guess, nor can I tell you what stated understanding they may have with one another, but I can predict confidently that my cousin will never offer for your daughter. It is a pity she has waited so long for that event, but each passing day can only increase that pitifulness. In my opinion her only reasonable course is to break with Seabury, since he has not the honourableness to initiate such a proceeding himself.

With the greatest respect, I remain yours etc.

Amy Meredith

Lord Safford, violently annoyed with Seabury's long hesitation, rocked back on his heels, glaring at his visitor. "Does Lady Susan know of this?" that young gentleman finally asked.

"She does not," snapped the marquis, "I thought it best to hear you out upon the subject before I disturbed her with it. I am not hearing much," he added ominously.

"I do not know what to say," the other replied weakly.

"By God, tell me if it is true!" exploded Safford.

"I cannot—I do not—my lord, I have ever looked upon you as a father, and of course...Lady Susan..." His voice trailed off. His throat felt dismally dry. "I have had every intention, naturally, of making Lady Susan my wife, if she will have me."

"Do not come the innocent with me, Seabury. You know Susan would have said yes to you any time these past seven years. What kept you from asking? What keeps you from it now? You call me a father, and—yes," he went on, his voice breaking suddenly, "I have regarded you as a son. But by Heaven, if you have been playing my daughter for a fool all these years I will deal with you as with my bitterest enemy. Now answer me, man!" he concluded, recovering his full fury. "Is this letter true or not?"

Seabury swallowed hard. "It is not true," he said.

Some of Safford's rigid passion left him. "This is more satisfactory, sir," he said.

"Unhappily," Seabury took up again, so reluctantly that the very room seemed to sway before him, "it is not entirely false either."

This revelation struck Lord Safford with as much force

as if it has been an actual blow. He felt the wind had been knocked out of him, and dropped instinctively into a chair. The two men were sequestered in Safford's study, a room in which they had weekly passed many hours together ever since Seabury first sat in Parliament. The bond between the gentlemen was a strong one; it was sentimental as well as political, and had been nourished constantly since its inception by a continuing fund of shared experience. Lady Susan being his only child, Safford had often and keenly felt the lack of a son. Seabury had filled that gap, and gladly, since his own father had been more like a child to him than anything else. From earliest childhood he had been blushing for Romby's imprudent, sometimes scandalous, activities. Lord Safford, a patient, upright, powerful mentor, had given him (though belatedly) the guidance and support Romby could never impart. It was no little gift. It was so great, in fact, that out of mere gratitude Seabury was still prepared to marry Lady Susan. Slowly, carefully, he said as much to Lord Safford.

"But I am to understand, then, that you do not love my daughter?" Lord Safford queried at length.

Seabury answered with painstaking precision. "It is not so much that I do not love her, sir, as that my love for her is—that of an old friend. Lady Susan is very dear to me; she must be dear to me for your sake if for no other reason—"

Safford interrupted, "And there is in fact no other reason?"

"No, I should not say that, my lord. I am so much in the custom of—"

"Ah!" Safford broke in again shrewdly, "Custom. There is custom. There is habit."

Lord Seabury nodded regretfully.

"And when this is said then all is said. There is me and there is habit," summed up the older gentleman.

"There is a certain—fondness," Seabury murmured faintly, but with very little conviction.

"I wonder if Susan still loves you," the marquis said, chiefly to himself. "She did once, I believe."

Seabury felt such a conjecture to be beyond him. After

a moment Safford roused himself and spoke more briskly. "What of this Lady Caroline, then?" he asked. "You find—you love her?"

"I do not quite know how to characterize my feelings towards her," he responded. "Whatever they are, they are strong. That is the difficulty, sir," he went on, miserable at being obliged to make such an admission to Safford. "She affects me very much, too much."

"Affects you, eh?" Safford repeated, with what almost looked like a smile, though it was full of weariness. "And can you resist this—this effect?"

"I have, sir."

"And can you for always?" pursued the other.

"I can," Seabury averred evenly. He felt certain of this as he said it, with Susan nearby and Caroline well in the distance.

"I presume Lady Caroline will be returning to the country at the end of the season?" Safford said.

"I believe she will."

"Well then..." he began meditatively. "Well then. Habit and friendship are not such a bad foundation for a marriage, my boy. They may seem a little dreary to you just now, but I can promise you they are a damned sight better in the long run than a strong and mysterious effect. If you truly believe you can put away this business of Lady Caroline, and be a good husband to my girl—well then, I think we ought to forget about this letter and go forward as we have always meant to do. I shall say nothing of the business to Susan. But you know, my old friend, you really must take this young lady in hand—your cousin I mean. She could do a great deal of harm, dashing off notes like this! A very great deal of harm."

Lord Seabury passed a restless night when, this interview closed and a seemingly interminable dinner dispensed with, he at last returned to Rucke House. He had no argument with Safford on any score: everything his lordship had said appeared to him to stand squarely on firm, dry ground. Certainly there could be no question that Amy must be taught some self-discipline; he had hopes her visit to the country would help, but it was possible she was simply not ready for society at all. Mrs. Henry was not adequate to the task of governing her charge; but at all events, that particular problem would prove soluble someday, he was sure. As to the ghastly triangle which had somehow materialized between himself, Lady Susan, and Lady Caroline—here solutions were scarcer. Lord Safford's view (and doubtless the only sensible one) was that Caroline might and must be forgot, whereupon Seabury and Susan could settle down to a long and satisfactory life together. He was absolutely right, in the viscount's opinion. Absolutely right; and yet the idea of forgetting Caroline, now that he had been advised to do so by the marquis, met up with a profound resistance in Seabury's heart—a resistance which swelled, as the night wore on, into a virtual mutiny.

An effort of will, he told himself, would release him for good and all from the tyranny of his irrational regard for Caroline—but how much easier, he could not help but reflect, if she should marry someone else and thus remove herself irretrievably from such consideration. Perhaps, he thought, she would accept Sir Sidney Pettingill. It was nearly a week since that young man had called to ask Seabury's permission to offer; he must certainly come to the point soon. It was cowardly on Seabury's part, this desire to wait until Caro herself settled the business for him; moreover, the idea of a marriage between her and Pettingill was not at all satisfactory. Still, his lordship's confusion was so great that he contemplated such an arbitrary end to his dilemma with what almost amounted to enthusiasm. Pettingill was not a bad fellow. He was enormously wealthy, for one thing, and—and perfectly kind and honourable. Caroline would do no worse with him than Seabury would with Susan, the viscount told himself. In fact he told himself this several times repeating it almost as if it were an incantation when he had said good-night to his man and had got into bed; she would do no worse, she would do no worse—and so thinking he fell asleep at last.

*   *   *

May 19th.

Dearest Angela,

It seems I must be living in a madder whirl of society than I knew, for having written to you only yesterday of your brother's latest offer of marriage to me, I have another to report. Before I do, however, I must take advantage of this opportunity to complain that somewhere in the middle of the more recent proposal I began to sneeze, and that since my suitor has gone away, I have manifested further symptoms to such a degree that I can no longer ignore the fact that I have got a cold—and a prime little goer it appears to be, too. I have taken rhubarb, and am quite awash in gargle, so I suppose the remainder of my sufferings can be alleviated only by vigorous whining—hence the exercise you have just read. I am tucked up in bed very nicely, in any case, and Windle (though she appears to be low in spirits, for some reason) looks after me with a solicitude that is at once exhausting to herself and to her patient.

Now for that offer. It came this afternoon at one o'clock, in the form of Sir Sidney Pettingill. I know I have written to you of him before—he is the one with the wavy red hair and the wet lips. There is enough of him to make one and a half Sir Sidneys, and enough of his chin to make three reasonable ones … well, suffice it to say that he looks perfectly stunning in twenty thousand pounds a year; or, if it does not suffice for you to say so, let it be noted that it certainly satisfies two or three dozen match-making mammas here in this great centre of civilization.

Now then! Any one of those aforementioned mammas would give their eye-teeth to hear said to their daughters what Sir Sidney has said to me today; but I only sneezed. "My dear Lady Caroline," he began (brilliantly original!) with a bow, "I should like to address you on a matter of some significance."

Thought I to myself, "I should like that too, but I can hardly suppose that what signifies to you will be of much moment to me." I held my tongue however, and simply nodded. I may remark, indeed, ere I go further, that I was an extremely good girl during this interview! I knew from his very bow—from the very seals he had chosen to wear, forsooth—that this was to be an offer of marriage. Those seals just wailed of marriage; I read them as easily as if they had been hieroglyphs, and I a practised scholar. Moreover, I felt this cold advancing—and you know how I abhor a cold. But in spite of these tribulations, in spite of everything nature and man could do to try me, I remained absolutely on my best behaviour, and was not only courteous but (with no more than a few exceptions) also graceful.

"It has come to my attention, dear ma'am—er, no, that is not what I mean," said my gallant, "I mean, it has been my honour to know you . . . er, to continue an acquaintanceship of growing personal intimacy . . . or rather, at least, in short, I have had the pleasure of having the pleasure of counting myself among those who count themselves among your warmest friends for some time. I suppose you are aware of it. I hope the position is returned. Dear ma'am!"

Angela, if I am exaggerating in even the tiniest degree how tongue-tied my admirer was, I hope I may develop pneumonia.

"I am afraid I do not entirely understand you," said I civilly.

"Deuce take this collar," said he, tugging at that article—which must indeed have cut very painfully into his over-sized chin. "What I mean to say, dear Lady Caroline, is that despite the difference between our ranks, I have taken the liberty of adoring—well, that is to say, of liking you very strongly . . . and that the proportions of that sentiment in my bosom having swelled to quite a great deal of—er, largeness, I am flinging myself headlong at your feet in hopes you will intervene before I—er, break my nose. Dear, dear ma'am!" Upon which he gazed at me with what I believe is called, by both the very religious and the very romantical, fervency.

"Dear sir," said I gently, and absolutely—I assure you—without laughter of any kind, "I should be very sorry were you to break your nose; and perhaps, in order to prevent such a catastrophe, I ought to interrupt you

now and inform you that it is not my intention to
marry—for I think your discourse drifts towards that
topic?—now or ever. If I have presumed too far, I beg you
will excuse my immodesty, which stems only from a desire
to avoid any painful scene. If I have—"

But at this point I was myself interrupted by Sir
Sidney, who burst out gaspingly, "You do not mean to tell
me that Seabury said nothing of this to you? I was
certain...I had understood...I thought you must be
prepared, dear ma'am—"

"Am I to understand that you addressed Lord Seabury
upon this head?"

"Certainly! Just last week. On Wednesday, in fact."

This intelligence gripped me queerly, dear Angela,
though it was not until after Pettingill's next remark that I
fully realized why.

"I told him all about myself," asserted he. "About the
Pettingills, how long we have been in Dorset, how much I
am worth in pounds a year, and all that! Did he say
nothing to you?"

Angela! What fools we mortals be—or at least, what a
fool *I* had been. I knew then, with dismal certainty, why
Lord Seabury asked me last week if I should not be sorry
to live apart from my brother—in Dorsetshire, for
example. And I had thought—well you can guess what I
had thought...and I have been well punished for that
audacity. I could have wept for an hour on realizing how
corkbrained I had been; but I had not an hour to weep in.
Sir Sidney continued to bear down upon his point in a
most insistent way, and it took me above ten minutes to
persuade him that Seabury had not informed me at all of
what I was to expect from the friendly baronet.

"Oh dear!" said he, when at last he believed me. "In
that case, I must repeat to you what I said to him, before I
ask you to do me the extraordinary honour which it was
my purpose in coming here to ask you to do me. There
have been Pettingills in Dorset, dear ma'am, for more
than an hundred—"

I broke in upon him and repeated what I had
endeavoured to say definitively before: that I could not be
persuaded to marry. I found this easier, you will

understand, than saying I could not be persuaded to marry *him*.

"But my dear Lady Caroline," said he, with a dismay almost touching to see, "this upsets all my plans!"

I apologized for the necessity.

"But you simply cannot . . . it never occurred to me that you might . . ." He kept silent for a brief moment, utterly confounded at being refused—which was undoubtedly the thing that had never occurred to him. Then, as if he had had an inspiration, he broke out suddenly, "You do not refuse me because I am too young for you, do you? I hope not, dear ma'am! Believe me, I am aware of your exact age, and it does not discourage me in the least! As I told Lord Seabury, I need only one heir after all, and so long as you—"

"I beg you will cease," said I, feeling that the interview (never promising) had taken a decided turn for the impossible. "I am certain any number of young ladies in London would be delighted to figure in your plans, and would moreover perform their duties in that capacity more than adequately. For myself, as I believe I have said already, I have no intention of marrying regardless of who may honour me with such a petition, and even regardless of that unknown person's age. I am sorry to disappoint you when you have been so kind as to consider me as—as a candidate, dear sir, but I must respectfully decline."

Do not scold me, Angel, for using the term candidate. I am convinced that is how he himself has thought of the hopeful young ladies round him all season. He was evidently crushed, however, and had I not by then been sneezing with a regularity that was quite astonishing (I have edited out the sneezes, as you see, having considered you forewarned) I might have sat with him a few minutes longer while he recovered himself. I really felt decidedly invalidish, though, so I excused myself from his company after begging him to feel free to stay in the drawing-room as long as he cared to, until he was more composed.

Dear me, Windle has just bustled in and out of here wearing a drearier expression than any I have ever seen on her. It is a bit too much, I think to ask me to deal with a woeful Windle when I myself am so moped. I scarcely dare ask her what is the matter; on the other hand, she is casting out martyr-like signals that simply beg for an inquiry. Oh dear, oh dear. Who would have thought a pair of blue eyes could cause me so much confusion? I wish I could read their expression as easily as I can Windle's. I see this letter is plummeting into inexcusable self-indulgence. Farewell, then, before it worsens. Remember me (mildly) to our dear Edgar.

Ever yours,
C.W.

The mystery of Miss Windle's martyr-like expression would have been no mystery at all to Caroline could she have known what was occurring two doors away from the drawing-room where she herself received Sir Sidney, and at the very same hour. Miss Windle, to put in succinctly, had finally cornered Lord Romby in the Gilt Saloon and had closed in for the kill. The old man, though he was not fond of the Gilt Saloon, had come there when Sir Sidney Pettingill's arrival in the long drawing-room made him see the wisdom of quitting that particular place. When Miss Windle found him he was reading an illustrated journal and muttering over it profusely. "Scoundrels! Rogues and sapskulls!" were his exact words when she entered, after a light knock. "What is this?" he went on, looking up. "Oh. No need to interrupt myself for that, is there," he concluded, though (fortunately for her) Miss Windle could not make out his garbled words.

"I hope I do not intrude upon you, sir?" said she timidly.

"If you hoped with real devotion you would avoid the risk altogether by not coming in," he remarked.

"I do intrude, then?"

"See how far behind you you have left the door, and judge for yourself," he suggested.

"Oh dear, my lord! You speak in such witty riddles sometimes that it is all I can do to keep up with you!"

"I should have said you did a fine job of keeping up with me today; it is keeping away from me you need to work at."

Miss Windle laughed a delicate, desperate laugh from behind her green silk fan and protested, "One can never take you at your word, dear sir. I know, if no one else does, how true that is. May I sit down?" she added, advancing to a chair just opposite to his.

"Certainly," he answered. "And may I stand up?"

She gave another helpless giggle. "I hope you will not."

"You are simply bursting with these little hopes today, madam. Be careful, or the sheer weight of probability will ensure your disappointment."

"Ah!" said she wisely, smoothing the skirt of the green silk morning gown it had taken her a month to make. She had bespoke the fan to match it, and had moreover purchased (at no little sacrifice, for her means were slender) a pair of green silk slippers to add to the effect. The cap on her greying locks was laced with long green ribands, and she carried a reticule of the same hue. All in all she looked a little like a sea-weed. "I place the greatest of my hopes in such kind and capable hands, that I fear not of so sorry an end to it. I wonder if you know what I mean," she brought out diffidently, almost blushing.

"Wonder no more, in that case: I have not the slightest notion."

"Oh! I must explain myself better, then."

"Not at all; I beg you will feel under no such obligation, madam. I am not curious."

"Oh, la! You men are such jokesters!"

His lordship looked slowly over one stooped shoulder, then over the other. "We men?" he echoed when he had done so. "Is there someone invisible in the room, or do you address me in the plural?"

"Oh, naughty creature!" cried she, shaking her fan at him playfully. "Are you never serious?"

"Never, madam," he assured her. "I live at this same giddy pace year in and year out, and am likely to die of hilarity at any moment."

Perfectly delighted with this account, she gave a peal of laughter. "But my dear sir, I must beg—I must implore you will be serious, nonetheless, if only for an hour."

"By God, I have been gay so many years, I can hardly

tear the smile from my lips; but for you, madam, I shall attempt it." He glared at her unpleasantly while awaiting her response.

"My lord, I hope you will not think me bold if I say that, having watched you carefully above a month now, I believe I can discern behind your self-sufficient exterior a lonely and mournful gentleman."

"There are those little hopes again, madam. You ought to watch *them* more carefully, I protest."

"I am not afraid to hope," said she meaningfully, "where the benefit, if granted, means so much happiness."

"Well, if it means so much happiness to you as all that, I agree not to think you bold. There! Are we done? Is that all? Are you happy?"

"Dear sir, really, I must plead for a trifle more seriousness; indeed I must!"

"Oh, very well then" he grumbled. "Go ahead and plead."

"My lord, really!"

"Spit it out, spit it out!" said he, reaching for his stick with an intuition that he might soon need to pound it against the floor.

"It is a little difficult—" she faltered.

"Then give it up, my good woman!"

"No. I must have my say," she replied, feeling harassed to a degree but also resolute. "Lord Romby, it is my impression that you are in need of a—a friend. A helpmeet who will stand by your side and share your little sorrows and your little joys. A person, in short, who will sympathize with you in your goals, encourage you in your endeavours, strengthen you in your weaknesses, congratulate you in your triumphs. You have been alone too—"

"I have a valet," he interrupted.

"My dear sir, that is not my meaning!"

"What *is* your meaning?" he demanded.

"It is, that you are in need of a wife, Lord Romby. And no matter how you deny it, no matter how you hide your loneliness behind that brave, crusty shield, I shall always know you are sad and sorry until you have a wife to aid you. A wife to comfort you, as the tender ewe comforts her lambs! A wife to bear you up, as mighty beams support the roof! A wife to—"

"How will it be if I simply round up a piece of mutton and some trees?" he broke in. She ignored him.

"A wife to shelter you, as—as the skull does the brain! A wife to nourish you, as the sap does the towering elm. A wife—"

"Sap and skulls, eh?" he cackled. "Now you begin to arrive at the heart of the matter!"

"Lord Romby, you are incorrigible! How long will you refuse all human warmth?"

"Oh, *human* warmth!" he exclaimed. "Now this is more promising! You suggest I chase after the old petticoats again, eh?"

"Hardly, dear sir."

"I was quite a champion in that line at one time," said he reflectively, while his companion hid behind her fan. "Naturally that was some while ago—though I fancy there are still a few ladies here and there who would not be sorry to find my card sent up to them late one night. If I had a bit more blunt to work with, you know, I promise you I could do great things—but I wax poetical and bore you, I see."

Miss Windle was too much discomposed either to affirm or deny this hypothesis.

"You know, Miss Windle, you surprise me," Romby went on. "I never figured you for such an understanding gal. Most ladies faint at the very mention of—"

"My lord, I pray you will not continue!" cried the poor good lady, feeling herself very near to tears. "I know you are teasing me, but it is very bad of you to carry the joke so far."

"Joke? Teasing?"

"Please, sir, I scarcely know how to continue in the face of such raillery."

"Raillery?"

"Lord Romby!" she burst out suddenly, with a kind of authority only a former governess of little boys can command. "I shall not be trifled with an instant longer. Lord Romby, I know how difficult it is for you to

confront your—more tender sentiments, and because I
know it, and because I can read into your soul a little
better than—than certain other people—I am come to
offer myself as—" her voice threatened to fail her but she
recovered it by a savage effort and concluded, "as your
wife!"

There was a pause; then, "No!" exclaimed his lordship.

"Yes!" she affirmed.

"No!" he repeated.

"But yes, I do," asserted she.

"By God, I know you do," he snapped out. "What I
mean is no. You offer and I say no!"

"No!" she gasped out. "You are not serious."

"But yes," he insisted.

"Not—ever?" asked she incredulously.

"Not ever. You might even say never."

"Never?"

"Just so. Now you have gone and said it, just as I said
you might."

"This," she began, then checked herself and was silent a
full minute. "This," she repeated at length, "is very bad."

The old man looked at her warily at first, but presently
his glance softened. "I am sorry," he brought out gruffly,
to his own surprise.

Miss Windle did not appear to hear him. She sat
staring at the fireplace, which happened to be before her,
and was absolutely still. After a good three minutes of this
(during which Romby had started to believe she was
dead) she roused herself suddenly, rose without a word,
and quitted the drawing-room. Lord Romby, with more
tact than he had exercised in the entire twenty years
previous to this moment, waited until the doors were shut
to burst into laughter.

Frustrated lovers abounded that day in London. Sir
Sidney Pettingill, more stunned than saddened, had
wandered away from Rucke House that morning to find
himself, not a very long time later, in Conduit Street.
Perhaps he had slipped into an invisible groove formed,
through the years, by Lord Seabury's many passages from

one place to the other, for Pettingill somehow discovered himself directly before the Marquis of Safford's establishment, and had no sooner made note of this circumstance than he found himself actually knocking on Lord Safford's door. Mildly surprised, he observed vaguely that he had sent his card and compliments up to Lady Susan, and even the ten minutes he waited for that gentlewoman in the small drawing-room did not, somehow, provide sufficient time to orient himself. He was not in the least alarmed when Susan came in—no, not alarmed at all; but her arrival did come as something of a minor shock. He was positive, thinking about it later, that it was not something he had planned. It was pleasant to see her, at all events.

That bright look about her hair which he had first remarked in Hampstead he now saw again, and saw with delight. What a lovely smile the girl had, too! Somewhere he had heard—had he not?—that she was over five-and-twenty years old; but he could scarcely believe such a tale looking at her now. "My dear ma'am," he said genially, taking the hand she extended and making a portly bow above it. "I am so glad you are at home!"

There was a particular sparkle in Sir Sidney's eye that immediately made Susan feel quite as cheerful as her caller. "I should have been sorry to miss you," she answered demurely. She seated herself and begged him to do the same. She was prepared to embark upon the usual round of polite inquiries and devoirs when Sir Sidney burst out with extraordinary enthusiasm.

"My dear Lady Susan," he exploded, without other prologue, "will you do me the honour to be my wife?"

"My dear sir!" Vastly confused, Susan blushed and averted her eyes. Presently she added in a murmur, "You are in earnest?"

"Perfectly," he said—or rather, a spirit within him caused him to say, for it seemed to him that he had utterly lost control of his own behaviour. He waited breathlessly.

"You have spoke to my father?" she asked.

"Not at all. I—" His speech became a little halting as the mysterious spirit seemed, momentarily, to desert him. "I am afraid this is—well, it is all rather spontaneous, if you follow me. Will you marry me, Lady Susan? I should be the happiest man on earth. I know I do not deserve you," he tacked on as an after-thought.

"Not deserve me! Oh dear! I must ask Papa," said she, all in one breath. Literal-minded as she was, she assumed he referred quite plainly to the fact that his rank and family were of less consequence than her own. She had no very clear idea of what constituted a good match, but she was pretty sure that whatever it might be, it was what her father wished her to make. She could not guess, moreover, how the marquis would receive the notion of a son-in-law other than Seabury. She must ask.

But Pettingill instantly objected, "No, it is I who must ask his lordship. I ought to have done so before. I wonder why I did not? Is his lordship at home?"

Lady Susan was about to pull the bell-rope and send a footman to find out when a better thought struck her. "You truly desire to marry me?" she asked, facing him. "You will not run off the moment you are left to yourself?"

"Certainly not," he replied, almost indignantly.

"Then I must go and find Papa myself. Wait here," she said, vanishing before he had time to protest. With a sense of boldness that invigorated her as nothing had ever done before, Lady Susan marched through the house on Conduit Street looking for her father. Sir Sidney was not a handsome man; she did not deceive herself on that point. He was not a brilliant man, or an ambitious one. In all these aspects he was distinctly inferior to the man her papa had chosen for her, Lord Seabury—but Sir Sidney had one advantage the viscount could never hope to have: he adored Lady Susan. Heretofore when Susan had read of love gleaming in a young man's eyes she had been quite at a loss to understand what could be intended by the phrase. After meeting Sir Sidney's glance this afternoon, however, it made sense to her. This was the first and, as it happened, the last time in her entire life that Lady Susan made an independent judgement of what was best for her—but she did make it, and it is to her credit that she did not attempt to suppress or ignore it. On the contrary, she sailed directly into her father's presence (he was examining accounts in his study) and announced, "Sir Sidney Pettingill is here, Papa, and wishes to marry me. I should like him to do so very much, sir, if you have no objection."

That the marquis was surprised need not be mentioned here; nor, indeed, need all his initial remarks be detailed. They were what they ought to be: how could this be, why should she wish to marry Pettingill, what of Seabury and so forth. Mostly they were interrogative in nature, but when he had obtained some answers he took time to make a statement of sorts. "I desire you to be happy, my dear, and it is on account of that desire that I do not dismiss this extraordinary proposal out of hand. However, I think you must take some time to consider; I must speak to your mother and Pettingill—and to Seabury, for that matter, if you decide to accept Sir Sidney—"

He would have continued but she broke in, "Why must you talk to Lord Seabury, Papa? He and I are not betrothed. I gave him a perfectly good opportunity to come forward in Hampstead, you know, and if you want my opinion, he purposely resisted. It was not terribly kind of him, either. Perhaps he has decided to remain a bachelor."

"You seem to know your own mind on this matter, my dear," said Safford, much struck since her entrance to the study with just this observation. "How will you feel if Lord Seabury continues to be received in our house, if I still work with him in Parliament? Will you then not feel painfully the force of what once existed between you? Does it amount to so little as that?"

She thought for a moment. "Frankly, Papa, I do not expect I shall pass much time in London once I have married Sir Sidney—if I do marry him, that is. He has a lovely estate in Dorset you know—he told me all about it when we met in Hampstead—and I expect I shall chiefly reside there. I hope the loss of me would not weigh heavily upon you and Mamma. Of course you would always be welcome in our home."

He was silent. Then, "You are not afraid to disappoint Seabury?" he asked.

"Dear Papa—I know it is only natural for you to be a

little prejudiced in my favour, but quite candidly I think Lord Seabury has given us some reason to believe he does not really wish to marry me. Seven years is . . ." she paused delicately, "a long time to wait, after all."

Safford squinted at his daughter, who squinted back. "You truly suppose you will be happy with this young man?"

"I am certain of it."

"Well then, my dear, you had better arrange for me to speak with him myself." As he said this he reached across his desk for her hand, and presented her with a wide smooth cheek to kiss.

"Oh Papa!" she cried, availing herself of this opportunity. "I am very happy indeed!"

                                        Rucke House, May 21st

Dearest Angela,

I have but a moment to write before the coach leaves. My next letter will come to you from Bessford, since that is where I am going. Little Amy Meredith has run away! Seabury thinks it may be with Mockabee, as I do too— only privately, for I do not wish to alarm him any more than need be. What a morning we have had!

Seabury at first refused to let me come to Bessford, but Lady Beatrice intervened in my behalf. Her friend Walfish will follow us later. Windle comes too; perhaps the excitement will make her heartache easier to bear. My cold is all but gone, so have no fears on that head. Oh dear, they are looking for me—

                                        Best love to all,
                                        Caro

P.S. This is all in confidence of course. Officially we are in Hampstead.

                        C.W.

Chapter XII

"I simply cannot credit it," Lady Beatrice said for the third time that day. Lord Seabury's coach and four, with Seabury, Windle and Caro inside, was just in the act of pulling away from the marchioness's house in South Audley Street when her ladyship decided to repeat her phrase a fourth time and then to burst out impatiently, "I instructed you two to separate Amy from Mockabee. How can you have allowed this to happen?"

"For one thing, dear ma'am, just because Mockabee is out of town at the moment does not prove that it is he who has abducted Amy," said Seabury, not entirely in the best of spirits himself. "And for another, how could Lady Caroline and I have prevented it? We had not the slightest hint of it."

"Actually," Caro brought out with reluctance, "I did wonder why Amy was so very cheerful when she left London. Such a catastrophe as this, however, was quite beyond—"

"Ah, you see!" Beatrice cried, jumping in upon this admission. "She did have a hint after all. Why, Caroline, why did you not mention it to me? Why? It is most vexatious!"

"Lady Caroline, as I imagine she was about to say,

205

could have had no notion of such a disaster as this one; it is a thing that could not occur to a gentlewoman," Windle defended her. "Begging your leave to say so, madam," she added, with an injured glance at the lady opposite her. Caro and Windle shared a seat; it was Seabury, across from them, who was obliged to make room for his majestically proportioned aunt.

Lady Beatrice returned Miss Windle's gaze with a regard not altogether kind, and went on (pointedly addressing Seabury), "None the less, I entrusted Amy to your care. I hope you will not deny that you have failed dreadfully.

"This sort of bickering can achieve nothing, madam," said his lordship coldly. "I pray we may desist from it, particularly since we are not likely to reach Bessford before sundown."

"What a stick you are, Seabury. It is your least attractive trait."

The viscount steadfastly refusing to be drawn into another quarrel, Lady Beatrice eventually recovered her temper and confined her remarks to milder topics. Conversation was something less than brilliant nevertheless, since no one in the coach could really be interested in anything other than Amy Meredith's disappearance. The note from her aunt informing them of the disaster had revealed very little of use, other than that the girl was gone. Apparently she had simply packed up and removed all the clothes she had brought from London, leaving not even so much as an explanatory letter. Her disappearance had been noticed about midnight, when she failed to come home from the house of a family in the neighbourhood, where she had said she was dining. The neighbouring family, when questioned, disclaimed any knowledge of a dinner invitation to Amy—and so the trail stopped dead. Seabury had made his decision to hurry to Bessford not so much because he had real hopes of picking up her scent in that locality as for lack of alternatives. Of course the innkeepers near Bessford and Canterbury should be interrogated; but if that resulted in nothing he would be obliged to try something more desperate, perhaps even to call upon the gentlemen of Bow Street.

All the time Lord Seabury's coach was bearing down upon Bessford, the Marquis of Safford was frantically endeavouring to find its owner. When he received no answer to the notes he sent round, he visited Rucke House himself. He was told that his lordship had gone to his house in Hampstead. The marquis sent a letter there, and toyed with the idea of calling in person; however, political business prevented his quitting London. He urgently wished to speak to Seabury before the announcement of Lady Susan's impending marriage should appear in the *Gazette*. He desired to explain the matter to the younger man face to face, and to preserve if he might the friendship they had shared for so long. He would never have given permission for the item to appear so soon if he had imagined Seabury might be out of town. Late at night he yielded, though sadly, to the inevitable, for the announcement would appear the following day.

The object of all this concern, utterly ignorant of it, arrived in Bessford with the rest of his party a little after eight o'clock in the evening. The older Miss Meredith greeted them with tears on her cheeks; she had scarcely stopped crying (Mrs. Henry informed the newcomers) since the younger Miss Meredith had vanished. Lord Seabury attempted to comfort her, and at the same time to draw out from her any helpful information she might have forgot or overlooked. She was not, after all, an especially clever old lady: there was some possibility that she would deem inconsequential a detail that would later prove crucial. His lordship, however, succeeded in eliciting to such intelligence from her; she had absolutely nothing to offer, save a heart full of self-reproach and remorse.

In the area of remorse, however, she could not surpass the redoubtable Mrs. Henry. Miss Windle, on first gazing into the eyes of her ancient competitor, expected to find there some vestige at least of her customary hauteur; but she found none. She discovered instead as meek and rueful a glance as could possibly survive in an eye habitually so icy; in fact, Mrs. Henry looked positively mortal. Of course there is no failure more violent and spectacular, if one is a chaperone, than to have one's charge run off with a person or persons unknown; still, Miss Windle had expected Henry to stand up to the crisis with a trifle more spirit than she manifested now. The cause, at least in part, of Henry's extraordinary mildness was revealed to Windle, during a private interview, within an hour of her arrival in Bessford.

"I am afraid you must be very tired, Miss Windle," murmured Mrs. Henry to that•lady while the others clustered round Miss Meredith, "but I shall make so bold as to request a word with you alone in spite of that. I hope you will not disappoint me. It is a matter of some significance."

Miss Windle, exhausted by the journey indeed, was nevertheless surprised and curious. "As you like," she returned obligingly, but not without a distinct sensation of continuing mistrust of Henry. The two ladies slipped off into a tiny dining-room downstairs. This was, indeed, the only common room in the house besides the one Miss Meredith and the others occupied, that place being made to serve as drawing-room and sitting-room, music-room, library, and study. The house was really hardly bigger than a cottage.

Mrs. Henry very civilly offered Miss Windle a chair; she herself remained standing, and paced throughout the chief portion of the interview. "This is not a pleasant matter for me to discuss," Henry began, beginning also her wanderings through the cramped room, "but I am advised by my priest to do so, and do so I shall."

Miss Windle's curiosity doubled.

"The human animal," said Mrs. Henry after a long, deep breath, "is a peculiar creature. We are all of us subject, Miss Windle—as I trust you will agree—to our little caprices and humours, our prejudices and our, er, passions. It is the duty of society as well as the individual to attempt to...to control these little whims so that civilization may, ah, push onwards. Where would England be, for example, if our monarchs were in the habit of making laws in a fit of pique or, er, let us say, ordering the execution of various persons under the influence of envy, or wrath? And yet, some few things are done under these influences, both within the government and outside it... and the best one can hope for after having committed such a rash act is— forgiveness. Yes, one must ask—"

"Mrs Henry, I beg you will forgive me—while we are on that topic—for interrupting, but I am very tired. Is there something you particularly wished to say to me?" Miss Windle disliked Mrs. Henry to the point where she did not mind being rude to her.

The lady lost some of her colour before she replied, "There is. I was coming to that. Miss Windle, I think it will not surprise you to hear that I have sometimes... experienced emotions in regard to you which were not altogether charitable."

Miss Windle nodded slowly.

"It may, however, surprise you to learn that I was sometimes so carried away by my—emotions that I... I did some damage to your property."

"You do not mean—!" she exclaimed, startled.

"I am afraid I do," said Mrs. Henry, in a hushed voice and with eyes downcast for very shame. "It was I who destroyed your needlework."

"Mrs. Henry, I was aware of a certain friction between us," said the good lady after a pause, "but I confess I had no idea it affected you so deeply as that! What did you hope to accomplish by such means?"

"I hoped, quite simply, to annoy you."

"You could have achieved that in a subtler way," Windle pointed out. "You have cost me months of work."

"I am very sorry," said Mrs. Henry, with only the slightest trace of her habitual stiffness. "I have always had an uneven temper. Sometimes I cannot govern myself. It is to this fault in me that I attribute," she swallowed hard against a rising emotion, "poor Amy's disgrace! If I had been firmer with her, calmer with her! Oh, how I envied you Lady Caroline—how I envy you. That is why..." But Mrs. Henry, overcome by recent events, could not continue and actually broke, instead, into a long, dry sob.

"Dear me," Miss Windle murmured kindly, much disconcerted. "This will never do." She reached out to Mrs. Henry with the intention of patting her hand, but that lady (who had sunk down momentarily into a chair)

sprang up again and resumed her frantic wandering about
the room.

"When Amy disappeared I went to my priest. I
consulted with him...I told him my doubts. He
suggested that I speak with you on this head. I thought it
might help, that it might somehow...bring Amy back.
Merciful Heavens, I hope it may!"

Miss Windle, whose kind soul had by now utterly
forgot the wrongs Mrs. Henry had done her, echoed
solemnly, "Indeed I hope it may too." She then settled
down to giving Henry whatever comfort she could offer
(Mrs. Henry, soon recovering a good deal of her
characteristic haughtiness, would not accept much) and
to drinking a cup of tea to sooth her own jangled nerves.
Their *tête-à-tête* was interrupted by an abrupt knock at
the door, followed directly by the appearance of Lady
Caroline Wythe, distinctly in alt.

"News!" she cried.

"From Amy?" Mrs. Henry demanded, rising, and it
was pitiful to hear the involuntary eagerness of her tone.

"From Mockabee," Caro answered grimly. "He has
had the impudence to send a note from Morton Hall
informing Miss Agatha Meredith that—I believe his
words were, that he imagines her friends will like to visit
him there soon, and that they may do so at their
convenience. Seabury is seeing about the coach now."

"He mentions Amy?" Mrs. Henry asked, while at the
same moment Miss Windle cried out, "The poor man! He
will be exhausted."

"Poor fiddlestick," said Caro. "I am going too, and so
will you if you please, my dear."

"Oh Caro, I scarcely think I can," groaned Windle,
while Henry repeated her unanswered question.

"Mockabee says nothing of Amy," Caro told her
finally, "and Seabury says he is anxious on the subject. In
my opinion, it is only to be expected. It is very clear to me
he has got her with him; he simply chuses not to write
down as much. Such a piece of evidence could be very
awkward for him someday."

"Pray God she is well," said pious Mrs. Henry.

"I think she must be, or Mockabee would not entangle

himself any further in the business. Come, Windle, run and put on your cloak. The night is chilly."

"My dear, you do not really intend to accompany his lordship! Does Lady Beatrice countenance the scheme?" inquired the fatigued Miss Windle.

"Oh, she is too tired to care. She stops behind to wait for Mr. Walfish. If you are absolutely dead on your feet I suppose Miss Meredith's abigail or some such could—"

"Miss Meredith does not employ an abigail," Henry broke in, "and if she did I doubt if she could spare her. I do not know what Morton Hall may be, or where it may be, but if Amy is there I shall be more than happy to travel there with you, Lady Caroline. I shall be grateful, in fact."

"Oh, dear!" Caro was not, at least not immediately, mad for the notion. She delayed by explaining that Morton Hall was Mockabee's country seat, in Berkshire. "It is a matter of an hour, no more, from Two Towers—that is my brother's house, you know. We shall stay there, of course."

"I had forgot the baron was a countryman of yours," Mrs. Henry murmured, not altogether pleasantly.

"I hardly like to admit any connexion with him whatever," said Caroline, with a civility she did not feel deeply, "but I cannot deny that one."

"Indeed," said Henry. Then, in a much softer tone, "Will you permit me to escort you? Miss Windle will be able to rest, and to look after Lady Beatrice and Miss Meredith tomorrow. Miss Windle is dreadfully tired."

"That is so," Caro assented.

"I shall not mind the hardships of the journey at all," Mrs. Henry said, "so long as I may be of service to Amy."

Lady Caroline cast an interrogative glance at Windle, who gave an almost imperceptible nod in return. "Of course you may escort me, Mrs. Henry," said her ladyship. "It is good of you to offer."

Mrs. Henry did not pause to complete these courtesies, but instead left the room with a quick bow and a whispered "Thank you" and went directly to her bedchamber to pack. She was downstairs no more than fifteen minutes later, a small valise beside her. "I am prepared to leave," she announced quietly.

It being out of the question to continue with the horses they had used during the last stages, Seabury had been busying himself with finding fresh ones—not an easy task at nine o'clock at night in a provincial village. He succeeded in finding a team not wholly inadequate, and was himself in the act of bidding his aunt and Miss Meredith farewell when Mrs. Henry came down the stairs.

"Now Seabury, be sure you box that hoyden's ears when you see her, and tell her whose regards you convey when you do so," Lady Beatrice instructed him. "I should prefer to wring her neck, but I save that pleasure for when I see her myself. And if Mockabee has married her, be certain—well, find a priest anyway and see what may be done about it. If he has *not* married her, tell them both—"

"My dear ma'am, I hope I shall know how to deal with whatever situation greets me," her nephew interrupted impatiently, "at least as well as the next person. I trust we are agreed that Amy's safety is to be attended to first, next her reputation, and after that her immediate happiness. Having agreed to that," he continued hastily, without leaving time for anyone to agree or disagree, "I think we have done all we can until the facts are known in detail. Lady Caroline?" he added, turning to take her arm and hand her into the carriage.

"Good-bye dear Windle," said she, kissing that gentlewoman. She made brief farewells to the others assembled too. Lady Beatrice gave her a piercing look when they parted.

"Be careful of Seabury, my dear," she murmured. "Do nothing rash. Good things come to those who wait, remember."

Caroline, a little nettled by this unsolicited advice, replied that she would try to conduct herself suitably.

"Not suitably, my dear. Wisely," said the old lady. "We must all look for wisdom, Caroline." On these words, which were uttered in a strangely choked voice, the marchioness pushed her young friend towards Seabury's waiting hand. An instant later they were in the coach and travelling.

It was an extremely wearing journey. The weather,

happily, had been fine during the past week, so that the roads were not muddy; but it was a long, hard distance to traverse, particularly since time was short. In all likelihood (they told themselves over and over) nothing could happen to Amy Meredith in the next twenty-four hours that had not happened in the last forty-eight. Nevertheless, a sense of urgency nagged at each of the travellers. Though they were on the road in excess of eighteen hours, they paused no longer than forty-five minutes, and that only twice. They slept in the coach, when and as they could, and even had a sort of pic-nic in the carriage between breakfast and their arrival at Two Towers. It was far from a festive occasion, however. No one could think of anything but Amy. Each passed the hours considering to what extent the girl's unspeakable adventure was his responsibility, and pondering what he might have done to thwart it. Lady Caroline was perhaps the least to blame in this respect, but even she could not help thinking that if she had taken a different tack with Amy—befriended her a little better, or cultivated her confidence—she might have prevented the catastrophe. Besides that, there was the awful likelihood that Mockabee had selected Amy as his prey in order to spite Caro and Seabury. What concerned her most was Seabury's inevitable distress. Naturally he would deem himself accountable for the disaster. She might have spared him that pain! Mrs. Henry's thoughts were equally mournful, and Lord Seabury's certainly were not gayer; and so a very crushed and weary, and extremely doleful and anxious party reached Two Towers a little after five in the afternoon on Thursday, May 22nd.

They arrived unannounced, for it had been the general feeling that a messenger could not have come sufficiently in advance of the party itself to make much of a difference.

"Merciful powers!" were Lady Lillian's first words on being summoned to meet her unexpected callers. "What on earth does this mean?"

Lord Seabury shook the hand of the sister he had not seen in six years. Lady Caroline embraced her, and Mrs. Henry was introduced.

"Dear me, how very grim you look, Oliver!" exclaimed Lillian.

"I am afraid we come on a rather distressing errand," said he.

Lady Lillian had begun to lead the newcomers into a drawing-room, but now she stopped suddenly. "Not my father again, I hope! Was there ever such a reprobate—"

Seabury broke in, looking even grimmer than before, "No, not my father. He is very well, thank you."

"I am certain of that; he will outlast us all. I only thought he might be behaving..." her words trailed off into silence.

"Badly again," her brother finished. "No, dear Lillian, it is not that." He paused to sit down heavily on a plumply cushioned chair; Lady Caroline, watching him, wondered at the bitterness in his tone when he addressed Lillian. She had not expected them to be effusive with one another, but the conduct she was witnessing was scarcely even civil. Naturally she had many other things to consider: these were her first moments home in nearly two months. Still, her exhausted brain could focus on only one thing at a time, and for the nonce she was concerned with Seabury and Lillian. "We are chasing Amy Meredith," his lordship finally resumed. "No doubt you remember her?" In as few words as possible he explained Amy's disappearance, the party's removal into Kent, the note received there, and the purpose of their visit to Two Towers. In the middle of this recital Lord Inlowe entered the room, accompanied by their little ladyships his daughters, Delphina and Theresa. All was confusion for a while, as Caroline flew to hug her brother, and then to embrace her nieces. Lord Inlowe was a tall, lean man, with thinning brown hair and the same large green eyes as Caro. He was also an intelligent and sensitive man, and he at once knew that something grave was afoot. After a short interval, therefore, he sent his daughters from the room and begged his brother-in-law (now encountered for the first time!) to say what might occasion his unexpected call.

Lord Seabury repeated the tale. "I must ask you, if I may, to lend me a horse to ride to Morton Hall. Our haste is in vain if I do not go there at once. It is impossible to say what Miss Meredith's situation may be now."

A sob escaped Mrs. Henry, whose fatigue had robbed her of her self-control. She was soon prevailed upon by Caroline to be assigned a bed-chamber and to go there now and rest. "Though I shall not sleep a moment until I hear of Amy; I know I shall not," she insisted, even as a yawn and a tear appeared together on her haggard features. Lady Lillian escorted her to a guest room herself, with a graciousness perfectly correct, if not warm. Left alone with Caro and Seabury, Lord Inlowe asked permission to accompany the viscount.

"That Mockabee is a misery to his neighbours," he said. "It would be a great satisfaction to me to meet him under these circumstances."

"Humphrey might be very helpful to you, Seabury," Caro urged. "He will show you the quickest route to take. In fact, I should like to come along myself—"

"Out of the question," said Inlowe immediately, while Seabury announced at the same moment, "Impossible."

"Well, who is to look after Amy when you get there?" Caroline asked, disliking to be excluded. "You will need a woman with you."

"Nonsense," said Seabury, while Inlowe pronounced, "Fustian."

"Good Heavens," exclaimed Caroline, with a semblance of peevishness. "Quite a little coalition you two have formed, is it not?"

"Be sensible, Caroline. You do not wish to be a part of such a business as this. There may even be some danger in it," Inlowe reasoned, while he rang for a servant and instructed him to have two horses made ready at once.

"Faugh," said Caro. "Mockabee will have done nothing to Amy; I am perfectly convinced of it. Nasty he undoubtedly is, but a fool he is not."

"Pray God you are right," said Seabury.

"Faugh," repeated her ladyship in disgust. "You are so busy feeling culpable and anxious, you have had no opportunity of considering the thing calmly, Seabury." Then, "Oh, dear!" she cried, clamping her hand to her

mouth as she remembered her vow not to speak rashly—
especially to the viscount. "I am dreadfully sorry. I must
be very tired. That is my only excuse. Of course you have
every reason to be concerned."

But Seabury showed no sign of having been offended;
on the contrary, he was gazing at Caroline with a look at
once penetrating and admiring. She found the effect
pleasant but disconcerting. "I hope you can forgive me,
sir?" she asked uncertainly.

"Not at all," he said slowly. "You are entirely correct,
no doubt. I ought to have seen it myself. My one fear now
is that he has married her."

"Angels defend us from *that* calamity!" exclaimed
Lord Inlowe, hurriedly kissing his sister before he rushed
from the room, explaining over his shoulder that he
needed to change his clothes for riding.

"I had better do so too," said Seabury, still fixing Caro
with that piercing look. "Would you be so good as to
show me to a chamber?"

"Oh, absolutely!" Caro said, rousing herself from what
had almost been a revery. The journey must have wearied
her more than she knew, she told herself, for she was
obliged to fight an extraordinary desire to march directly
up to his lordship, take both his hands in hers, and cover
them with kisses. And, moreover, he did not look much as
if he would have minded it. At least, he did not look so to
her. "Ridiculous," she told herself sternly, battling
valiantly against the awful impulse. "Show him to a
room," she instructed herself, and accomplished that aim
with the help of a footman and the butler. When she left
him she did so with a subdued farewell, and the assurance
that she would stay awake until he and her brother
returned. The viscount never lost that strange light in his
eye, but he said nothing out of the ordinary. After she
quitted him, Caro went to her own bed-chamber, where
she found her own dear Jeannie awaiting her. With
Jeannie and with her nieces she whiled away the
remainder of the afternoon; at supper she entertained
Lady Lillian with a complete account of all the latest
London *on-dits* and fashions; but at last Lady Lillian
(who was not strong) went to sleep, taking her nieces with

her; and a little time later, Jeannie—accustomed to country hours—could no longer suppress her yawns. Caroline, succumbing to the inevitable, dismissed the girl and prepared herself to keep what remained of the vigil alone. She sat up, so employed, nearly till midnight.

Chapter XIII

"Inlowe!" ejaculated Baron Mockabee when, having been summoned by his butler to the Green Saloon of Morton Hall, he presently entered that room. "This *is* a surprise."

"Where is Amy?" Lord Seabury demanded, without prologue. His hatred of the man with whom he was obliged to deal was such that his handsome features contorted involuntarily into what almost amounted to a sneer.

"Amy?" said the other vaguely.

"Damme, man, you have played with us long enough. If Amy is not here tell me where she is. If she is here, produce her, or by God, I will—"

"You will what?" Lord Mockabee inquired, smiling his sharp, lupine smile. He had become even thinner than he was habitually; in his gaunt face the eyes glittered and the lip curled more malevolently than ever before. Lord Seabury was ready to fly at him and knock him to the ground, but Inlowe restrained him with a firm hand.

"Is Miss Meredith here?" he asked quietly.

"My dear sirs," Mockabee said emphatically, "I think it well to mention—for official purposes of course—that Amy Meredith is not now, nor has ever been, in my custody." Even as he said so, however, he beckoned to a waiting footman and gave him a meaningful nod. The man disappeared.

"By God, Mockabee, what manner of trick is this? Do you suppose I have come all this—"

Lord Inlowe interrupted his brother-in-law with a loud and significant cough. "My good friend, I think perhaps you had best wait a moment longer," he suggested.

"Lord Inlowe is very wise, very wise," said Mockabee. "May I offer you gentlemen sherry?" He began to pour, but did so clumsily and spilled a few drops. His right shoulder was still sore, so that he was obliged to use his left hand.

Within minutes the footman reappeared, with him Amy Meredith.

"Amy!" cried Seabury, with an instinctive movement towards her. The footman, rather than releasing her however, placed himself between the two. Mockabee commended him.

"You see, my dear Seabury, it would be foolish of me—I am sure you will agree in a moment—to give you my, er—what you have come for, that is, before I receive what . . . what I require."

Seabury cursed.

"Dear me, what an excess of temperament! I am certain our lady-friend has heard no such language before. Not, at least, from me."

"I can imagine," muttered Seabury. "How do you feel, Amy? Are you well?" he questioned eagerly. The man who held her made as if to whisk her away, but Mockabee stopped him.

"Let him assure himself as to her condition," the baron instructed. "Go ahead, Seabury. You will find she has come to no evil—no thanks to herself I may add."

The viscount's fury with his host was great indeed, but it was not stronger than his desire to know Amy was safe. She looked very pitiful: her clothes were soiled, her hair unwashed and uncombed, and her usually rosy cheeks were unnaturally white. She insisted, however, that she had not been harmed.

"Did he tell you to say so?" Seabury asked.

"Yes, dear cousin," she said, beginning to weep as soon

as she spoke. "But it is true in any event. Please take me away from here, please!"

"Are they hurting you, Amy?" his lordship continued urgently.

"No," she said, though her tears seemed to contradict her answer. "I pray you, take me away from him! I know I have been wicked, terribly wicked—"

"Did he force you—did he..." Seabury's throat choked against the words and he glanced at Mockabee dangerously.

"Be easy," the baron said unpleasantly. "She is just as pure as when I made her acquaintance—however pure that might be, gentlemen."

Amy looked so woefully confused by the turn the conversation had taken that Lord Seabury tended to believe her captor. "He has fed you well?" he asked in a calmer voice.

"I suppose so. Well enough. Please, dear Seabury, please take me away!" She was going to continue her petition, but at this point Lord Mockabee nodded to the footman and he conducted her out of the Green Saloon again.

"Do not fret, Amy," the viscount advised her retreating form. "I shall not quit this place without you."

Mockabee smiled at these words. "I am glad to hear you say so, my lord. I expected you would feel that way."

"Of course he does," Lord Inlowe broke in impatiently. "Now name your price and let us have done with these theatricals."

Seabury, whose exact sentiments could not have been stated more succinctly, faced his adversary in silence.

"Ten thousand pounds," Mockabee said.

"Good God!" cried Inlowe, without meaning to. "Mockabee, you ought to swing for this."

"Done," Lord Seabury said faintly.

"Done?"

"I shall write him a promissory note of hand at once. Mockabee, have your man bring me some writing paper."

The baron, prepared for this need, showed Seabury to a small escritoire in one corner of the large, lavishly appointed saloon.

"Seabury, you do not mean to pay the man his sum!" exclaimed Inlowe. "You cannot believe he expects it! Come, come sir. This is very madness."

"Every penny," Seabury replied in a low tone. "I was prepared to pay twice as much."

"In that case—" Mockabee commenced, grinning.

"No," Seabury shot back. There was something so threatening in his intonation that the discourse stopped there.

"But what on earth...why on earth should you do such a thing, Mockabee?" Lord Inlowe asked while the other wrote—not an unreasonable inquiry when one had seen the opulence of Morton Hall. Its owner surely did not seem to be short of money.

"Losses," the baron said lightly, "in the West Indies. Perhaps you heard of them; it seems half London did. Disastrous, if you consider my fondness for velvet. And lace. And sherry," he added, draining what remained in the crystal glass he held. "These things are expensive," he continued, shaking his head as if the thought saddened him. "Ruinously expensive. Ten thousand pounds, however," he went on, brightening, "will purchase a very great deal of sherry. Inlowe, are you acquainted with Miss Amy Meredith?" he appended.

Lord Inlowe owned, mistrustfully, that he was not.

"I think when you are," Mockabee resumed deliberately, "you will see how the scheme of abducting her might—might almost suggest itself, as one may say, to a mind otherwise idle. She is a young lady just perfectly made, if I may say so, to be a dupe. She seems rather to scream for it."

"Mockabee, one more word from you and I will request your presence on a duelling-ground—see if I do not!" Inlowe exploded.

Seabury, however, was strangely patient under this onslaught. "Miss Meredith is not...it is quite true that she is extremely silly, and gullible. Your own sister attempted many times to persuade her to ignore this—this man, but to no avail whatever."

"Ah, your sister, Lord Inlowe! Another story altogether!"

"What the devil do you mean?" asked Humphrey.

"Nothing, dear sir, nothing," said the baron with a mockery of a bow. "Only ask her someday about card parties, and the game of brag. Her answer should afford you a pleasant half-hour's entertainment."

"What the devil does he mean?" Humphrey repeated, turning this time to Seabury. The viscount shrugged.

"Best to leave it be," he said gently. "Now, Mockabee, here is your note. Where is my cousin?"

"Ah, my dear sir! You do not suppose I shall hand over your precious jewel before I have converted this—no doubt excellent—piece of paper into cash?"

"I certainly do suppose it!"

"Hardly businesslike, dear sir. I should not have expected it from you."

"Mockabee," said Inlowe, fairly bursting with anger, "you had best chuse something you will accept as a pledge, and you had best do so immediately. We shall not leave tonight without Miss Meredith, if we have to arm a band of the citizenry and bring her out by main force."

"Ah, and expose the poor dear to the cold eye of the public! Unthinkable," pronounced Mockabee, with heavy sarcasm.

"Then you had best decide, sir, what you will accept for security," muttered Inlowe menacingly.

"Lady Caroline?" said the baron lightly.

"Damn your eyes," Lord Seabury burst out, "if you do not come up with an answer in ten seconds, I shall murder you outright. I swear I will, on—on this ring. Take this ring, Mockabee! It has been in my family ten generations and more. Take it and hold it until your wretched cash arrives. Will you?"

"Inlowe, have you no little bauble to contribute?" the baron inquired. He had already received from Seabury the massive gold ring, thickly encrusted with emeralds.

The Earl of Inlowe removed from his right hand an heavy signet-ring. "I have never parted with this since my father gave it to me twenty years ago. Now send for Miss Meredith, or I shall not answer for the consequence. Mockabee!" he thundered suddenly, with a resonance surprising in one so slender.

The baron pulled the bell-rope as if galvanised. When the manservant appeared he was instructed to fetch Miss Meredith.

"If ever I hear another whisper from you, Mockabee," Seabury told him fiercely after the footman left, "or even so much as half of a whisper, I shall bring you to trial regardless of the hardship to my family. Is that understood? This trick succeeded once: it cannot again."

Lord Mockabee bowed and gestured largely, if vaguely, with his hand. "Naturally, dear sir, this marks the end of our intercourse."

"See that it does," said Inlowe briefly, but eloquently.

Miss Meredith appeared a few moments later, without baggage.

"Where are her things?" Seabury asked, though he hardly cared.

"I should guess," said Mockabee, with one eyebrow expressively raised, "in some shrubbery in Kent. Unless someone has moved them. They were a trifle . . . obvious."

Lord Seabury wrapped his cousin in her travelling cloak (ornamented since the night of her escape from her aunt's with a long rent down one side) and bundled her towards the doorway.

"Good-bye, my dear," said Mockabee, with a low bow. "Your acquaintance has been—an enriching one."

Inlowe tossed the man one last furious glance, but Seabury did not even deign to turn. He quitted Morton Hall without another word, put Amy up upon his horse, mounted it himself, and was five miles closer to Two Towers before he spoke a syllable.

Even then he said little. Amy wept during most of the ride to Lord Inlowe's estate; she was so distraught that she could scarcely even grasp who Lord Inlowe might be. She understood, however, that Mrs. Henry awaited her at their destination, and this soothed her tremendously. Seabury, beyond satisfying himself that she was safe and sound, did not care to converse much with her just then. He was vastly, overwhelmingly tired, nor was it the ordeal he had just lived through that concerned and exhausted him. Certain ideas, certain thoughts would not be laid to rest in his weary head: they insisted upon calling attention to themselves, standing up (as it were) and demanding consideration. In spite of these thoughts being intimately connected to Lady Caroline, he hardly even saw her when the small party at last reached its destination. He nodded curtly to her, handed Amy into Inlowe's care, and staggered off to bed—though not before giving thanks, in simple but deeply heartfelt words, to his brother-in-law.

"I suppose Mrs. Henry is asleep?" said that gentleman to his sister when the viscount had disappeared up the staircase.

"Yes, I think so," said she, peculiarly chilled by what had just passed. "I should not like to wake her. Amy, will you allow me to put you to bed?"

Amy dropped a few extra tears on being denied the presence of her indulgent chaperone, but she quietly acceded to Caro's request none the less. Caroline felt rather like crying herself, as she privately reflected while helping Amy to climb under the covers. She had asked Inlowe to wait up for her, and went down, after bidding Amy a final good-night, to find him in the library. She had never imagined Miss Meredith could be so docile and tender; indeed, the girl had actually asked for a hug from her before she left the room. Caroline mentioned the fact to Humphrey after he had recounted to her what had passed at Morton Hall.

"Dear me yes, the poor little thing has been through quite an adventure," said the young earl. "Practically melted in your friend Seabury's arms, you know."

"Not my friend," said Caroline stiffly.

"Not your friend? Seabury? I hope you do not mean to say you have taken him in dislike, Caro? He seems the devil of a fine fellow to me!"

"Do you like him, Humphrey? I do too. Oh Humphrey, I have been such an idiot!" she cried abruptly, allowing her weary head to drop into her hands and hiding her brimming eyes.

"Dear me, Caroline! What is the matter?" He rose and went over to her to pat her head gently. "I am sure it cannot be so bad as all that. It is something to do with Seabury?" he prompted, when she did not answer.

Caroline broke out into what can only be described as a sob.

"What a lot of tears we have had tonight," exclaimed poor Inlowe, quite at a loss as to what could trouble his sister. "Have you offended Lord Seabury, my dear? You say he is not your friend. I am certain you have but to speak to him, and he will forgive you. He seems an extraordinarily fine fellow, Caro! I am sorry not to have made his acquaintance sooner; I cannot think why Lillian avoids him."

Caroline said "Oh Humphrey" several times.

"Really my love, you must tell me a little more than that if I am to help you. Caro, perhaps you are just tired. Perhaps you ought to sleep a while, and when—"

"No, no, there is no cure for it! I have been an idiot, and he will never ever love me," she burst out, more frantic each moment. She was, in truth, terribly exhausted.

"Who will never love you? Seabury?" asked Inlowe, bewildered.

Caro raised her tear-stained face to his. "Yes," she said. "Yes, Seabury—and I love him so much! Oh Humphrey!" she repeated, and lapsed into a fresh set of sobs.

"Oh dear," murmured her brother, feeling quite unequipped to deal with such an extremity as this. "You—are you perfectly certain he does not care for you, pet? If I recall correctly, he objected rather—well, violently, when Mockabee remarked he would accept you as a pledge. A vulgar joke of course, but I did not think it required quite so wild a retort. He damned Mockabee's eyes, you know, and threatened to kill him."

"Did he?" said Caro, her tears ceasing for a moment. "But he is very chivalrous; you do not know him as I do. He would do the same for Windle, believe me."

Inlowe shook his head slowly. "I am not so sure," he said vaguely; then, "by the way, this reminds me. What did Mockabee mean about you and card parties, Caroline? Something to do with brag, I think? Or was it faro?"

Caroline's eyes flew open and she stared at her brother. "Good Heavens, Humphrey, tell me what he said!"

"But he did not say anything. Or rather, he said *you* would have something to say about it. You certainly look as if you do, my dear."

"Promise you will never breathe a word of this."

"Promised."

Caroline straightened herself in her chair, clasped her hands firmly in her lap, and told her brother the story of her quarrels with Baron Mockabee. "You see, this is precisely the sort of thing," she concluded fretfully, "Lord Seabury could not forgive. My behaviour was inexcusable throughout the whole affair. It may even have given Mockabee the idea of using Amy in his plot—as a sort of revenge upon the family, you know. And Humphrey, you have no notion how I have regretted my conduct! When I found Seabury had risked his life to defend me . . . and all because of that wretched poem . . . and that because of my stupid scheming! Well, you can see the chain of events goes on for miles, but in the end one cannot help but assign the blame to me. It *was* my fault, all my fault," she practically wailed, while Inlowe sat down again and gazed gravely at some indistinct point before him. This was his habitual attitude for hard thought, and when Caro saw him that way she fell silent and watched him expectantly.

"Caroline," he said finally, shifting his gaze to her, "there is no getting around the fact that you were imprudent in your early actions. Not inexcusable, mind you—but imprudent."

Lady Caroline nodded sad assent.

"However. As regards your subsequent behaviour, I do not think it can be faulted. Having recognized your mistakes, you endeavoured at once to correct them. Sorely tried by your adversary, you kept your tongue and bore your trials gracefully and patiently. Frankly, I think that is the end of the matter. This business of Amy Meredith's abduction is nothing to do with you, my dear. From what I understand, she brought it upon herself entirely."

"Oh but Humphrey, even if Seabury could be brought round to that point of view," she objected, "he knows perfectly well I have been indiscreet. Why, he saw me that night in men's clothing! Indiscretion is what he cannot bear. You saw how brief he was with me tonight. Oh dear, he is going to marry that horrid Susan Manning and while away the rest of his life in dreadful, killing tedium!"

"Susan Manning?" echoed Inlowe thoughtfully. "Now

where have I seen that name before? Just recently, it seems..."

Caroline interrupted his concentration by asking, "Oh, what does it matter anyhow? My life is ruined."

"Oh my, Caro; that is a little harsh, I protest," said he.

Exhausted though she was, Caroline's good sense told her (after a very little reflection) that he was right. "Of course—I do not know why I exaggerate like that. I had better go to sleep after all, my dear. Oh Humphrey!" she said for the twentieth time that night. "You are the most wonderful brother anybody ever had. I have not even asked you how you are!" She hugged him, new tears standing in her eyes.

"Well, well...I am perfectly fine, in any case," he murmured. He kissed her forehead. "Very glad to see you too, my dear, no matter what may have brought you home."

With a few more phrases they bade one another good-night. Caroline fell into bed without so much as brushing out her hair, and slept at once. She awoke hours after the family had breakfasted, and finding her eyes uncommonly puffy as a result of the previous night's weeping, was reluctant to seek out the others. Instead she had Jeannie bring her some chocolate, which she drank in bed. She then attired herself in her old riding habit (blue, for which she was heartily thankful—she was sick to death of rose), slipped out of the house, and rode over to Gaworth to visit Angela. She was not at home, therefore, when Lady Beatrice and her party arrived, a little before two in the afternoon, and completely missed the explosive reunion between the marchioness and Amy Meredith.

"Brace yourself, young woman," said Lady Beatrice when, all necessary greetings and information between visitors and hosts having been exchanged, she had succeeded in shutting herself and Mr. Walfish into a sitting-room with Amy. Lord Seabury had been invited to join this festive little group, but had declined, preferring instead to accept another invitation (this from Lord Inlowe) to have a look round at the grounds. Miss Meredith appeared properly cowed when her aunt continued, "I have been angry in my time, my good gal, but never, never have I been so angry as I am with you now. What fever so diseased your brain as to make you attempt such lunacy as this? What snake persuaded you—no, never mind; I know the answer to that! But what possessed you, Amy Meredith?" she demanded, pretty much at the top of her voice, while she rose to tower majestically over the victim of her inquisition. "I must have an explanation!"

Amy wept. As a rule, Amy did weep these days, except when she was sleeping. She had been shedding tears continuously almost since leaving Canterbury with Mockabee, for it was then she had discovered her stupidity. Certainly she had cried all this morning—first with joy on seeing Mrs. Henry, and later with fright at the idea of Lady Beatrice's arrival. Her worst fears were being justified even now, and she cried all the harder. "I do not know," she finally brought out.

There was a silence; then, "I do not know? I—do—not— know?" parroted Lady Beatrice nastily. "Idonotknow?" she fairly shrieked, spitting the words out all in one piece as if they were a charm to invoke Satan, or someone of similar qualities. "I," she pronounced with terrible distinctness, "I *wish* to know. I *want* to know. I *must* know, Miss Amy. I *will* know!"

Ansel Walfish looked upset. "Dear ma'am, really," he dared to say, at the same time nervously fingering the cords on his Brandenburg buttons. "Might you not be—ah, coming it a trifle strong? The poor girl—" he added, gesturing awkwardly at Amy, who certainly was a sorry sight.

"The poor girl?" shot back the marchioness. "And what of me? Or you? Or Seabury? Obliged to chase about for days through the countryside! Obliged to tell stories to all the world, only to protect *her* miserable little name? Obliged to pay ten thousand pounds to retrieve—"

"Ten thousand?" gasped Walfish.

"Ten thousand?" echoed Amy, who until now had not heard the sum.

"Yes, my dears! Ten!" thundered Lady Beatrice. She flung up her fat fingers and waved them at the other two. "This many, my dears! Ten thousand."

Her audience sank into awed silence. Finally, "Who paid it?" asked Amy hoarsely.

Lady Beatrice fixed her with a dreadful stare. "Seabury."

"Oh my!" whimpered Amy.

"No, not 'oh my,'" Lady Beatrice pounced again. "Oh Seabury! That is who deserves your exclamations. Amy Meredith, you have disgraced, distressed, and seriously discommoded us all."

Revitalized wailing answered this charge.

"Well may you weep!"

Amy wept.

"Well may you grieve!"

Amy grieved.

"Well may you—"

"Lady Beatrice, pray stop a moment!" Mr. Walfish burst out at last, rushing up to his old friend. "I entreat you, I implore, dear ma'am—sit down, be calm. I can bear no more of this; no, indeed I cannot. Does it not occur to you—dear friend, forgive me, but does it not occur to you that part of the blame is yours?"

"Is . . . mine?" In spite of her outraged intonation, her ladyship accepted the chair Walfish offered.

Miss Cecelia Windle, who was crouching in the corridor to listen to all of this through the keyhole, breathed a sigh of profound relief.

"Yes, dear ma'am. I regret it infinitely—I have magnaregrets, if I may say so; I am omniregretful—but I am compelled to give it as my opinion that you are at fault as well as Miss Meredith." He stood watching her almost fearfully, quite astonished at his own forthrightness.

"My dear Walfish," said Lady Beatrice in a low tone, "please enlighten me as to the justification of your interesting opinion."

"Well," said Walfish, noting with surprise that he was experiencing a sort of mild exhilaration, "I think you ought to have taken Miss Meredith into your house in the first place. It was foolish to leave her with Seabury. A bachelor cannot be expected to know how to manage a young girl. I should not know how, for example."

"Your ignorances, my dear Mr. Walfish, are your own

affair. Is this the end of your reasoning?"

"Not entirely," he said bravely.

"Pray complete your remarks, in that case," said she, breathing ice.

"It is my conviction," he resumed resolutely, "that Miss Meredith never was old enough to come out in the first place. In spite of her years, I mean. It is not her age which is objectionable; it is the fact of her not having been educated properly. She needs taking in hand—which is what I am obliged to submit, with apologies, you should have done, dear ma'am. She wants sophistication." On these words Mr. Walfish made a little bow, to signify that his oration had come to a close, and seated himself again.

Contrary to his expectations, Lady Beatrice did not spring at him the instant he finished. In fact, she did nothing for some minutes. She sat, wordless and still, with very much the air of a person who is considering things. Mr. Walfish waited on tenter-hooks—though not more so than Amy Meredith, who dared to imagine at this juncture that her hour of trial might be ended. She also dared to smile—just a very faint and fleeting smile—at Ansel Walfish. Mr. Walfish smiled back.

"My friend," Lady Beatrice said, after quite some time had passed, "there is much truth in what you say."

"Not really!" was the phrase which escaped Walfish's lips.

"Yes, really. You are as surprised as I at the notion—and yet, dear Walfish, I am obliged to confess your point is well taken. Indeed I ought to have kept Miss Meredith with me, or I ought not to have countenanced her visit to London at all. I am an old and selfish woman, Mr. Walfish, but I hope I am not too old and too selfish to admit when I am wrong."

Ansel Walfish found himself in the unusual situation of not knowing what to say.

"I think what Amy must do now—providing her reputation can be kept intact, which will be a miracle considering all our antics these past few days—is to come home with me to South Audley Street for the remainder of the year. I shall teach her—with your assistance, Mr. Walfish, I hope—how she must conduct herself in society.

Evidently it is perfectly useless for her to pass any more time with her Aunt Meredith. You will not, however, be *in* society, young lady," she continued, rounding on Amy, "until you have shown yourself capable of mature and reasonable behaviour. Do you understand? If you are not ready next season, you will simply be obliged to wait until the one following it; and if you have to wait until you are forty, I do not care. I shall not risk another scandal like this one, is that clear?"

"Very clear," said Amy, beginning to cry again.

"Now then, my dear, no need for more tears. I suspect you have tormented yourself tolerably well these last days, eh? Take my hand, then, and let us speak no more of it," she added, quite kindly. Miss Meredith fell upon the hand she extended and rather covered it with kisses. "Oh, la, my dear! Leave something for the gentlemen!" laughed the marchioness presently. She smiled somewhat wearily upon Amy. "What a task we have before us!"

The young lady gathered up what little courage was hers to gather and, in trembling accents, made a request. "May Mrs. Henry live with us and help me too?"

Lady Beatrice was not delighted with the notion, but she said she would reflect upon it—and Mr. Walfish winked at Amy as if to indicate that he would see to it her wish was granted. Miss Windle, still stationed at her keyhole, tightened her lips sceptically, but was scarcely in a position to voice her opinions to anyone. "I must confer with Seabury now," she heard Lady Beatrice say, and afterwards made out the unmistakable sound of skirts rustling. It was time for Miss Windle to be off, no doubt about it; she sprang up, but was still in the corridor when the others issued from the sitting-room. She was obliged to employ deception in order to escape being found out: with a weak smile, she murmured something vague about a volume of Herrick, and swept gently past Lady Beatrice towards the library.

"Listening at the door," Lady Beatrice whispered to Walfish after she had gone, and shrugged. "I know these lady's companions; eavesdropping is eat and drink to them. They could not survive without it. Ah well," she shrugged, "I hope she heard something interesting!"

*   *   *

Lady Caroline had been so full of her own news, when she first arrived at Gaworth, that it was above an hour before Angela Gilchrist could mention what she had been burning with curiosity to ask about from the start. She had plenty of privacy, at least—if she had not the opportunity—for the two young women were alone, Baron and Lady Trantham having exchanged pleasant but brief courtesies with their daughter's bosom beau and then having retired diplomatically. As for Edgar, he was nowhere in sight. "He never is anymore," Angela at last replied to Caro's question on that head. "Do you know, I think he has conceived a *tendre* for Maria Halley! Papa is awfully pleased; you know what he and Colonel Halley are to one another."

"Maria Halley!" Caro said, surprised but not at all stung that Edgar's heart should have turned in that direction. "With her teeth! Our Edgar must be grown a man at last, for this can only be true love, I trust."

Miss Gilchrist made a disapproving, clicking sound with her tongue. "Maria is very, very sweet," she pointed out.

"Very sweet!" agreed the other, her hands flying up to indicate her blamelessness in anything said against Maria Halley. "I am delighted for Edgar. Only I am a little curious," she added, more quietly, "as to what *I* shall do now. I seem to be throwing off prospects at a perfectly ripping pace."

"Dear me, Caro, you are not sorry about Edgar and Maria are you?" asked Angela, concerned but puzzled. Her pretty face showed her bemusement as she remarked mildly, "I suppose it is painful to lose a suitor even if one did not want him; but you looked positively crushed, my darling! I should have thought you would be very cheerful just about now, Caro. After all!"

"I am cheerful, believe me," said Caroline, striving valiantly not to cry. "Very cheerful indeed. Edgar and Maria Halley...is that so? Very wonderful, very very lovely—" But she could not continue.

"No, not that, my love. Really, this is fascinating,"

Angela said. "When I saw the *Gazette* this morning I thought immediately of you—how happy you would be!"

Caro looked up, her sadness checked for the moment by curiosity. "The *Gazette*?" she inquired.

"Well certainly. Humphrey sends it over every day from Two Towers you know, after Lillian is done with it. He always has, my dear. Had you forgot? What a very long time you have been away!"

"Naturally Humphrey sends it over," Caro said, her brow furrowing, "and he is very glad to do it; but what has that—you must understand, my dear, I have been much too busy these past three days to look at the *Gazette*. What is there—"

"Why, Lady Susan Manning of course," Angela retorted. "You do not mean to say you have not heard!"

"Not heard what, my dear? Tell all." exclaimed Caro, suddenly aching with impatience.

"Why, that Lady Susan Manning is betrothed to Sir Sidney Pettingill. Caroline, you really did not know?"

"Good Heavens!" was her only answer.

"My dear girl, do you desire some tea? Some water? A cordial? Caro, you look positively ill!" cried Angela in some alarm, heading for the bell-rope.

She held up a hand in a vague gesture. "No, no. I need a moment to take it in, that is all," She was silent again.

"I am sorry to have blurted it out so abruptly, my pet. I simply never imagined . . . I wonder—do you suppose it is possible Lord Seabury does not know either?"

"I have no idea," said Caroline woodenly.

"Well somebody ought to tell him. He may wish to do something about it."

"I cannot fancy his not knowing," she murmured.

"I cannot fancy his knowing and not mentioning it," returned Angela; "unless the picture you have drawn of him is very false indeed."

"Perhaps Lord Safford asked him not to say anything," hazarded Caroline. "Are you quite certain this is true?" she asked a moment later.

"Absolutely. See for yourself," she said, crossing the room to a small Pembroke table laden with journals and papers. "Now where can that have got to? I was sure I put it—"

"Never mind, my dear Angel," Caroline broke in. She had risen hurriedly and followed her friend, and now she gave her arm a quick squeeze. "Forgive me, pray; I must fly. I do not need to see it for myself, but I must ask Seabury—I am sorry. Give my love to Edgar . . . Do not bother to show me to the door, really—" And with this phrase, flung carelessly over her shoulder, Caroline was gone.

Chapter XIV

"Well, my dear," Lady Beatrice commenced drily, "how do you like your sister these days?"

She addressed her nephew, Lord Seabury, whose ride round the park of Two Towers had but recently ended. Indeed, he still wore his riding boots, complete with mud—but Lady Beatrice was too impatient to wait while he changed.She had grabbed him the moment he and Inlowe returned, and more or less dragged him to that same convenient sitting-room where Amy Meredith and Mr. Walfish had lately been closeted with her. Miss Windle, as before, hovered silently outside the door.

"Lillian," Seabury replied haltingly, "seems well."

"Always was a fine actress, that gal," her ladyship said musingly. "She is simply furious at our descending upon her, you know. I am surprised she does not poison our tea."

"I trust her feelings are not so violent as that."

"Oh, one can never tell," she said carelessly. "In any case, that is not why I wished to speak to you."

"Pray speak on, then," said Seabury quietly. Little though he cared for his sister, he liked even less to hear the situation joked about. It was painful to him that he and Lillian had grown so far apart. If the cause of their quarrel had not been even closer to his heart, he would have done much to achieve a reconciliation.

"Seabury, I should like to pay Amy's ransom," Lady Beatrice brought out flatly. "I think it my duty, in fact."

His lordship could not help glancing at her in surprise. "Your duty, ma'am?" He smiled in spite of himself. "I do not recollect your ever referring to such an entity in—well, ever!"

She looked flustered but continued determinedly. "None the less, I feel I am at—at fault in this matter, and should like to make what reparations I can." She went on to explain her plans for Amy's future, ending with a repetition of her initial request.

Seabury stood and walked the length of the room. "My dear ma'am," he said presently, returning to look down upon her, "I am grateful for your generous offer, but the difference between your estate and my own—in short, it is out of the question. Your circumstances would be considerably reduced by such an expense, would they not?"

"Somewhat," she admitted.

"And mine scarcely at all," said he. "I think you had best keep your money. If you desire to help Amy with it, give her part as a dowry and the rest as a legacy; that is my advice."

"Seabury," Lady Beatrice said slowly after a moment; "Seabury, you are entirely—revoltingly—good. That money might have been left to you!"

He shrugged and turned away. He was not feeling terribly well, for some reason. It disturbed him that his first and only visit to Two Towers took place under such peculiar circumstances. There was something depressing in the fact that he liked Lord Inlowe so much; indeed, he liked him more than anyone he could remember meeting in years, and felt as if he had known him forever. What good did it do, though, when he and Lillian got on so badly—and when, moreover, he was under orders from Safford to put Lady Caroline utterly out of his mind? A stay at Two Towers ought, by rights, to have been supremely pleasant to him; instead, he felt as if he had no business enjoying it. As for Lady Beatrice's extravagant offer, it was positively absurd, and rather irritated him than anything else. She was saying something to him now, in an unusually grave tone; he forced himself to listen.

"You like Lady Caroline very much, do you not?" she was asking rhetorically. "In fact, my dear, I have a strong idea you love her. Well, you ought to offer for her, Seabury. It is perfectly preposterous, this business of sacrificing your happiness to the Marquis of Safford. Marry her, my dear; do."

In his present humour, this interesting suggestion was as much balm to Seabury's soul as salt is to a wound. "In the name of all that is reasonable," he spat back sharply, "I beg you will stop trying to make my life pleasanter. I have enough trouble without that."

"What troubles have you?" asked Beatrice, surprised. "Seabury, I know it is not the sort of thing one is in the habit of doing, but will you confide in me?"

He turned to her with a weak smile. "I thank you," he said patiently, "but as you say, it is so far from my habit . . . in any case, I stand in no need of a confidante. I know what I must do; I only require . . . the strength to do it." His nerves were so much strained by this time that as he said these words Lord Seabury felt tears starting to his eyes. Preferring not to show them, he went at once to a window and gazed out upon the lawn. His back was still to the door when it burst open and Lady Caroline bounded in.

"Oh, here you are at last," she said breathlessly, rushing to give Lady Beatrice a welcoming kiss. "I have been looking into every room in the place. Lady Beatrice, I hope you had a pleasant trip? Lord Seabury, did you know Lady Susan is to marry Sir Sidney Pettingill?" As these sentences came out all in a jumble, it was necessary for her to repeat the last one several times before the others could make sense of it. While she did so she untied the ribands of her cap and tossed it upon a chair, for she had entered Two Towers in too great a hurry to attend to that detail before.

"It was in the *Gazette*," she explained, then added conversationally, "you know, I practically tripped over Windle in the corridor. Lovely to see her again, of course, but I do hope you were not discussing anything confidential."

Lady Beatrice waved vaguely to indicate that they were not. "You are absolutely certain of this?" she asked.

"Oh, positively. Did you know nothing of it, sir?" she continued, turning to Seabury.

"Nothing at all."

"I hope you are not—I hope it does not—"

At this juncture Lord Inlowe, happening to pass the open doors of the sitting-room, entered and was told the news. "Of course," said he, striking his fist against his palm, "that is where I saw her name. Remember, I said I had seen it?" he remarked to Caroline. "Lady Susan Manning and Sir Sidney Pettingill. And I remembered *his* name because Angela told me just the other day that he had offered for y—Oh dear," he checked himself. "Probably a secret, hey?"

"Rather," said Caroline, while Seabury burst out, "He did offer for you?"

Lady Caroline affirmed that he had.

"And you refused him?" he pursued.

She gave him a puzzled glance. "Naturally. You do not suppose I could be happy with such a man as that!" she said, candidly if not delicately. "Not but what Pettingill is a very agreeable gentleman," she hastened to add, regretting (as usual) her initial, spontaneous reply. "Very agreeable. Lady Susan ought to be very hap—Are you quite well?" she broke off suddenly, as Seabury sank down into a chair and buried his head in his hands. "Oh my dear, you are—what an idiot I am, springing it on you ... oh dear!" She looked frantically from Lady Beatrice to Humphrey, but neither of them seemed to know what to do either. "Seabury," she exclaimed, dropping to one knee before him, "is there something I can give you? Oh, forgive me, forgive my wretched tongue. I was so full of the news I never stopped to—dear sir, are you crying? Seabury, you are crying!"

This was incontrovertible, for when his lordship looked up his blue eyes were quite awash with tears, and more had slid down his handsome cheeks to the very edge of his rugged jaw. One tenacious droplet trembled at the

corner of the cleanly-moulded lips Lady Caroline
admired so much. "I cannot . . . I wish . . ." As he struggled
with these words, Lord Seabury broke into a brilliant,
entirely involuntary smile. "Absolutely in confidence," he
brought out at last, in a shaky voice, "I have never been
more relieved in my life. Good heavens, if it is only true!"

"But it is true," Caroline insisted, so fascinated with his
behaviour that she forgot to rise, and still knelt by him.

"I do not know how to believe it."

"Believe it, believe it," urged Lady Beatrice, who did
not care whether it were true or not, so long as Seabury
took it to be so.

"This is . . . most embarrassing," Seabury roused himself to say, grinning despite the awkwardness of the
situation while he wiped the tears from his face with the
lace-edged handkerchief Caroline offered him. "I think I
had best excuse myself . . . compose myself . . ." He
continued to sputter obscure phrases as he moved past the
others to the door, but regained some coherency before he
made his exit. "This is a very extraordinary piece of news
to me, as you may perhaps imagine. I hope you will all be
kind enough to excuse this—unusual display on my part.
It took me by surprise as much as any of you, believe
me—" he murmured, descending again into muddled
words as he finally left the company.

Lord Inlowe was the first to speak in his absence.
"Does he do that often?" he asked mildly. "I protest, I
should never have taken him for so sentimental a fellow.
He practically had me crying myself!"

Caroline assured him the viscount's outburst was
completely out of character.

"An astonishing man," Lady Beatrice pronounced.
"Astonishing. I have known him all his life, and he still
surprises me. Do you know he refused to let me pay Amy's
ransom? Not only that, he advised me to give the money
to her instead of himself! It is positively unheard
of—especially in this family. No one on earth is greedier
than Romby—and I daresay you have noticed a
certain . . . fascination where money is concerned in
Lillian, hey?"

Lord Inlowe conceded that he had. It was of interest to

him to hear of Seabury's generosity, but it did not surprise
him. He had formed as good an opinion of his lordship as
Seabury had of himself, and would have had difficulty
believing any ill of the other man whatever. Lady
Caroline, though, heard in this little anecdote a reminder
of how rashly and foolishly she had judged the viscount.
Imagine her having supposed he allowanced Romby to
safeguard his own inheritance! The reflection, though it
had occurred to her before, was more lowering than ever.
She sank into the chair Seabury had so lately vacated and,
as he had done, hid her face in her hands.

"What is this?" demanded Lady Beatrice.

"Caroline thinks Lord Seabury does not like her,"
Inlowe explained quietly.

"Oh phoo! I never saw such sapskulls as these two.
Agreeable ones though," she added, with a smile at
Humphrey and a pat on the shoulder for Caro.

"I had better go to my room," Caro said in a muffled
voice, for the events of the morning had already been so
confusing as to exhaust her all over again. With little
more ceremony, she quitted Lady Beatrice and her
brother and wandered sadly up to her bedchamber, where
a tenderly maternal Miss Windle comforted her and
urged her to rest for a while. She slept until it was time to
dress for dinner, and awoke a good deal more tranquil.

"You know, my dear," said Windle, while she watched
Jeannie brush Caroline's abundant hair, "I have become
convinced of late that the key to happiness in life is not
romance and adventure but good works and fine
thoughts. It is fine thinking, my dear, and not impas-
sioned dreams, which signify in the end. Fine thoughts, I
may say, are rocks in the river of life. Good works, I
consider, are the sand that underlies them. Young hearts
may flow like the swirling waters; young breasts may
churn and throb; young mouths may gush like river
deltas; but the bottom of all is the river bed, and this, I
conceive, is the very stuff of life, its core, its centre!"

Lady Caroline correctly interpreted this speech as
signifying that Miss Windle had put Lord Romby out of
her heart. She nodded politely and listened with what
patience she could muster to her companion's continued

development of this philosophical theme, but she could not help but rejòice when, properly dressed and coiffed, she was ready to go down and join the others. She was wearing one of her favourite old dresses, a white satin chemise dress edged with lace ruffles; she carried a fan cut in ivory. She was much more at ease in this gown than she had ever been in her London wardrobe; and feeling so, she carried herself to more advantage. Lord Seabury noticed the change at once, though he could not be certain whether it was actual or only the product of his imagination.

He had been much refreshed by his period of solitary reflection, and sat down to dinner with a healthy appetite. He could not make this morning's news accord with the impression he retained of his last interview with Safford, but he had already written to that gentleman to felicitate him on his daughter's impending nuptials as well as to ask (as tactfully as possible) if anything he had said or done had given offence. Beyond his fear of losing Safford's friendship, the newly announced marriage agreed with him uncommonly well, and he was more cheerful at table than Caroline had ever seen him.

Unfortunately, the repast was marred, and Lord Seabury's spirits considerably dampened, by a dispute which sprang up during the second remove between Lady Lillian and her brother. It began with her inquiry as to their father's whereabouts.

"He is in London, naturally," said the viscount; "or at least I suppose he is. I hope he is," he added with a laugh, draining a glass of claret.

"Hope indeed!" she returned, with unaccountable frigidity. She had not been blessed with her brother's good looks and when she was angry (which was often) her cheeks flared with a blotchy, unattractive pinkness. They did so as she continued, "I scarcely think it was wise of you, Oliver, to leave him unattended."

"He is hardly that," objected the other mildly, with a smile. "He has a whole houseful of servants to abuse, and is probably enjoying himself immensely at it."

"But he ought not to be permitted to do so," she insisted, much too loudly for his taste. Amy Meredith, for one, was listening to them, without any pretense of doing otherwise, and he suspected Ansel Walfish was too.

"My dear Lillian, when a man passes the age of—oh, sixty or so, it is my feeling he ought to be allowed to do pretty much what he pleases. In fact, it would be difficult to say who has authority to stop him."

"You have always been soft with him, Oliver," Lillian pursued. "You have always been on his side. He bullies you, and you permit it. It is shameful."

"My dear, perhaps—" He was reluctant to go on, but there seemed no other choice. "Perhaps we may discuss this some other time? Surely there must be gayer subjects than—"

"You ought to have allowanced him ages ago. You ought to have done it the moment you reached your majority. I told you so then and I was perfectly right." Her voice was gaining volume at an alarming rate; she seemed to have lost all government of herself.

"Dear Lillian, I have always done what I thought was best at the time, you know," he defended himself quietly. "It is very hard on him to be controlled by his children; it would be for anyone. Even now I sometimes contemplate restoring him to his original—"

"Oh, you are hateful!" she cried out, with as much petulance as either of her little daughters could have manifested. "You know how he always despised me, and yet you defend him—! How can you sit at my table and accept my hospitality and still persist in . . . persist in . . ." But she did not have the opportunity to say what Seabury persisted in, for Lord Inlowe—quite alarmed by this exhibition—chose this moment to go to his wife and insist upon her leaving the table.

"You are not well, my dear," he murmured kindly, as he urged her gently from her chair. "You must have a dreadful headache, I am sure. Do come with me, and let me see what I can do for it." With this and similar encouragement, he led her from the room: it was not the first time she had had such an outburst. Generally, however, her temper was directed at Caroline—very occasionally at her children. He had never seen her lose her head this way among company however. He found it disconcerting.

"Been that way from a child," Beatrice murmured to Caroline later, when the ladies had withdrawn from the table. "Her mother spoiled her dreadfully."

Lady Caroline, though she naturally had a thorough and intimate acquaintance with Lillian's fits, found this one peculiarly illuminating. It had never occurred to her that Romby might be the cause of the rift between Seabury and his sister. She had certainly never imagined that Seabury might have defended his father against even greater restrictions than the ones he himself had eventually imposed. Lady Lillian never spoke of her father at all. It was another example, undoubtedly, of her own odious jumping to conclusions. The observation was not cheerful.

Lord Inlowe, meanwhile, had left his wife to the care of her abigail and returned alone to his guests at the dining-table. He poured some excellent Madeira for Mr. Walfish and Lord Seabury, and sat back to enjoy a glassful himself. His nerves were still jangled by the *contretemps* at dinner, but the wine soothed them pretty efficiently. "You know, Seabury," he said presently, "I feel as if I must apologize for Lillian, only I cannot think how."

The viscount waved this remark away. "Not at all necessary," he said, feeling a trifle better for the Madeira himself. "This is hardly the first time Lillian has . . . ah, vented her spleen in this direction."

"You are very good to take it so calmly," Inlowe replied. "I wish I could."

"Frankly, dear sir, I suspect I can take it in stride because I know I shall probably not see my sister again for another six years or so. It does distress me, though, that we get on so ill with one another."

"I certainly hope it will not be another six years," Humphrey returned warmly. "Now that we have finally met, I do not mind saying I should like to continue the acquaintance. Yours too, Walfish," he added politely.

Mr. Walfish bowed smilingly and accepted another

glass of Madeira. "I'm afraid it will be another six years before Lillian will receive me," Lord Seabury said regretfully. "Otherwise, I protest I should be tempted to move in with you, so pleasant do I find these surroundings."

"But really, Seabury, Lillian does not mean to flare up like that. I am sure she loves you, despite all appearances. She only . . . she seems to need someone to be angry at. Before you came it was Caro. And she actually likes Caroline too, believe me!"

"I am sure she does," said Seabury. "I fail to see how she could do otherwise, indeed."

"I am glad to hear you say that, old fellow. Caroline seems to feel—" But he checked himself mid-sentence, having just remembered that Ansel Walfish (quiet though he was) still remained in the room.

Mr. Walfish, however, was far too alive to the feelings of others not to understand at once what was happening. Dining at the tables of friends almost every night of his life had made him sensitive to the needs and desires of his companions, and he had learned that where he was not tactful, he did not get invited to dinner again. Therefore he rose, graceful and unalarmed, and excused himself from the room with the ease of a professional. "If you do not mind, dear sirs—I feel a bit super-nourished; you see what I mean. I believe I shall take a stroll out on the grounds, if you can spare me. Deuced delicious Madeira," he added, and he polished off his last glass and bowed himself from the dining-parlour.

"Mr. Walfish is a natural diplomat," Seabury smiled.

"Bless him for it," the other returned. "I am anxious to discuss this business of Caroline with you, you know. I hope it does not make you uncomfortable?"

"Not at all," said Seabury, whose jubilant mood had led him to drink three times as much wine as he was accustomed to, and who consequently could only be made uncomfortable by a natural disaster, or perhaps a political crisis of major significance.

"Caroline thinks you dislike her," Humphrey said flatly. "What do you say?"

"Ridiculous," came the response.

"Just as I thought," Inlowe pronounced with satisfaction. "More wine?"

"Please."

Lord Inlowe filled his guest's glass and his own, which he then raised and drained. Seabury followed suit, upon which Inlowe bespoke a second bottle. When it arrived he dismissed the servants from the room. "Now look here," he resumed, pouring freely. "I have no idea how to persuade her of what you say. She is convinced you could never approve of her. Thinks she is too flighty for you, or some such thing. Indiscreet—that was it."

"Ah," said Seabury, thoroughly foxed by now. "She *is* indiscreet."

"Exactly," agreed the other. "Always was."

"But charmingly so."

"Precisely! Entirely!"

"A delight merely to be acquainted with her. You too, Inlowe," he added, gesturing at the other with his glass and drinking up immediately afterwards.

"I was sure of it! I knew it. You must tell her so," said Humphrey.

Seabury considered this. "No," he finally brought out.

"But why not?"

"Might lose my head," he explained. "Might kiss her. Excuse me, Inlowe; I hope you do not mind."

"Mind!" exclaimed the other. "On the contrary!"

"Well you see," Lord Seabury murmured confidingly, leaning over the table, "I think I might ask her to marry me."

"And then what?"

"Then what? Disaster!" affirmed the other.

"Indeed? But why?" demanded the lady's brother.

"Rebuff. Rejection. I cannot bear it. Too hard on me, old fellow. Forgive me. Otherwise—no question about it."

"But . . . would she refuse you?" asked Inlowe, his head hopelessly muddled. "I do not think so, dear sir. I think she loves you."

"Oh, phoo," said Seabury. "If I may borrow a phrase from my aunt."

"Why should she refuse you? Really, old fellow, tell

me. I am dying to hear," said Humphrey, who actually
had forgot what he knew of the subject.

"She hates me!" said he. "I heard her say so myself. She
thinks I am the greatest beast in nature. Well she did think
that, anyhow. Maybe she tolerates me now. I could not
say, exactly."

"Oh, phoo," Inlowe retorted. "If I may borrow from
your aunt as well."

Seabury vouchsafed permission; then, "But I swear it
to you, dear friend," he said. "It is true: she thinks I am
cold and rigid and dull. She would laugh at me."

"She would not. She would accept you."

"Never."

"Absolutely."

"Impossible."

"Beyond question."

"Not believable."

"Fifty pounds she will."

"An hundred she will not," said Seabury.

"Done!"

"Done," the viscount agreed, shaking his brother-in-
law's hand firmly. There was silence at the table.

"Better go ask her," Inlowe advised.

"Tonight?"

"Why not, old fellow?"

"Frankly," said Seabury slowly, "I think I may be a
trifle bosky."

"Best time!" the other recommended.

"You really think so?"

"Indubitably!"

Seabury pushed his chair away from the table. "Off I
go, then," said he resolutely.

"Good man!" encouraged Humphrey.

"Just a—just a few minutes and we shall know,"
muttered Lord Seabury, his head reeling as he stood.
"Know for certain," he refined, staggering to the door.
"Know for good and all." He walked out of the room.

"Inlowe," he said, entering the dining-parlour again a
moment later.

"Yes, old fellow?"

"Where do you suppose the ladies have got to?"

Lord Inlowe stood and tripped over to his new friend. "The violet drawing-room, I expect. Follow me." He gestured vaguely and led Lord Seabury through the intricate passageways of Two Towers. "There she is," he said, jerking his chin towards Caroline, who sat just inside the open doors of the room he had named. "Go to, go to!"

Lord Seabury stumbled forward and arrived, a short time afterwards, at Lady Caroline's chair. "Come with me, please," he said sternly, extending an arm for her. Caro knew at once something was amiss with him, but it was not in her power to refuse his invitation. With a puzzled glance at the others, she rose and took his arm. "Outside," he murmured, beginning to move towards the door.

She turned to Windle, who nodded vigorously, and then to Lady Beatrice, who gestured as if to push her through the door. "Very well," she answered at length, looking in surprise at Humphrey, who still stood on the threshold. He smiled approvingly as the pair passed him. "Good man," he repeated in a low voice. Lord Seabury made for a set of French windows he had noticed, and opened them for Caroline.

"Where are we going?" she inquired, stepping through.

"Let me show you."

"There is nothing out here but the kitchen-gardens," she told him.

"Never mind, my dear. I know what I am about."

"You are drunk, are you not my lord?"

"Absolutely. Best time," he said, leading her along a row of plants.

"Best time for what?" asked she.

"Best time. None better," he repeated, finally stopping to lean up against the stone wall of the garden.

"Yes, but for what?" she insisted, mistrustfully allowing him to take possession of her hands.

"Kiss you," said the poor man. "Ask you to marry me. Caroline, please, will you marry me?"

"Good heavens," was her answer, while the viscount gathered her up to take the kiss he had promised himself in any case.

"Very good. Very good," said he, pulling away from

her a little to gaze into her green eyes with his extraordinary blue ones. "Now, will you marry me? *Please* say yes," he entreated hoarsely. "One hundred pounds says you will not."

"Well, I will," she heard herself answer. "Who wins the hundred pounds?"

"Your brother." He closed his arms round her again and kissed her forehead, then her cheek, then her mouth. "Never was so happy to lose a wager. Devil of a fine fellow, your brother."

"He feels the same way about you," she murmured, feeling rather as if she were floating than standing upon the ground.

"Well I feel the same way about him," said he unnecessarily. "And I love you, Caroline. Very much."

And Caroline, gently kissing each of his fine blue eyes, said she loved him very much too.